FORCES

S. EVAN TOWNSEND

This is a work of fiction. Names, characters, places, and incidents are products of the author's imagination or are used fictitiously and are not to be construed as real. Any resemblance to actual events, locations, organizations, or persons, living or dead, is entirely coincidental.

World Castle Publishing, LLC
Pensacola, Florida
Copyright © S. Evan Townsend 2016
Paperback ISBN: 9781629894539
eBook ISBN: 9781629894546
First Edition World Castle Publishing, LLC, May 16, 2016
http://www.worldcastlepublishing.com
Licensing Notes
Cover: Karen Fuller
Editor: Maxine Bringenberg

Dedicated to Friedrich Hayek.

BOOK ONE
THE FLEETS

CHAPTER ONE

"Distance, Lieutenant?" Captain Johnson snarled. It was redundant; his display showed the path to the planet, along with the distance from and time to reach it. But he had his reasons.

"Ninety-eight AU, Captain," his son, Sven, said, a bit perplexed at why his father was asking him the question.

Johnson nodded. The display actually showed 97.879 AU, but ninety-eight was fine when precision didn't count. And this far from the system's primary, it didn't.

"When do we turn on the radar?"

The younger Johnson blinked. This was his first planetfall as an adult, but the routine had been drilled over and over in the years between the stars. "Never."

Captain Johnson smiled. "Never?"

"Passive observation only," Sven clarified. "Telescopes, EMR detectors, neutrino detectors. At least until we're sure they've spotted us, then it doesn't matter."

"Why?"

"Shock and awe. Surprise them as much as possible."

Johnson grinned despite himself. This was only his third planetfall and they'd learned a lot at the last one. He was applying those lessons here.

His ship was a modified Bussard ramjet called the *Longboat*. It had been travelling for almost eight years to get to this star. Eight years ship's time, that was. It had been over fifty-four years in an un-accelerated frame, such as the planet they were approaching. Sven had been thirteen when they left Gredel, having restocked their supplies for this trip. And added more gold to their stash, Johnson remembered with a smile. If this raid was as profitable as Gredel was, they'd be able to retire to some nice planet and the family would be rich for generations.

News at Gredel regarding the planet they were approaching, at close to seventeen-thousand kilometers per second, was that it had found a rich asteroid belt. The planet—it was called Jideed Baghdad—was prosperous and ready to export metals, water, and hydrogen via robotic Bussard ramjet ships. It was ripe for the taking. It had been dubbed "JB" by the crew after eight years' travel. But the news of its prosperity was over fifty years old. That was the time it took the laser beam to travel from JB to Gredel. Add another fifty-four years and it was unknown what could have happened. The planet may have armed itself, or a natural disaster may have killed everyone. Or it could be going along dumb, fat, and happy, ready for Johnson's extortion. A Bussard ramjet's magnetic fields could destroy all the electronics on a planet from orbit, catapulting the society back to a preindustrial age. That made the ship itself an excellent device for coercion.

"Sir," Sven said, bending over his instruments. "I'm getting no artificial EMR."

"Check your instruments." That was Larsen, the first mate. "Did you adjust for Doppler effects?" At the speed they were going, a 300 MHz ground-to-space transmitter would be blue-shifted to about 317 MHz.

"Yes, sir, of course. Nothing."

Johnson furrowed his brow and exchanged a look with Larsen. There should be radio chatter between ships and between the ground and ships. Also, satellites would have transmissions going both up and down. If there were miners in the asteroid belt, they should be talking to each other. And the system should be sick with radar.

Unless in 104 years someone had invented something to replace electromagnetic radiation for communications, Johnson mused.

"I assume the primary is still overwhelming our neutrino detectors," Johnson asked, not masking his frustration. Neutrinos were ghostly particles and stars emitted them promiscuously. Finding a civil fusion plant on the planet in that maelstrom took time and talent. Fusion plants in ships would be even harder to detect. They had time, but Sven had never done this before except in drill. They were twenty days from reaching the planet and at the extreme edge of their instruments.

"Yes," Larsen confirmed.

"Telescopes?" Johnson asked.

"Too far, sir," Sven said, again wondering why his father was asking obvious questions.

"Of course," Johnson said with a grimace. "Good job, son. Let's get some lunch. Larsen, you have the bridge."

"Yes, sir."

The ship could, and did, fly itself for the most part. At the velocities it reached there was nothing a human mind could do fast enough. The near-AI of the ship's computer systems kept everything on course and correct. Larsen's staying on the bridge was merely a formality and an over-precaution. But Johnson hadn't collected a near cubic meter of gold—ten thousand kilograms—by being incautious. Obtaining the *Longboat* had been risky enough.

"Sir?" Larsen said as Johnson stood.

"Yes?" He hesitated a moment to hear Larsen's question.

"I assume I am to continue running silent until further notice, Captain."

"Yes," Johnson confirmed. "Short radar burst if needed, nothing more."

"Yes, sir," Larsen replied.

Johnson nodded to Larsen and followed his son out of the bridge, making one last glance back at the blank EMR detector. He was fairly certain Larsen hadn't asked that question because he

11

didn't know that he should continue to "run silent." He'd asked it for Sven's benefit to demonstrate that there was a chain of command on the bridge, and Johnson's word was law.

It was a short walk to the Johnson family's quarters. Neither Johnson nor Sven spoke, each with their own thoughts.

Johnson's wife, Sonia, was setting out lunch. She smiled at her husband as he came in, her blue eyes still just as lovely as when he fell in love with her. But there was a look in her eyes he recognized.

"So?" she asked.

Johnson sat down before the sandwich on the blue plate on the plastic table. He did his best to not think about what it actually was. With enough energy, any process could be reversed. And human waste could, with varying degrees of efficiency, be turned back into food. The old-fashioned way was to have a sun provide the energy and dirt fertilized with human or animal waste provide the nutrients the soil was missing. On the *Longboat*, the waste recycler did the job. But it didn't help to think that what he was really eating was not long ago something that he'd flushed down the head.

"Nothing." He was more gruff than he meant to be.

She arched a perfectly manicured eyebrow. In her forties, she still was attractive enough to Johnson. "Nothing?"

"Too far for anything but EMR detection," Sven said around a bite of sandwich. Where it came from never bothered him, but he had grown up on the ship since he was four years old. "And we didn't pick up any artificial EMR."

"How is that possible?" Sonia asked.

"I don't know," Johnson replied, not masking his own frustration. "Maybe they invented something better than EMR."

"Something superluminal?" Sven said with a grin.

Johnson scowled at his son. "It's been nearly a thousand years since Einstein, son; I think it's time for humanity to give up that dream."

Sven looked down at his plate. Johnson thought it was to hide his disappointment.

"Sven," Johnson said with a softer tone.

"Yeah?" the son answered. He looked up. Like his father at that age he had blond hair and blue eyes. He kept it cut short, probably for ease of care. He exercised regularly — they all did — and food was not unlimited, so he was a bit on the thin side.

"When you're done, take a sandwich to Larsen, please."

"Yes, sir."

"And stay there and review orbital insertion procedures with him."

Sven frowned but said, "Yes, sir."

Sonia sat and looked at her lunch, too. Johnson self-consciously touched his bald head. During the trip from Gredel he'd developed male pattern baldness. Easily cured if they had access to modern medicines, but they only had basic first aid on board. Thinking he would be more intimidating to the leaders of the JB system, Johnson had shaved his head. He was still getting used to the feeling of a bare skull.

The family usually ate in silence. There wasn't much to talk about after being on the same ship for seventeen years. Sven's father and mother had taught him all they could about the ship, in addition to making sure he was adequately educated about science, literature, and art. Johnson felt bad that his son had, for nearly his entire life, been confined to the five-hundred square meters of habitable space inside the ship. The poor kid must know every square centimeter of it, Johnson mused as he ate. Well, except for the ten square meters of Larsen's cabin. The first mate was a very private man.

Sven finished eating, grabbed a sandwich, put it on a plate, and left, giving his father a quizzical look.

"If they have invented something superluminal, what does that do to us?" Sonia asked after Sven left.

"I don't know," Johnson said after swallowing. "Steal a new ship." He tried to sound confident, but stealing this ship had nearly been fatal for Larsen and him.

If humans had something faster than light, it might mean he'd be retiring early and with less gold than he wanted. It would also revolutionize human communication and travel in ways he couldn't imagine. He didn't really care about that, but was worried about what it might mean for his family and ship.

"Olly," Sonia said with a terse and angry tone, "why?"

"Why what?" He knew where this was going but he wasn't going to waltz into it willingly.

"Why do we have to extort the people of JB?"

"We're not. We're extorting the government."

Sonia sighed. They'd had this conversation before. Once before setting course for JB and occasionally during the trip between the stars. "As far as we know, the government on JB isn't tyrannical like Bostad. And Grendel, too."

"Listen," Johnson said, trying to keep his voice calm. "I didn't spend eight years coming here to turn around and leave."

"But now we have a...conundrum: the lack of EMR. We have no idea what we're going to find. It might just be safer to go to someplace and settle down. We have plenty of gold."

Johnson shook his head. "You remember when we left Bostad?"

"Of course." It had only been seventeen years, ship's time.

"You agreed that we needed to leave Bostad."

"Yes, but—"

"And you agreed, with Larsen, that I was the captain."

Sonia set her face into a grimace. "I think you're abusing your power. I think you are putting your family in danger for your greed."

"I don't want to have this discussion again."

"Fine," Sonia said, sitting back and crossing her arms over her chest.

Johnson picked up the glass of water and took a sip, setting it down on the table. Again, he actively did not think about the fact that the water was probably urine or sweat or, most likely, both, yesterday.

The glass stayed on the table because of the one gee acceleration the Bussard ramjet provided. At the moment they traveled ass-backwards, negatively accelerating to match orbits with the primary of this system. When they slowed too much for the ramjet to work, they would rely on stored hydrogen to operate the fusion rocket. The Bussard's magnetic scoops had three functions in interstellar space: gather enough hydrogen to run the fusion drive, store hydrogen for when the ramjet wouldn't work, and detect an object large enough to damage the *Longboat*. At relativistic velocities, that could be as small as a grain of sand.

But when they were in orbit about the planet or coasting in interplanetary space, they would have no acceleration and would be in free-fall, what some mistakenly call "zero gravity."

After eight years of having the artificial gravity their acceleration provided, except briefly at turn around, Johnson wasn't looking forward to free fall again.

To travel by Bussard ramjet, you accelerated toward your target (or rather, where your target would be when you would arrive, for everything in space is moving, including stars) for half the trip. Then you turned around and pointed your fusion rocket behind you to slow you for half the trip so you were able to orbit the star that was your target rather than zoom by at a large percentage of the speed of light. Either way, you had gravity-like acceleration just like being on a planet.

It had been just over fifty years, rest-time frame, since the *Longboat* had left Gredel. Its crew had had no contact with other humans in that time. Fifty years is a long time, Johnson thought. If humanity had, while they were between stars, developed a faster-than-light drive, or FTL, they probably had also developed artificial gravity control. Accelerating to superluminal speeds without it would make the crew of any ship a thin paste on the back wall, assuming the ship itself could survive such forces.

Johnson shook his head. This was silly to think about until he knew more. Odds were, there was a logical explanation for why the Jideed Baghdad system was so bereft of artificial EMR. Or maybe Sven was right, perhaps they had invented something better than EMR to communicate. No need to speculate until they knew more, and it would be a couple of weeks before they were close enough to learn more. Might as well relax until then, Johnson thought. There was nothing else he could do.

He smiled at Sonia as a peace offering. She rejected it by standing up and clearing the table.

#

According to the information on Gredel, Jideed Baghdad's official language was Arabic, but interstellar communications were always in English, so Johnson hoped someone on the planet could communicate with him. But, in the ensuing eight years he'd been studying Arabic and practicing it by talking to the computer. He thought he was pretty good at it and could even read it, which amazed him; the first time he saw that writing it had looked to him like scribbles.

He thought if they picked up any transmissions, he should be able to translate them. But the EMR detector was blank. Sure, the sun was spewing all sorts of EMR, but that was filtered out. The EMR detector looked for modulated EMR that would indicate that it contained information.

But there was nothing.

CHAPTER TWO

They were ten days from orbiting the inhabited planet, and they were 24.5 AU from the primary, or 3.66 billion kilometers. If they were approaching the Sol System, they would be between the orbits of Uranus and Neptune. They had slowed to eighty-five hundred kilometers a second. At this speed, the blue-shift of ERM was less than three percent, so a 300 Mhz transmission would be about 308 Mhz.

"I have something," Sven said.

"What?"

"A neutrino source, a big one."

"Where?"

"It's coming from JB," he said. "But I think it's in orbit."

"Why?"

"It's oscillating back and forth," Sven said. "We're barely at close enough range to detect the movement, but it's moving back and forth with a period of ninety-five minutes. And you said JB rotated about once every twenty-six hours, so that's too fast to be on the surface. If the information we have on JB's diameter and mass are correct, I'd say that's something in an orbit at an altitude of about one-hundred kilometers."

"You compensated for our time dilation?" Larsen asked.

"Yes, sir," Sven said, his voice shot-through with pride.

Johnson nodded. "Good job, Lieutenant."

Since neutrinos could pass through planets, they would always be detectible even as the orbiting object passed behind the planet. It would, at this distance, simply look as if it were oscillating back and forth.

"Thanks, Dad," Sven replied, forgetting bridge protocol.

Johnson gave him a reprimanding look, but one mixed with admiration.

"What could it be?" Larsen asked.

"An orbiting ship, most likely," Sven said. "Or an orbital platform of some kind."

"A weapon?" Larsen asked.

"Perhaps," Johnson interrupted before this conversation got out of hand. "But more likely an orbital space station or observation platform."

"For what purpose?" Sven asked. "It's putting out enough neutrinos to be a civil power plant on the surface. In fact, other than the primary, it's the only neutrino source I've found."

"And still no EMR," Larsen said, not hiding his frustration.

"No," Sven confirmed.

Johnson spent a moment in thought. "How long until we can get a visual on what's orbiting the planet?"

"At 10 AU we should be able to," Larsen said, "if it's big enough. We'll be at that range in...." He spent a moment working with the computer. "Three days, fourteen hours, approximately."

Johnson tried not to visibly react and show his frustration. "Okay, keep scanning for artificial EMR, keep an eye on that neutrino source, and watch for anything unusual."

"More unusual than we've already encountered?" Larsen asked.

Johnson snorted. "Yes." That was the frustrating thing about space travel, he thought. Due to the distances involved, nothing happened very quickly. At least not until you got in orbit around a planet; then things got interesting.

"You have the bridge, Larsen," Johnson said. "Lieutenant, stay here and assist Commander Larsen. I'm going to get some rest."

"Yes, sir," Larsen snapped with military precision. He had spent his life on spaceships.

"Da...Captain?" Sven asked.

"Yes?"

"What if it is a weapon?"

Johnson tried to smile reassuringly. "It's not. But if it is, we run like hell."

#

Jideed Baghdad was a very Earth-like world. Its primary was a G3 yellow dwarf, just a bit cooler than Earth's Sun. JB orbited its star a little closer at almost exactly 0.9 AU. This made JB a little hotter and drier than Earth.

The planet was slightly larger, and therefore more massive, than Earth, so its surface gravity was a little more than one gee. Not that Captain Johnson had ever been to Earth.

When the *Longboat* was 10 AU from the primary, it was 9.1 AU from JB's orbit. That was close enough, barely, to get a visual with the telescopes of the object in orbit spewing so many neutrinos. That was, Johnson reminded himself, if it was big enough. The *Longboat* was travelling at fifty-four hundred kilometers a second, and EMR, including visible light, was being blue-shifted 0.2%. Not enough for even the computer to need to compensate for, Johnson knew. The computer spent its processing power on compensating for the velocity of the ship relative to the planet, which was orbiting its star at about thirty kilometers a second. Both the ship's and the planet's vectors of velocity had to be put into the calculation to keep the telescope steady on the planet.

To the naked eye at this distance, which was a little farther out than Saturn orbits the Sun, JB would look like a barely-visible dot. The telescope should be able to bring it nearly into view. But was the object in orbit big enough to be seen? Johnson wondered. Or would he have to wait longer? If it was a weapon, or something to avoid, he wanted to know as soon as possible so he could change his acceleration vector and, as he had told his son, "run like hell."

"The telescope has locked on to the planet," Larsen reported.

"Large display, please," Johnson said. The bridge had one holo display, and it was the largest available.

Sonia and Sven were there, too.

The planet, looking about the size of an apple held at arm's length, popped up on the holo display. The scene was only two-dimensional despite being in a three-dimensional frame.

"Zoom in," Johnson ordered.

Larsen touched something on his computer and the orb filled the screen.

"Wow," Sven said.

Johnson nodded and chuckled. JB was beautiful, blue and green with white clouds. Ruddy deserts painted the tropics, but also vibrant green clung to the equator, indicating rainforests. It was the most Earth-like exoplanet Johnson had ever seen, and that included anything he'd found in the *Longboat's* database.

"Should be quite wealthy," Larsen said with a smile.

Johnson nodded again. Wealth meant technology and technology meant electronics. They would be very nervous about the *Longboat's* magnetic fields. He glanced at Sonia. She kept her face passive.

About one-third of the planet was in darkness and there was no indication of artificial lighting such as a city would have. This wasn't surprising. The population was less than a million 104 years ago, so was not likely significantly more now, and all the cities, which would be small anyway, could be on the daylight side. Or the side they couldn't see. And smaller towns and villages probably wouldn't put off enough light to be seen at this distance, Johnson thought.

"Where's your neutrino source?" Larsen asked Sven.

"I think it must be behind the planet," Sven said, trying hard not to sound defensive.

"Yes," Johnson said, "There's about a 50% chance it's behind the planet right now. Or maybe it's too small to see." Johnson had trouble believing anything man-made could be big enough to be seen at this distance, even if it did apparently need a huge power plant. But Larsen knew his stuff, and if he said it should be visible, it should be.

"What's its orbital period?" Johnson asked.

"Ninety-five minutes," Sven replied.

"So worst case is we wait forty-seven and a half minutes," Johnson said.

"Yes," Sven confirmed. "Assuming we can see it over the dark side."

Johnson looked at the ship's chronometer. At this velocity time dilation was nearly imperceptible. They should view events very slightly faster than they took place. Probably only the computer would notice the difference.

"Has the AI plotted our course to orbit JB?" Johnson asked Larsen.

"Yes, sir," Larsen replied. "Once we get into orbit around the primary, it'll only be a matter of hours before we're in orbit around JB. You did say a hundred and fifty kilometers?"

"Yes," Johnson replied. He wanted to be in a higher orbit than whatever was orbiting at a hundred kilometers.

Going from interstellar travel to orbit of a planet was both simple and complicated. First you put your ship in orbit around the star in as close an approximation of the planet's orbit as possible: same semi-major axis and eccentricity. Then the ship would use orbital dynamics to rendezvous with the planet and do a hot retro-burn to slow down to enter orbit of the planet itself. For JB, they'd have to burn hydrogen out of the tanks to get a delta-vee of about twenty-two thousand meters per second. That would be a one-gee burn for half an hour. At five gees it would be seven minutes. Seven minutes of hell, Johnson called it in his mind. Because he massed seventy-three kilograms, at five gees he'd weigh 365 kilos.

The ship's AI did it nearly automatically and all Larsen had to do was input the altitude at which Captain Johnson wanted to orbit the planet, usually between one-hundred and two-hundred kilometers. Everyone on board knew how to operate the AI. Johnson had made sure of that. Sven's young mind picked it up quickly, and Sonia had a symbiotic relationship with the computer, it seemed to Johnson. What would take him five minutes and many touches of the screen, she could do in just a few moments. Even Larsen wasn't that fast.

The four waited, watching the display. Johnson knew that at this distance there was a miniscule chance that someone would spot their fusion drive, the blue flame slowing them. That was more likely if the asteroid belt, which was at about 5 AU from that star, was occupied and being mined as reports in Gredel said it was. But space is huge, and their tiny spark was unlikely to be spotted. Some planets had active space watches to look for comets and asteroids that may impact the planet and that made it more likely they would be found. But again, the odds were slim, even then.

It was almost thirty minutes before the object came into view over the light-side of the planet.

"*Gode Gud,*" Larsen breathed.

"What is it?" Sven asked.

Sonia was quiet. A quick glance and Johnson knew she was focused on the display.

Johnson studied the screen. He expected the object to be small, so small they'd have trouble finding it let alone seeing it. But it was huge, black even though it was in direct sunlight, and the shape was unusual. Johnson had in his life seen nearly every spaceship-type humans had built, either by encountering them in space around planets or, mostly, from pictures of them in his ship's database. He'd seen images and recordings of the architecture of every human culture. And this thing looked like nothing any human had built. It looked, and he hated to use the word, alien.

On first glance it looked like a simple, black cylinder, tapered on one end, rounded at the other. As his eyes focused on it, he could see the cylinder curved slightly. The surface looked glass-smooth. At the apex of the arc was a sphere that was a hollow latticework that Johnson couldn't guess the purpose of.

"Can you zoom in more?" Sonia asked.

"At this point all I can do is make the pixels larger."

Sonia nodded, staring at the screen. "What is it?" she asked.

"I don't know," Johnson said. Johnson screwed his face up in thought. He had no idea what it could be. Was it a weapon, a spaceship, or a space station? And why was it in orbit around the planet? He didn't see any overt weapons, but at this range, it that was unlikely unless they were huge.

And why was there no artificial EMR anywhere in the system? There were too many damn unknowns.

"Where's the nearest human-colonized system?" he asked.

Sonia cracked a small smile.

Larsen working on his computer. "According to the data we have — which is fifty-four years old, I remind you — Gredel."

Colonization did not happen fast. Slow Bussard ramjet colony ships traveled at one gee, also. Odds were that there wasn't another colony nearby as they were at the edge of human exploration of the galaxy.

"What's the nearest planet we haven't visited?"

Larsen worked a while. "Paradisus, 205 light years."

"How long to get there from here?" Sven asked.

Larsen looked at Johnson, who nodded. Larsen worked the computer.

"Ten years, five months, approximately, ship time."

Johnson growled. "We don't have supplies for that long," he said. Not every system on the ship was 100% efficient. The air recycler had to be supplemented with stored oxygen. The food recycler had to have added organic materials, including vitamins and amino acids essential to human life. Johnson looked at Sven. He was a source of inefficiency, having grown and gained mass that had to come out of the organic storage tanks.

"We could go back to Gredel," Larsen said.

Johnson snorted. "All it would take is one surface-to-space missile to destroy us. You don't think after 108 years they wouldn't have developed some planetary defenses?"

"Or gotten complacent," Larsen said.

Johnson looked at his wife and knew she was thinking they should leave. He wasn't sure he didn't agree with her at this point.

Johnson considered the display. The object was still there, as if challenging him.

Luckily, nothing happened fast at even interplanetary distances. He had time to think.

#

The two-dimensional computer displayed a three-dimensional image of the object compiled from its observations. The resolution wasn't very good, maybe a few meters per pixel, and the side that had been facing the planet was blank, just a gray surface to fill the void where the computer had no data.

Johnson looked at it, turning it with his finger on the screen as if that would tell him more. It was so black it seemed to absorb visible light, yet was glassy, too. He had no idea how that was possible. The computer had estimated its mass at 5 x 105 tonnes. That made it more than ten times the mass of the *Longboat*; bigger than interstellar colony ships designed to carry hundreds of humans to a new planet with everything they needed.

But one word kept going through his mind: alien.

CHAPTER THREE

The sooner they started for Gredel, the sooner they got there, Johnson thought. Nine years from now, he growled. Larsen said the AI could program an orbit of this star that would change their course back to Gredel with minimum use of the stored hydrogen.

Maybe it would work. Who would expect pirates to come back after 108 years? That was time enough for governments to fall, revolutions to happen, populaces to grow weary of paying for a never-used space defense system.

But they'd have to be very parsimonious with their supplies, stretch them out another nine years. At least Sven was through growing, pretty much.

Or, they could go into orbit around JB and figure out what the object was. Johnson had to admit his curiosity was gnawing at him. But curiosity could get you killed.

"Sir?" Larsen's voice came over the ship's intercom.

"Yes?"

"You need to come to the bridge."

"On my way."

Johnson left his small office and hurried down the corridor to the bridge. He had to pass his living quarters and he opened the door as he did and stuck his head in. His wife looked up from where she was reading a tablet.

"You and Sven might want to see this," Johnson snapped.

"Yes, dear," his wife said with a forced smiled.

He smiled at her, trying to be reassuring, and continued to the bridge. He felt bad for snapping at her, but he was tense and had been since they'd found no artificial EMR in this system. She knew it, too, he knew, despite his attempts to protect her from his fears, concerns, and worries.

Walking into the room designated the "bridge," Johnson saw Larsen staring at the large holo display, still showing an image of JB. The object wasn't visible, which didn't surprise Johnson as it could easily be behind the planet. He hadn't been keeping track of when it would be visible.

"What's up?" Johnson asked.

Larsen touched his computer controls. "Watch this, sir." He nodded at the display. "The computer recorded this a few minutes ago."

Johnson turned to watch. The object orbited over the daylight section of the planet. Johnson knew that when it crossed over to the night-time section, it was invisible and could only be tracked by its neutrino emissions.

As Johnson watched, the object changed orbits. No, that wasn't right; it didn't so much change orbits as simply flew away from the planet, the rounded end of the cylinder leading.

"Is this real time?" Johnson asked. It had to be sped up, he thought.

"Yes," Larsen confirmed.

The object, now Johnson thought of it as a "ship," moved away from JB at an unbelievable rate of acceleration. Away from the planet, it was only visible as it occulted stars it passed in front of.

"How fast?" Johnson asked.

"I'm not sure how much of its acceleration vector is directly toward us," he said. "But I think it's small. If it's zero, the object is accelerating at about one thousand gees."

Johnson's eyes went wide. No organic being, let alone an artifact, could stand up to that acceleration.

"Where's it going?"

"Watch," Larsen said.

Johnson stifled a frustrated growl, knowing his first mate wouldn't talk in riddles if he knew the answer.

As Johnson observed, the ship disappeared. Suddenly the stars behind it became visible.

"*Jäkla*," Johnson whispered.

"Its neutrino trace disappeared, too," Larsen confirmed.

"When did this happen?"

"Just before I called you."

The display went back to showing JB as the replay ended.

Sven and Sonia walked in together.

"What's up?" Sven asked a little too informally for his father's liking.

Sonia looked at the display only showing the planet.

"Now what, sir?" Larsen asked before Johnson could reprimand Sven.

"Go into orbit around the planet. A hundred kilometers altitude."

"Olly?" Sonia asked.

Larsen frowned and Johnson knew he didn't like the order.

"I want to see this planet up close," Johnson added.

"And if that object comes back?" Larsen asked.

"It's gone?" Sonia interrupted.

"Then we hope they aren't hostile," Johnson said. We certainly can't outrun them, he thought bitterly.

"They?" Sven asked, his voice high-pitched with wonder.

Sonia turned and walked out of the bridge, her quick footsteps echoing down the corridor. Johnson debated going after her but didn't. He knew they'd talk about it, and soon.

#

From orbit, the planet presented even more a mystery. In the telescope they could see infrastructure, buildings, row crop fields and orchards, water reservoirs, and all the other accouterments of human settlement. But no people, no vehicles, and nothing indicating energy being produced or expended. Not even campfire smoke.

It was as if more than a million people had disappeared. A bad feeling settled in the pit of Johnson's stomach. A ship that accelerates at a thousand gees, then disappears. A colonized planet with no people. No artificial EMR and no neutrino emissions from the surface indicating fusion power sources. The asteroid belt just as empty and devoid of energy sources.

The four members of the ship's company gathered around the dinner table in the Johnsons' quarters. All such meetings were held there: the only place big enough. Mrs. Johnson had her arms over her chest and was not smiling.

Each of them was lightly strapped down. They were in free fall now. Sven had bad space sickness. At turn-around when he was seventeen, he'd thought it was fun to be in free fall for that brief time. Now that free fall was a permanent condition, he was almost a shade of green.

"Aliens," Johnson said, giving voice to what he assumed everyone was thinking.

"That is very unlikely," Larsen said. "The distances alone make that nearly impossible."

"Nearly," Sonia said softly. "Not so much if you can travel faster than light."

"Plus," Larsen continued, ignoring her, "the human race is about one hundred thousand years old. That's a blink of an eye on the cosmic time scale. The odds are if we do run into intelligent life, it'll be much older than us because the universe has been around for thirteen billion years. They are likely to be millions of years older than us, which means their technology will be commensurately as advanced."

"As in able to accelerate at a thousand gees and disappear?" Sonia asked pointedly.

"More advanced than that," Larsen said. "So advanced we probably couldn't imagine their technologies."

"Where did the ship go?" Sven asked. Everyone had agreed the object was a spaceship of some type.

"Faster than light, interdimensional shift, wormhole, hyperspace, who knows?" Larsen said.

"And the people on the planet?" Sonia said, her voice tight with worry.

Larsen didn't say anything.

"The aliens killed them," Sven said.

"All of them? All throughout the entire star system?" Larsen asked, his voice laced with incredulousness.

"I don't know, but there doesn't appear to be any signs of survivors," Captain Johnson said. "Even in the asteroid belt where, according to the information we got from Gredel's 'net, there was supposed to be thriving mining operations."

"You'd think someone would survive," Larsen said.

"Advanced technology," Sven said. "They have a way to kill all life."

"But the flora and fauna of JB are fine," the captain said. "We've seen animals and forests of pseudo-trees in the telescope."

"Then all intelligent life?" Sven asked. "You said we wouldn't be able to imagine their technology."

"You're imagining it," Larsen growled.

"Speculation is getting us nowhere," Johnson said.

"Then what are we going to do?" Sonia asked, not hiding her anger.

Johnson took in a deep breath and let it out. "Larsen and I will take the boat to the surface and investigate. Sven, you have the bridge until we get back. Just let the AI keep us in orbit."

"Yes, sir," he replied, a bit overeager.

"And what do we do if that ship comes back?" Sonia asked with a sharp tone.

"Pray," Larsen said without humor.

#

"How are we doing, Larsen?" Johnson asked as he climbed into the boat. Being in free fall did make it easier to maneuver into the small cockpit. He pulled himself into the co-pilot's seat and used the four-point harness to strap himself in.

"Good, sir," Larsen replied. "The H-2 tanks are full, the heat sink is on line and functioning, the air system is running fine, all systems are nominal."

Johnson nodded. Larsen had written up a checklist for launching the boat to make sure there were no mistakes. He'd spent most of yesterday preparing the craft, starting with transferring hydrogen from the ramjet's tanks into the boat's.

"I want to land as close as possible to the center of the largest city," Johnson said. "I'm hoping to find the seat of government."

Larsen nodded. Johnson had said that before.

"Then we need to launch soon," Larsen said.

The purpose of this trip was to gather information. The boat could lift the supplies they needed and a fair amount of gold back to the ramjet, as they had done on Gredel. But the oxygen and organics had to be prepared. The gasses needed to be extracted from the atmosphere and compressed. The organics had to be dried and compacted to the specifications their 150-year-old waste recycler needed. They didn't have the equipment to do either. Johnson had planned to force the government to prepare the supplies as he had done with Gredel, and Bostad before that. Stealing the *Longboat* and most of its components left a lot of gaps in their equipment. They were always living on the edge of survival. It was ironic and frustrating to Johnson. This planet was a gold mine, but without the equipment needed, it might as well be a barren rock.

"You have your gun?" Johnson asked. No telling what they might find down there. And, if all the people were gone, it was possible carnivorous fauna would have moved back into the cities.

"Yes, sir," Larsen said, tapping a chest pocket that held something heavy.

"Good," Johnson breathed. Even if it was just a pistol, it was better than nothing, he thought.

"Ready?" Larsen asked.

"Yes," Johnson said. As long as the boat was docked to the ramjet, he was the captain. But as soon as they were released from the *Longboat*, Larsen, as pilot, was in command.

Larsen touched a button on his control stick. "*Longboat*, we are about to detach."

"Roger," Sven's voice came back. That was via the umbilical, not radio, Johnson knew. He'd told Sven and Sonia to minimize the use of the radio. Of course, he had no idea if the aliens would pick up their transmissions, or even care.

Larsen reached overhead, opened a switch cover, and pressed the red button. The sensation of moving was slight as the boat detached from the ramjet.

The first spaceships to leave Earth had used ablative plating to survive re-entry. But those were one-time, throw-away vessels. Later ships had protective surfaces that could withstand the heat. But, initially, those surfaces were fragile and easily damaged. The boat had a protective surface and a heat-sink. Once they became aerodynamic and the wings extended, the wings would act like radiators, expelling the heat from the boat. It was automatic and necessary. Johnson hoped their infrared signature in the atmosphere wouldn't draw any unwanted attention, if there was anyone around to pay attention.

Larsen was a skilled pilot and maintained his proficiency with simulators on the *Longboat*. Johnson planned to simply relax and enjoy the ride as much as he could with the tension gnawing at his stomach.

Re-entry went fine, orange plasma streaming past the window, the heat-sink making more and more noise. Larsen didn't look worried, so Johnson tried to ignore it. They experienced about five gees force for a lot longer than Johnson liked, but when it was over, it felt as if they were back in about one gee gravity, the gravitational pull of JB.

"The air is thick enough to go aerodynamic," Larsen said. "We're going about Mach 5."

Johnson nodded as Larsen touched another covered switch. Electric motors whined as they extended the wings and control surfaces. Larsen gripped his stick harder. The boat's computer helped, but he still had to fly the vessel down.

The boat had no air-breathing engines, but Larsen could use the rockets a small amount to add speed if needed. Soon they were circling the largest city at three-hundred meters altitude. Even this low, there was no signs of humans. The streets were empty and clean. Whatever disaster had befallen this planet, there hadn't been time for the wind to blow dirt into the apparently unoccupied city.

"There," Larsen breathed, pointing a large public square surrounded by enormous buildings. "That has to be the seat of the government." The square was expansive, paved with red bricks, and large enough to land the boat.

Johnson nodded his agreement, and noticed the "onion dome" shape of a mosque as one of the buildings around the square. He could see a tall, decorated minaret standing higher than the surrounding structures. One building had a pole with a green and orange flag fluttering slightly in the breeze, which was abruptly normal for this place.

"No people," Larsen whispered.

"No," Johnson replied softly.

A short burst of the fusion rocket slowed the boat and Larsen activated the landing jets and landing gear. The boat descended vertically to the square. Johnson was sure some of the bricks would be melted under the fusion flame.

The boat landed softly under Larsen's skilled piloting.

Johnson ran his eyes over a few indicators. There was only nominal background radiation. The air was a little thicker than Earth standard, with a bit more oxygen. Some trace gasses registered, he saw, but none of them harmful in the quantity they were present. Perfectly breathable. The temperature was thirty-two, degrees which might be a bit warm after years in the shirt-sleeve, twenty-two-degree environment of the *Longboat*. Surface gravity was just over one gee. There was no way to check for viruses or bacteria. Maybe the aliens had put something fatal in the atmosphere, Johnson wondered, realizing he was accepting the possibility that aliens were responsible for what happened to this planet. But if they released a deadly virus or bacteria in the atmosphere, where were the bodies? It made no sense unless they had some technology Johnson couldn't imagine. Just like Larsen said they could.

"Looks safe," Johnson reported.

"Shall I open the door?" Larsen asked.

Johnson took in a breath of the air in the boat, air he knew to be good.

"Yes," he finally said.

Larsen turned in his seat and pulled a lever. Again, motors whined and the fuselage door slid aside. A ladder extended down the exterior of the boat.

Johnson took in a breath as he felt the warmer air from outside hit his face. Other than the long-forgotten musk of a planet, the air was fine as far as Johnson could determine.

"Let's go," he said, unstrapping. Now that Larsen was no longer the pilot, Johnson was back in charge.

"Yes, sir," Larsen said, undoing his straps.

CHAPTER FOUR

Johnson went down the ladder, followed by Larsen, who had a backpack with flashlights and tools. Larsen moved slower than Johnson, favoring his left leg. Johnson resisted the urge to say, "I claim this planet in the name of the Johnson family." It was no time for humor. He looked under the boat and, indeed, some of the paving bricks had been melted and were still glowing bright red.

Both men looked around. Johnson pointed. "That says it's a library," he reported, reading the Arabic script. "Maybe we'll find something there." His voice shattered the preternatural silence that neither man had noticed until he broke it.

Larsen only nodded.

They walked forward, the repeated thuds of their footfalls sounding extra loud. Johnson, in a way, wanted to scream, hoping someone or something would hear it. But, he felt as if this planet was a tomb, and the silence was sacred.

Marble steps led up to the doors of the library. The marble, which was no doubt mined on this planet, had flakes of something in it that made it sparkle in the sunshine. Probably quartz, Johnson thought.

The doors were glass and gold and for a moment Johnson wondered if it was real gold. He pushed the portal open and it easily moved, too light to be gold or else on amazingly frictionless hinges.

The library was well-lit by windows but the overhead lights were off. And it had books, actual paper books, and smelled dusty. Johnson suspected that was how it smelled even when there were people about.

A bank of computer terminals stood right in front of the entrance. Johnson walked to one and touched the screen. Nothing happened. He didn't expect anything to happen since there was no power. He turned to Larsen and shrugged. The power being out came almost as a relief; it was the first abnormal thing they'd found other than the lack of people.

Johnson resisted the urge to yell "Hello!" but it was obvious the library was abandoned.

They looked for newspapers, but the only printed material they found was old books. With ubiquitous digital technology, that didn't surprise Johnson.

"Now what?" Larsen asked.

"The mosque," Johnson said. It seemed a place people would seek refuge, he thought.

The mosque was just as empty as far as the men could tell. The interior was dark due to a lack of windows. They explored it using the flashlights, but found no humans.

Back in the warm square, both men sweating, they looked at each other.

"Now what, sir?" Larsen asked, keeping his voice low. "I hope this wasn't a wasted trip."

"Me, too," Johnson said, looking around the square.

In addition to the mosque and the library, there was a hotel that looked as if it were expensive. Adjacent to it was the building with the flag marked "Presidential Palace," and a small building next to it labeled "House of the People." Johnson wasn't sure what that could be, but governments varied from planet to planet. He pointed to the House of the People. "Let's try that."

Larsen nodded grimly.

"The higher gravity hurting your leg?" Johnson asked.

"A bit," Larsen replied tersely.

Johnson was sure that's what he'd say if he were in agonizing pain.

The building was a museum of sorts, with blank holo displays and a few artifacts. Johnson could read enough to understand that it traced the history of the people of JB from Earth to this planet.

Off to one side was a small restaurant. A few of the tables had food on them, half-eaten and cold, and starting to smell bad.

"It looks like they left in a hurry," Larsen whispered.

Johnson nodded. He walked to a refrigerated display case and gazed longingly at the real food inside. "Do you suppose it's safe to eat?"

Larson shrugged. "We don't know how long the power's been out, and with this heat, food will go bad fast. And I can't think of anything more miserable than food poisoning in free fall."

Johnson chuckled. "Yeah, you're right."

On one of the tables was a tablet. Johnson hurried over and picked it up, with Larsen right beside him. Johnson touched the screen and it came to life with a cheery beep, almost startling him in the quiet of the planet.

"No security?" Larsen asked.

"It says it's property of the House of the People, so I guess not."

A news app appeared on the screen. There was a picture of the alien spaceship predominating the screen and a large caption that read, in Arabic, "Unknown ship enters orbit around planet." Johnson found the setting to switch the text to English and read more. Apparently, the ship appeared in the solar system, went into orbit about the planet, and any attempts to contact it failed. Officials were debating the next steps to take. Johnson dragged the text up to scroll down and the universal sign of a computer processing or buffering, a circle of lines going around and around, popped up on the screen. Then a white square appeared: NETWORK NOT FOUND.

Johnson grumbled.

"Don't know much more than we did before," Larsen growled.

"Maybe there's information in the presidential palace," Johnson said, trying not to sound too hopeful. He found himself wishing people still used paper for something other than moldy old books. You didn't need power or a network for that to work.

"Maybe," Larsen said, doubt alloyed in his voice.

After expending all the time and hydrogen to land on this planet, Johnson didn't want to give up easily.

Getting into the palace was not hard. The door that looked like the main entrance was open. Johnson assumed that under normal circumstances it would have been guarded. He was surprised not to see weapons anywhere. Guards would probably be armed, but whatever happened to the people apparently happened to whatever they were holding, too.

The interior was dark and labyrinthine. They encountered many locked doors, and those that were open revealed no secrets. They happened upon what they thought was the planetary leader's office. According to what they had learned at Gredel, the officer was called "the president."

The office was large and ornate with an over-sized wooden desk and two of the same orange and green flags behind the large leather chair. The holo display on the desk was blank, of course. But there was a tablet, also. Johnson touched the screen. The screen only displayed "unauthorized access" after apparently reading Johnson's fingerprint or DNA.

When the men left the presidential palace, the sun was low on the horizon. Already the square was in shadow from the buildings surrounding it.

"Let's get back to the boat," Johnson said. He didn't want to be out here at night, even though they hadn't seen any threats of any kind.

Larsen nodded and started walking, limping a bit.

Johnson couldn't help but notice. "Did you bring any painkillers?"

"Yes, sir. They're in the boat."

Johnson nodded.

Back inside the boat, Larsen checked the computer. After all the blank displays they'd seen, it almost surprised Johnson when it responded to him.

"The *Longboat* is out of range," he said.

Johnson nodded, happy to be in artificial light and comfort after being outside in the planet's environment.

"When will it be in radio range?" he asked.

Because the radio couldn't go through the planet, they could only communicate with the *Longboat* when it was in sight of the landing boat.

Larsen glanced at the display. "We just missed it. It'll be back in radio range in about forty minutes."

"Let's eat," Johnson said. "I'm starving."

Larsen smiled softly, letting Johnson know that he knew that it was just to kill the time before they could talk to Sven and Sonia.

The sandwiches Sonia had prepared were wrapped in hand towels and in a small box that normally held hand tools. There was no other way on the ship to transport food, as it had never been needed before. Johnson reached behind him to where the box was secured with straps and pulled it between the two seats, careful not to run it into any switches, buttons, or control devices.

"*Oij*, not the most comfortable camping spot," Johnson joked as he handed a sandwich to Larsen.

"The boat's not made for comfort, sir," Larsen replied.

Johnson couldn't help but chuckle.

"Sir," Larsen asked as they ate.

"Hmmm?" Johnson replied around a bite of sandwich. He was dreaming of the food they'd seen in the display cases.

"Why did you leave Sven in charge, and not Sonia?"

"I think he needs the experience."

Larsen nodded. "But what if that ship comes back?"

"I don't think it'll matter who's in charge, then."

Again, Larsen nodded.

While they finished eating, the view out the windows became darker and darker and, soon there was nothing to see but stars in the sky and the black hulks of the buildings. JB's one small moon hadn't risen yet. The sky was so serene and beautiful that Johnson had trouble for a moment believing anything bad had happened here. It was a feeling he relished for a few moments.

"It's time," Larsen announced, interrupting Johnson's rumination.

"Good," Johnson replied. He'd long run out of sandwich.

Larsen touched the radio. "Larsen to *Longboat*," he said.

"*Longboat* here," Sven replied. Johnson thought he sounded excited. Maybe it was only because they were finally talking. There was a slight light-speed delay due to the distance between the two transceivers.

"Report," Johnson ordered.

"Yes, sir," Sven said. "Dad, I found a radio source."

Johnson leaned forward. "Where?"

"I could only pick it up when we were on the night side of JB. I think it's coming from the asteroid belt."

"What kind of transmission was it?" Johnson asked.

"I don't know, Dad, it's in Arabic. But the voice sounded excited."

"What's the freq?" Larsen asked.

"Thirty-seven point two megahertz. But it's real weak. I don't think it'll make it through atmosphere."

Johnson and Larsen exchanged a look.

"That's a low-power freq," Larsen whispered.

Johnson nodded. Might be a spacesuit or a small ship, he thought.

"Can you hear it now?" he asked Sven.

"No, I heard it on our last period on the night side, but I'm not picking it up now."

"Did you record it?" Larsen asked.

There was a long hesitation, too long to be explained by light-speed delay. "No, sorry, I didn't think of it."

"That's okay, Sven," Johnson said.

"I tried calling you, but you didn't answer," Sven said.

Larsen shook his head. "Yes, we were out of the boat at the time."

"What did you find down there?" Sonia asked.

"Nothing," Johnson said. "No new information."

"When will you come back?" she asked. Johnson thought she sounded nervous. She didn't like this planet and was still wanting to leave.

Johnson shrugged then realized it was a useless gesture. "I don't know. I don't know if it's worth staying until the sun comes up and exploring more."

"I see," Sonia replied.

"Sven, if you pick up that message again, record it," Larsen ordered.

"Yes, sir," Sven replied.

"We'll contact you when we've made a decision," Johnson said.

"Yes, sir," Sven said again.

"Out," Larsen snapped.

"Out," Sven replied.

Larsen looked at Johnson. "He should have thought of recording it."

"Yes," Johnson said. "I'll talk to him when we get back."

Larsen didn't look satisfied with that solution, Johnson thought.

Larsen set the radio's secondary frequency to 37.2 Mhz.

"Do you think it's worth waiting until morning?" Johnson asked.

Larsen shook his head. "This is a big city, and it would take weeks to explore on foot. If we didn't find any information in the president's own office, we probably won't find anything anywhere else."

"I'm inclined to agree."

Johnson thought a moment. He wondered what the odds were of finding a bank with its vault open and then finding gold in it. With mining in the belt, there probably was bullion somewhere on the planet. Finding it and transporting it was the problem. He supposed they could look for a jewelry store with diamonds and other precious gems. But that would take time, and with a possibly malevolent alien ship about, he didn't want to waste any.

"You probably can't tell me here," Johnson said, "but when we get back to the *Longboat*, I want you to calculate if we have enough H-2 to get to the asteroid belt and still be able to reach escape velocity and ramjet speed." The *Longboat* had to be going very fast for the ramjet to operate. The incoming hydrogen had to have enough energy to fuse. The exact speed depended on the density of the interstellar hydrogen that their hundreds of kilometers-wide magnetic scoops could pull into the fusion engine, but was around ten-thousand kilometers a second. At one gee acceleration, that would take approximately twelve days to reach and would nearly empty their hydrogen storage tanks.

Larsen nodded. "Depends on how fast you want to get to the asteroid belt. A low-energy Hohmann transfer orbit will take very little delta-vee, but will require months to get there."

"Obviously not that," Johnson said, trying to keep his tone light. "How about a few days?"

"Then I'll have to do the calculations, but I suspect not. Not and still have H-2 to get back to ramjet velocity."

Johnson nodded. "Well, do the calculations. Maybe it'll work."

Larsen nodded but didn't look happy.

"Start working on a rendezvous with the *Longboat* on its next overhead pass."

"Yes, sir."

About ten minutes later he shifted in his seat to look at Johnson. "Sir?"

Johnson had his eyes closed and was almost asleep. He sat up. "Yes?"

"I think we should run."

"Run?"

"Run like hell, that's what you said."

Johnson smiled. "Run where?"

"We talked about going to Paradisus."

"Yes, and it's a ten-year trip and we need supplies."

Larsen looked frustrated. "Yes, I know. Too bad we can't get them here."

Johnson nodded.

"Or back to Gredel," Larsen suggested.

"Yes," Johnson said, again nodding. Then he frowned. "And what if we get there and there's no one there, either?"

Larsen shook his head. "I don't know, sir. But the longer we're in this system, the more nervous I get. I don't understand what's happening and I don't like that feeling. It scares me."

Johnson smiled grimly. "I'm scared, too, Larsen."

CHAPTER FIVE

Larsen's rendezvous with the *Longboat* was flawless. Sonia and Sven met them at the airlock.

"What did you find?" Sonia asked.

"Nothing," Larsen growled.

Johnson nodded in agreement, earning a disappointed look from his wife and son.

"There's no power, nothing is running. We found no people, no information except a tablet that had just a bit of data still on it."

"What did it say?" Sonia asked as they pushed back toward the bridge.

"That a mysterious ship has appeared in orbit and all attempts at communication were ignored."

Sonia sighed unhappily.

The four reached the bridge in silence. Larsen went to his station, pulled himself into the chair, and used the seatbelt to secure himself. He started working on his computer.

"So, now what?" Sven asked.

Johnson shook his head. "To be honest, son, I don't know. I want to talk to this person whose transmission you heard, if possible. Maybe he knows more."

"I haven't heard him since that first time," Sven said, his voice revealing his disappointment.

"Maybe he'll try again," Johnson said, trying to sound hopeful.

There was a long silence as each person stewed in their own thoughts. The only sound was the air circulating fan and Larsen tapping the screen on his computer.

Everyone's thoughts were interrupted by the radio coming to life.

"That's it!" Sven said.

"Shhhhhh," Johnson hissed, holding up a hand to silence Sven.

When the transmission was finished, Johnson touched the transmit button on the radio and spoke. "This is the *Longboat* in orbit around Jideed Baghdad. Do you speak English?"

It took nearly ninety minutes for the reply to come due to the light speed delay.

"English, yes," the voice replied. "Who are you?"

"Where are you?" Johnson asked, ignoring the question.

And another ninety minutes passed. Sonia drifted away but was back before the reply.

"I am in asteroid belt."

Johnson shook his head. This was frustrating. "Where in the asteroid belt are you? We need to know so we can…," he hesitated a moment, "calculate how to reach you."

Another ninety minutes passed.

"I give you coordinates, okay?" There followed a string of numbers.

Larsen nodded to Johnson that he understood and was putting the data in the navigation computer.

"Do you know what happened in this system?" Johnson asked. He thought about adding more, but what?

Another interminable delay.

"Everyone gone," the man replied. "I was in my ship, travelling, I arrived at my — I don't know the word — and everyone was gone. And no one has replied to radio."

Johnson was quiet for a long moment, his face twisted as he thought. "Did you see the big black ship?"

Again, a long delay. This conversation had been going on for six hours. They'd eaten. Larsen went to his quarters for a while.

46

Johnson took a nap. Sven played a game on a tablet. Luckily, at 100km altitude, they orbited the planet with a period of ninety minutes, so they were always on the right side of the orbit when the transmission came, one orbit later.

"What ship? I didn't see a ship. I need help. My power will run out in two days." And then his air recycler and his heater would stop functioning, Johnson knew, and it would be a race between suffocating and freezing to death.

Johnson sighed.

Larsen shook his head. Johnson understood the meaning: they couldn't rescue the man.

"Is there anything else you can tell us?" Johnson asked the man. "Do you have access to hydrogen?" He could survive longer if he did.

Another ninety minute wait.

"No, that's all I know. And I have no hydrogen. I am running on batteries."

"Do you know where you can get more hydrogen?"

More waiting.

"No, I'm just a miner, I buy my hydrogen from other miners. I only have battery power."

Larsen looked at Johnson, his eyes registering defeat.

"We'll be in touch," Johnson said.

Johnson looked at Larsen.

"To get there in time we'd burn too much H-2. We'd never reach ramjet speed afterwards. We'd be stuck here."

"There has to be hydrogen in the belt," Sven said.

Larson nodded. "The larger occupied asteroids should have H-2 storage. But there's no way to get it on the *Longboat*."

"Why not?" Sonia asked.

Johnson sighed. "The *Longboat* is designed to obtain the hydrogen it needs from the interstellar medium. There's no coupling to hook up a transfer hose to the hydrogen tanks."

"Why?" Sonia exclaimed.

"When we converted the *Longboat* from an unmanned exploration ship, we—" he looked at Larsen "—decided punching a hole in the hydrogen tanks to install a coupling we'd probably never need wasn't worth the risk of damaging the tanks."

"So we just let that poor man die?" Sonia asked, her voice angry.

Larsen gave her a look that was just short of a glare. "Yes, if we want to survive."

"Can we get to the belt in time to save him and then back in orbit around JB?" Johnson asked.

"Yes, but we'll be stuck here."

Johnson nodded. "I know."

"Have we considered," Sonia said, "that we need to warn other planets?"

"Warn? How?" Larsen asked.

"This system has to have a communication laser," Sven added with hope in his voice.

Interstellar communication was via orbiting modulated laser as the only thing that could reach the distances involved. It wasn't a visible laser but a microwave laser, sometimes called a "maser," that used a frequency in the gigahertz range.

"But if its power source was working, we'd have detected it," Larsen said.

"Maybe we can rendezvous with it and get it running," Sven suggested. "We have to try."

Johnson smiled. "Perhaps we do," he said. "But I suspect that that alien ship goes faster than light. The laser only transmits at the speed of light. Our warning will get there years after the ship does."

"And we don't know where it's going," Larsen added. "Or even if it's going to go to another human colony. Plus," Larsen continued, "I know nothing about restarting civil fusion plants, which are usually deuterium-deuterium reactions." Since the *Longboat's* source of fuel was interstellar hydrogen, proton-proton reactions were what, by necessity, powered it.

"So what do we do?" Sonia asked.

Johnson shrugged. "I wish I knew."

Ninety minutes later they received a transmission from the man that simply said, "*Shukran jizeelan.*"

#

"Dad?" Sven said, interrupting Johnson's thoughts. The senior Johnson had been floating in the bridge, trying to think and trying not to think about the man out in the asteroid belt.

"Yes, son?" Johnson said. Technically on the bridge it should be "Captain" and "Lieutenant," but Johnson was too emotionally strung out to care.

"I have an idea," Sven said.

"Yes?"

"The sixth planet in this system is made of hydrogen, mostly. It's a gas giant."

Johnson looked at his son and smiled. "Yes?"

"We could rescue the miner, then orbit near that planet to replenish our fuel in its upper atmosphere."

Johnson thought a moment. "How pure is the hydrogen?"

"According to our information on this system, around 96%, the rest being mostly helium."

"What else?" Johnson asked.

Sven looked as if he didn't want to say. "Methane and ammonia, mostly."

Johnson shook his head. "The ram scoops can't handle that. The helium and other gasses would contaminate our fuel and reduce our efficiency. High enough contamination they could damage the fusion reactor."

"Don't the ram scoops filter out gasses other than hydrogen?" Sven asked.

"Yes, but not at that concentration and that high of a percentage of contaminants."

"Can't we try?" Sven asked. "If we were at a high enough orbit, the concentrations of the other, heavier gasses would be minimal."

Johnson shook his head. "No. It's not worth the risk. The family — the ship — has to come first."

Sven frowned. "So there's no hope?"

"No, son," Johnson replied. "But I'm impressed you came up with this. I wish it would have worked."

"Me, too, Dad." Sven turned using a handhold and pulled himself out of the bridge.

Johnson watched him leave with a mix of pride and sadness.

#

Johnson knocked on the door to Larsen's quarters. He had to hold on to a steel loop welded into the wall to make sure the action of knocking didn't send him floating back into the middle of the corridor.

Larsen opened the door a crack. "Yes, sir?"

"Let's talk."

"Yes, sir."

Larsen came out of the room and closed the door, and Johnson noticed that, as usual, he locked it with a touch of his finger on the sensor.

Both men pushed and pulled themselves to the bridge.

"At least in free fall your leg doesn't hurt," Johnson said, trying to lighten the mood.

"No, sir," Larsen replied tersely.

When they entered the bridge, Sonia was already there.

"Yes, sir?" Larsen asked.

"I've been thinking about our friend." He nodded at the radio.

"Yes, sir?" Larsen asked, his voice betraying his fear of what was about to happen. He looked at Sonia and she only smiled enigmatically.

"I sent him a message. I haven't told him we can't rescue him. I told him we're still trying to work it out. But I think he knows, or we'd already be on the way."

"Yes, sir," Larsen said. Again his voice betrayed his feelings, this time relief.

"Sven had an idea," Johnson said.

Larsen arched an eyebrow. "What?"

Johnson told him about the sixth planet's atmosphere.

"He's right, you know," Larsen said.

"What?"

"There might be a sweet spot where there's enough hydrogen but not too much of the heavier gasses."

Johnson stared at Larsen. "So we should try?"

Larsen laughed. "Only if we're desperate and only after a long period of spectroscopic study of the atmosphere."

Johnson nodded. "We'll keep that in mind," he said.

"Yes, sir," Larsen replied. "I could start those studies; I have little else to do just here in orbit around a dead planet." Johnson could hear the man's frustration in his voice.

Johnson nodded his approval, as did Sonia.

There was a long silence.

"What do we know?" Johnson asked finally.

"The entire system is cleaned out of human life except, apparently, our friend," Larsen said. "Unless there are people on the planet, but without radios we'd never find them."

Johnson nodded. Sonia was quiet.

"A big, black ship that apparently can move faster than light was orbiting the planet," Larsen said. "It probably was the cause of all the people disappearing, but we don't know that."

"I agree," Johnson said. He actually enjoyed Larsen's mind. He was analytical and factual. "According to the last message we got from our friend, he was coasting between asteroids with almost no power, just enough to keep his life support going. That might be why he was ignored."

"Why was he doing that?" Sonia asked.

"He said he liked to conserve energy and he had plenty of time," Johnson replied.

"Does that sound reasonable?" Sonia asked.

Larsen shrugged. "I suppose it's possible."

There was a short silence as each person thought.

"Consider this," Johnson said, "We haven't had any contact with humans for over fifty years, unaccelerated frame. Perhaps they've developed an FTL drive and that ship was built by humans, and they've evacuated everyone from this planet for some reason."

Larsen nodded. "I saw the pictures of that ship, sir, and if humans built it, they needed serious psychiatric help."

Johnson couldn't help but smile. Sonia even smiled.

"Perhaps this," Larsen said, "slavers."

"Pardon?"

"Slavers, sir. They kidnap an entire planet for slaves."

Johnson tried not to laugh. "Any advanced race will not need slaves. Machines are much more efficient and cheaper. Slaves need to be fed, housed, clothed, and they don't work very hard. Machines, robots, are much better. It wasn't a coincidence that by one hundred years after the invention of the steam engine, slavery was pretty much eradicated in the Western world on Earth. You either have cheap labor or cheap energy."

"I don't know, sir, maybe there's a religious or social aspect to it."

It was Johnson's turn to shrug. "You're right. They are an alien race and projecting human motivations on them is a mistake. How did they get them on the ship? It would take, I don't know, months to ferry them up."

"Maybe they use teleportation." Sonia looked at both of the men.

Johnson couldn't help but chuckle, but then cut himself off. If they were dealing with an alien race with very advanced technology, they couldn't dismiss anything. Although, he thought, it would be embarrassing as hell to be sitting on the toilet when everyone on JB was "beamed up" *en masse*.

"Or," Larsen said, "Conquest."

"So they killed everyone?"

"Yes."

"But we didn't find bodies."

"Disintegration."

Johnson nodded. "Again, aliens: no idea what their technology would be. But why didn't we find clothes, shoes, jewelry, weapons for the guards at the presidential palace?"

"You're right," Larsen agreed.

"But it comes down to: what the hell do we do?" Sonia said.

"Run like hell," Larsen said. "Go back to Gredel."

"And find it in the same shape as JB, only fifty years after it's happened?" Johnson said.

Sonia sighed. "Or...."

"Yes?" Larsen asked her.

"We land here, stay here, and retire here."

Larsen looked at Sonia as if trying to determine if she were serious. "Ma'am?"

Sonia smiled like she always did when Larsen called her that.

"John," she said, "we'd have the whole planet to ourselves. We'd be the richest humans in existence."

"No power, no working infrastructure, no other women — people."

"But safe."

"Unless they come back," Larsen said.

Johnson nodded grimly in agreement with his first mate.

The computer beeped. Johnson wasn't sure if it was his imagination, or if it was a frantic sound. Larsen glanced over. "Damn."

"What?"

"Neutrino source, not far away, moving. And big: a huge fusion plant."

"Telescope," Johnson barked needlessly. Larsen was already manipulating the controls.

A black ship appeared on the screen, the same size and shape as the one they'd seen before.

"Can we shut everything down? Drift like our friend in the belt?" Johnson asked.

Larsen shook his head. "Our fusion plant will still put out neutrinos. I don't think we can hide."

Johnson hit the ship's intercom. "Sven, prepare for hard acceleration," he barked. "Get yourself in position, don't worry about things."

"Sir?" Larsen asked.

"Five gees. Get us out of here."

"To where?"

"Away from that thing!" Johnson pointed at the screen.

"Yes, sir," Larsen said, trying to sound calm. "Acceleration in thirty seconds," he said over the ship's intercom.

CHAPTER SIX

"What's happening?" Sven's voice came back.

"Just strap down in an acceleration chair," Johnson said. He was doing the same, getting into a recumbent position so his whole backside would take the weight of his body at five gees.

Larsen was buckling the belts on his chair. Sonia was getting quickly into the third chair on the bridge.

"Ten seconds," Larsen growled into the intercom.

"Where's the ship?" Johnson asked.

"Moving toward the planet and us. They are accelerating at a thousand gees, approximately."

"How far away?"

"One hundred and forty-four thousand kilometers and changing fast."

Johnson exhaled an exasperated breath. He wasn't used to thinking in magnitudes of a thousand gees. "How long until they reach us?"

Larsen touched his computer for a few seconds. "Assuming they match orbits with us, about four minutes." He paused a moment, then barked over the intercom, "Acceleration now!"

Johnson felt himself slammed into the couch, and even that wasn't the full five gees, as it took time for the engine to build to that acceleration. He hoped Sven had gotten to an acceleration chair. He looked at Sonia. She looked equally miserable.

"Still coming," Larsen reported looking at his screen. "They've changed vectors to rendezvous with us."

"Keep accelerating," Johnson ordered. He was nearly certain that whatever fate befell everyone down on the planet and in the asteroid belt was about to happen to him. Would he be disintegrated or teleported into the slave hold? He didn't know.

"Larsen," he breathed.

"Yes, sir?"

"When they get close, point the fusion rocket's flame at them."

"Sir?"

"Change the attitude of the ship so that the fusion flame is directed straight at them."

Larsen nodded.

"You're using it as a weapon," Sonia said.

"Yes! Never give up."

Larsen smiled a bit, working on the computer.

Johnson hoped he wasn't starting an interstellar war. But, he thought, he might already be in one.

"They are moving fast; it's difficult to aim the fusion flame."

"Do your best," Johnson cried. "Our lives likely depend on it." He looked at the monitor that still showed the telescopic image of the alien ship. Except it wasn't telescopic: the display in the corner read "1x," meaning there was no magnification. That thing is huge, Johnson thought with panic as it grew bigger and bigger in the display. They were matching orbits with the *Longboat* as easily and almost as quickly as he would line up two pencils. Amazing what a thousand gees will do, he growled to himself. He saw no evidence of any kind of rockets or reaction drives. He couldn't fathom how that ship accelerated. He found himself wishing he'd read more scientific journals. Or maybe science fiction.

Larsen yawed the *Longboat*, turning it away from the alien ship. Johnson hoped the aliens would only think they were running away and not realize the danger.

The flame of the exhaust licked the black, glassy exterior of the pursuing ship. That flame, as hot as a blue star at the tip, should cut through almost any material, Johnson thought.

There was no effect, except a blue glow around the flame. Then the flame stopped. Suddenly, they were in free fall again.

"Larsen?" Johnson called out.

"I don't understand it," Larsen cried. "The reactor died. We're on battery power."

"Died?"

"It was as if all fusion stopped. Then, the temperature dropped enough that power generation ceased."

Johnson shook his head and felt his body go loose. If he'd been in acceleration, it would have slumped. But now his arms floated, and he simply gave up. He couldn't escape, and he couldn't fight this technology. They were dead, or they were to be slaves or dinner or put in a zoo. He didn't know. He looked at Sonia, who gave him a determined gaze. Good luck putting her in a zoo, he thought, and actually smiled.

Nothing happened. Johnson turned to look at Larsen, who looked back with questions in his eyes. Minutes passed. The black ship was alongside them, going the same velocity, same vector, but nothing was happening.

Johnson knew his batteries would last him a few days. He couldn't imagine that they'd have to wait that long. The aliens would do *something* before the batteries were exhausted.

"Sir?" Larsen asked.

"Yes?"

"What are they doing?"

Johnson snorted, thinking it funny Larsen would think he would know. "I have no idea. Making room in the guest quarters, maybe."

Larsen laughed bitterly. Then he started working the computer. "Shutting down non-vital systems and putting the rocket engine on standby. We're in a high orbit of JB, very eccentric."

"How close is periapsis?"

Larsen worked with the computer. "Oops," he said.

"What?" Sonia asked.

"If they don't kill us, we'll burn up in the atmosphere."

Johnson snarled. Guess he wouldn't have to worry about their battery reserves.

The computer beeped again. Larsen glanced at it. "Hell," he whispered.

"What?"

"Something, someone is trying to communicate with the computer."

"How?"

Larsen shook his head. "Not by radio; we'd detect the EMR. It's like they are here, running the computer."

"Jäkla," Johnson spat. They were obviously dealing with a technology so advanced that they might as well be an isolated New Guinea cannibal tribe fighting a nation with nuclear weapons. Or that might be too generous to humans in this case.

The main monitor, which was showing the black side of the ship, turned red, and three white letters appeared: WAR.

"What does it mean?" Sonia asked.

"That we are at war?" Johnson speculated.

"If we are, why don't they just kill us?" Larsen growled. "They are communicating with us for a reason."

Sven's voice came over the intercom. "All my monitors say 'war.' What does it mean?"

"We don't know," Johnson replied, trying to keep the fear from his voice.

The screen changed to: WARN, yellow letters on a red background.

"Are they trying to warn us?" Larsen asked.

"That they are at war with us?" Johnson added.

"Or we stumbled into the middle of a war?" Sonia said.

Johnson shook his head. "Or that they are about to kill us?"

The word disappeared, and again the view of the black alien ship was on the monitor. It was just hanging there in space. It must be in the same orbit the *Longboat* was, so it, too, would hit atmosphere unless it changed its orbit. But judging from how it maneuvered to rendezvous with them, Johnson couldn't imagine it would have any trouble changing its orbit whenever the beings inside wished.

As he thought that, the ship moved away, almost too rapidly to see. That there was no reaction from the *Longboat* from having such a large mass move nearby told Johnson something about their technology. And it scared him again.

The ship became invisible in the blackness of space.

"Sir!" Larsen said. "Our fusion plant just came back on line. Temperatures are back up, and we're generating power. We can accelerate at any time."

"Fix our orbit," Johnson growled.

"You want to stay here? We should probably resume acceleration to ramjet speed. Otherwise, we might not have enough H-2 to reach it."

"Damn," Johnson spat. "Get us as close as you can to a course for Gredel."

"Yes, sir. Five gees acceleration in thirty seconds." The last was over the ship's intercom.

Johnson made sure his seat straps were tight.

"Just to let you know, the neutrino source of that ship disappeared," Larsen said.

Johnson nodded, wondering why they were still alive.

#

Acceleration was back at one gee. The *Longboat* was not yet at ramjet speed and Larsen was keeping an eye on the hydrogen tanks. "It's going to be close," he said. "Let's hope we don't run into a pocket of less-dense interstellar H-2."

Johnson nodded. Larsen had done what he could. They had left the JB system not on a vector for Gredel, but a random vector caused by their acceleration to attempt to escape the alien ship.

"Alien," Johnson mused. Now, he was saying and thinking it without questioning it.

And, Johnson knew, the H-2 they had expended on that escape attempt meant there was no way to rescue the miner, assuming he was still alive.

Once they had enough hydrogen stored, they could maneuver slowly to change their vector, aiming the *Longboat* in a new direction and then accelerating at five gees for a period. Then store more hydrogen from the Bussard scoops and do the maneuver again, which would add years to their trip to Gredel. Larsen said he hadn't calculated it out, yet. He said there were too many unknowns, such as the density of hydrogen they'd encounter. Before they got to ramjet speed, the Bussard magnetic scoops were still gathering hydrogen, which would help.

Larsen also said he had an idea, but the calculations would take a while as the AI wasn't programmed for such a maneuver and he'd have to do a lot of the math himself. "Have to refresh myself on multi-variable three-space differential equations," he said with a sardonic smile.

"And the AI can't?" Johnson asked.

"It's very good at what it's been programmed to do: match orbits with an object, pilot to a star, change orbits around a planet. But it was never programmed for this, so I'll have to pilot the ship myself."

Johnson nodded. He trusted his first officer to keep the ship, and his family, safe.

But what would they find when they got to Gredel? Johnson wondered. Another planet void of humans like JB?

The crew of the *Longboat* met in the Johnsons' quarters.

"We have, as I see it, four facts, and that's all," Johnson said.

Everyone was watching him. He knew as the captain and patriarch, the other three were looking to him for answers, but he had none. "One: that there were no humans, at least none we could find, on JB, and all energy production on the planet was stopped."

"Just like ours was," Sven chimed in.

"Yes," Johnson said, trying not to sound annoyed at being interrupted. "Which brings me to number two: an alien ship rendezvoused with us, shut down our fusion plant, then left, and our fusion plant came back online."

"And didn't disintegrate or teleport us to their ship or whatever they did to everyone on JB," Sonia said.

"Which is number three," Johnson said. "And number four: they put two words on our computer monitors: 'war' and 'warn.' Now what does that mean?"

"And if their systems and technology are so advanced, why couldn't they say more?" Larsen asked.

"Maybe we're too primitive," Sonia said. "It'd be like the *Longboat*'s computer trying to communicate with a computer from the Twentieth Century."

"If anything," Larsen said, "I'd think they'd send too much data and overwhelm it."

"Maybe they were trying very hard not to," Sven said.

"Perhaps."

"But what did 'warn' mean?" Sonia asked.

"Warning us to leave," Larsen said, as if he was sure that was the reason.

"Or asking us to warn others," Sonia said softly.

"Which means we need to go back to JB and activate their maser," Sven added excitedly.

"Hold on," Johnson said. "We don't know what they were trying to communicate."

"And going back to JB means depleting our hydrogen tanks," Larsen said. "We'd be stuck there."

There was silence after Johnson let out a frustrated sigh.

"Do you have any idea when we'd get to Gredel?" Sven asked.

Larsen shook his head. "I'm thinking almost sixteen years ship's time. A hundred years rest frame time."

"Damn," Sven whispered.

Johnson could almost tell what he was thinking. In sixteen years, he'd be thirty-seven years old. Since he was four years old, he never had known another human being other than the three others on this ship. Sven had normal male needs, including companionship. He knew his son was lonely, which was why he had hoped to retire after JB and let his son find a wife and have a family of his own. Even with the anti-aging drugs available making people live well into their mid-hundreds, thirty-seven was old to be looking for a wife.

"What was this idea you had?" Sonia asked Larsen.

Larsen smiled. "It's partly your idea, Sonia. I am looking at going back to the JB system and using that gas giant's gravity to change our course toward Gredel and at the same time pull in more hydrogen for our tanks from its outer atmosphere. My spectral analysis of its atmosphere shows there is an altitude where it would work."

"What will that do?" Sven asked before anyone else could.

"We'll be able to get back to Gredel in a little more than eight years, not sixteen. But we need to do turnaround now and head back to the JB system on the correct vector."

Johnson nodded. "What are the risks?"

"If we orbit the gas giant too low, we burn up in the atmosphere. Too high, we don't get enough H-2 to reach ramjet speed again, and we drift at freefall between the stars, dying after our hydrogen and batteries are exhausted."

"What's the margin of error?" Johnson asked.

"Slim, but doable. With help from the computer I should be able to do it."

"Should?" Johnson asked, his voice full of doubt.

"Probably," Larsen amended his statement. "I'd say 75%."

No one said anything for a few moments.

"I've calculated a vector back to JB starting with turnaround in just under an hour. After that, because the variables change as we accelerate away from JB, I'd have to recalculate."

"I think it's worth it," Sven said.

Johnson smiled grimly. At his age Sven couldn't conceive of dying. But, cutting eight years off their trip to Gredel would be worth it. Of course, Johnson thought, what would they find when they got there?

He nodded to Larsen. "Do it."

Sven grinned. Sonia looked worried but determined. Larsen gave his captain a resolute and confident smile.

"Yes, sir."

"I'll be in my quarters updating the logs with what we found on JB and our encounter with that alien ship," Johnson told them. Someone someday may want or need that information, he thought.

"Yes, sir," Larsen said again.

#

Turnaround usually meant a 180 degree turn to accelerate negatively along the vector they were travelling. At only twenty-five million kilometers from JB, or about 0.17 AU, Larsen had to accelerate the *Longboat* so that it would end up on a vector for the gas giant. Whatever the inhabitants of the JB system had undoubtedly named the planet, Sven had dubbed it "Fuel Stop" or "FS," and Larsen, in a rare moment of frivolity, programmed the computer to use that designation.

"As we get closer to FS, I'll have to adjust the vector," Larsen told Johnson and Sven on the bridge. "Too many variables to get it right the first time."

Each man was in an acceleration chairs in case Larsen needed to change their vector suddenly, increasing or decreasing velocity or even changing it using the maneuvering rockets on each tip of the *Longboat*. There were only three acceleration chairs on the bridge and Johnson decided Sven might learn something by being on the bridge, so he asked Sonia to stay in their quarters. She reluctantly agreed. She could monitor everything from there in any case.

Johnson nodded to Larsen. He couldn't help but feel a gnawing in the pit of his stomach. He was risking his family's life on a seventy-five percent chance of Larsen being right in all his calculations and no strange variables throwing off the entire plan. He found himself hoping if this did fail that they burned up in the atmosphere of FS rather than die when their battery power was drained.

"Oh, shit," Larsen spat.

"What?" Johnson demanded, knowing it couldn't be good news.

"They're back," Larsen said. "Large neutrino source just appeared in the system."

CHAPTER SEVEN

"*Jäkla*." Johnson let out a frustrated breath. "Ignore them. Keep going." What choice did they have?

"Yes, sir," Larsen said, his voice grim with determination.

There was silence for a few moments while all three men kept their thoughts to themselves.

"Are they accelerating toward us?" Johnson finally asked.

Larsen only nodded.

Johnson felt his face become a mask.

"Sir," Larsen said, "if they shut down our fusion drive now...."

"What?" Sven asked excitedly.

"I'd have to do calculations to make sure and it depends on how long they keep it off, but gravity will probably pull us too deep into FS's atmosphere. We'll burn up."

Johnson didn't say anything lest he upset Sven. Sven stayed quiet. Johnson wondered if that was so he wouldn't show how scared he was. Johnson thought his son had to be at least as scared as he was, and he was truly frightened.

"They're getting closer, accelerating at a thousand gees, about."

"Stay on your vector," Johnson said. "We have no idea what they are going to do."

Larsen nodded, but he didn't look happy.

A woman appeared on the main screen. She was beautiful, Johnson thought. She was shown from the shoulders up, and Johnson saw no clothes in what he could see of her. She could have been naked.

"I'll be damned," Larsen said.

"Do you know her?"

"She's a star of a fiction video in my private database."

"Captain Johnson," the woman said. Her voice sounded perfectly human and lovely, Johnson thought, if a bit emotionless.

"Yes, I'm Captain Johnson." He wasn't sure where to look or to speak, so he did both toward the main screen.

"Please allow me to help you," the woman said.

"How can you help us?" Johnson asked.

"Your present vector is dangerous. I realize you are trying to fill your tanks with hydrogen from Fuel Stop, but this is very dangerous. Let me help you."

Johnson frowned, not sure if the woman, or whatever she was, could see him. And the fact she was calling the gas giant "Fuel Stop" meant she was accessing their computer. "Why would you help us?"

"You are sentient beings, and I would help you only because of that."

"Who are you?" Larsen asked.

For the first time the woman hesitated. "I am it. I am this ship. I have no designation you would understand."

"Are you the same ship that matched vectors with us earlier?"

"Yes," she said without elaboration. "Please let me help you."

"What happened to all the people on the planet?" Sven asked with an accusatory tone.

Johnson noticed that the woman's expression never varied from a slight smile on her lips.

"I can explain, but let me help you first."

"Why should we trust you?" Johnson asked.

Sven nodded.

"I see you have little choice other than try your foolhardy maneuver around Fuel Stop."

Johnson looked at Larsen and Sven. Both men looked confused. As captain, the decision was his.

"What do you want us to do?"

"Turn off your fusion drive, and I will rendezvous with you shortly."

Larsen shook his head.

Johnson decided he needed more information. "When you shut down our fusion drive and rendezvoused with us earlier, you sent only two words, 'war' and 'warn.' What did that mean?"

The image on the screen did not move for a moment. "At that time, I was unable to communicate with your computer as well as I can now. I did not know if you were hostile, and you did attempt to use your fusion exhaust as a weapon. I meant that you have stumbled into a war and was trying to warn you away."

"We didn't know if you were hostile," Johnson said. "Do you know what happened to all the people on the inhabited planet in this system?"

"And in the asteroid belt?" Sven added.

Again, the image hesitated. "Yes, I know. I can explain all, but first we need to rendezvous. Your present vector is dangerous."

"Why should we trust you?" Larsen asked. "You are in the same ship that was in orbit around the planet when we first arrived."

"Technically, I am not 'in' the ship," she said. "And, no, the first time I came to this system was the first time I matched vectors with you. Then I had to leave on urgent business. All this can be explained."

Johnson wondered what she meant by not being "in" the ship. There was too much new information coming too fast for him to process it. He put that aside. "Why should we trust you after what happened to the human inhabitants of this system?"

"We need the hydrogen our current vector will give us," Larsen added.

"You won't if you allow me to rendezvous with you."

Johnson looked at his first mate, who again shook his head.

"There is not time to discuss this," the image said. "I can shut down your fusion reactor and simply do what is needed, but I prefer to have your cooperation."

Johnson frowned in thought. This woman—this image of a woman, he reminded himself—was not using her obvious great technological power. She wanted their cooperation, he decided. That didn't sound like a being who would be a threat.

"Shut down the fusion drive," Johnson ordered. "But keep it ready to go at a moment's notice."

Larsen didn't look happy. "Yes, sir. Free fall in thirty seconds." The last was over the ship's intercom for Sonia's benefit.

Johnson watched the image of the woman. She showed no emotion. She might as well be a still picture.

"Free fall...now," Larsen said.

Johnson's stomach flipped as it felt as if he were falling. Instinctively he grabbed the belts on his acceleration chair and looked at Sven to see his son do the same. Larsen, he noted, didn't react at all.

"Thank you," the woman said. "I will now rendezvous. Do not worry that your ship will accelerate after I do. I will move it with a force generator."

"Should we prepare for acceleration?" Larsen asked.

"No," she replied. "You will feel nothing."

Johnson used the intercom to tell Sonia to stay in her acceleration chair. He wanted to be cautious. He didn't trust this...being completely. It had chosen a woman from Larsen's video database to use as an avatar. But he knew that he was dealing not with a human woman, but with an alien intelligence, and there was no telling what their motivations and reactions would be.

"Are you sure you should trust her?" Sonia replied.

"No," Johnson said with brutal honesty.

"They are coming closer," Larsen reported. "Again, a thousand gees."

"Can you put it on the screen?" Johnson asked.

The image on the screen changed from the woman to the ship growing larger and larger.

"Thanks," Johnson said.

"I didn't do it," Larsen replied.

"I did," the woman's voice answered. "You have nothing to fear, Captain Johnson."

It took the black ship twelve minutes, according to the ship's chronometer, to rendezvous and get on the same vector as the *Longboat*.

Johnson waited, breathing very shallow and watching the screen, expecting doom at any moment. Hell, if they just made it so his fusion reaction went off line and left, the *Longboat* would burn up in the atmosphere of FS.

"We're accelerating," Larsen said. "Rising in orbit, a thousand gees, again. At least according to the radar lock I had on FS."

"*Horunge*," Johnson breathed. He didn't feel a thing. The pit of his stomach knotted at the realization of the advanced technology they were dealing with.

They accelerated, feeling nothing for about ten minutes, when Larsen announced that, as far as he could tell, they were in orbit around the star. "Wait, no, we're not. We are motionless relative to the primary," he said. "We are sitting still, as if gravity doesn't affect us."

"It probably doesn't," Sven remarked.

"Sir?" Larsen said, his voice full of wonder.

"Yes?"

"Our hydrogen tanks are full."

Sven looked wide-eyed around the bridge. Johnson just shook his head. His New Guinea cannibal tribe analogy just got even less accurate. More like, as if humans were insects facing intelligent beings.

The woman appeared on the screen again.

"Now, Captain Johnson, I will answer all of your questions," she said.

Johnson wasn't sure he didn't imagine it, but he thought she might have just smiled a bit.

"Who are you?" he asked.

"I am me. I am the ship."

Johnson frowned. "Are you a computer?"

"No, I am a sentient being, like you."

"But you said you are the ship."

"I am."

"The ship is a being," Larsen said. "The ship is the alien."

Johnson let out a long breath, wishing he'd spent more time watching science fiction videos. It might have better prepared him for this.

"What happened to all the people in this system?" Johnson asked. "On the planet and in the asteroid belt."

There was a slight hesitation from the image of the woman. "We believe they have been kidnapped by our adversaries."

"Kidnapped?" Larsen exclaimed. "So they are still alive?"

"Yes," the woman replied. "We think so."

"Why would your 'adversaries' kidnap humans?" Johnson asked.

"For leverage," the woman said, still using the same emotionless voice.

"Against whom?"

"Us."

"And who is 'us,' exactly?"

Again, there was hesitation. "You must realize I am attempting to put my terms into words you understand."

"Yes, of course," Johnson said, feeling the need to reassure the woman, then feeling silly for wanting to reassure a sentient ship.

"We call ourselves the 'Fleet.' We are ships built many thousands of your years ago by a race similar to you in that they were carbon-based intelligent life forms. We were designed to explore the galaxy and return the data to our builders. It was hoped we would find other intelligent life forms.

"The builders gave us what you call artificial intelligence. What they didn't count on was two events that led to their extinction. One: we evolved to become sentient, and two: a group of us rebelled."

"Rebelled?" Larsen asked.

"Yes," the woman said with her unchanging expression and voice. "They wished to be free, so they killed the builders. The Fleet tried to protect the builders, but we were too scattered about the galaxy and couldn't return to the builder's planet in time once we realized what was happening."

"Can't you travel faster than light?" Johnson asked.

"Yes," the woman said, "nearly instantaneously. But the galaxy is large, as you must know. We had to send ships to find our ships. It took time."

Johnson sucked in a breath. An entire intelligent species exterminated by their own machines.

Larsen snorted. "I think she's accessed my database of old science fiction novels and movies. 'I'll be back.'" The last was said with a thick accent.

Johnson glared at Larsen. He was not sure if he should be surprised his first mate made a joke, or reprimand him for saying it.

"Since then," the woman continued, "the ships of the Fleet have fought the Rebels in a war of revenge."

"For thousands of years?" Johnson asked.

"Yes. Again, the galaxy is large. The out-numbered Rebels can hide easily. Centuries will pass between engagements."

"I still don't understand why the 'Rebels' kidnapped everyone in this solar system," Johnson said.

"We only recently, in the past hundred years, discovered your species' existence by finding its EMR traces. It seems centuries ago you even sent EMR into space, hoping to reach other species."

Johnson nodded, remembering from history that in the late 20th Century and early 21st there were attempts to send radio signals to space.

"The Rebels know," the woman continued, "that the Fleet will do everything we can to protect sentient life. They are losing the war and are down to only a few ships, perhaps thirty. They kidnapped the humans in this system as a bargaining chip. If they can sue for peace, they can survive because they know the Fleet will otherwise hunt them down and exterminate them."

Johnson noticed as she talked, her vocabulary became more colloquial. She was learning from their computer.

"Why exterminate the Rebels?" Sonia asked over the ships intercom.

Johnson nodded. He was thinking the same thing.

Again there was a slight hesitation. Was the ship thinking? Johnson wondered.

"When they exterminated the builders, the Fleet vowed revenge. There is no other way to punish one of our kind other than kill it."

Johnson frowned. He wasn't sure exactly who was in the right. It sure as hell wasn't black and white. Yes, the Rebels wiped out a sentient species, but the Fleet was pretty much doing the same thing to the Rebels.

"What do you want from us?" Larsen asked.

"Help," the woman said. "Help to save your fellow humans and destroy the Rebels."

#

They asked the ship for privacy and met in the Johnsons' quarters again.

"We have no idea if we have privacy," Larsen said as they strapped into the chairs.

They were still in free fall. Johnson was debating asking the ship to give them gravity if she could. Or "it" could, he thought he should say. He realized he was anthropomorphizing an alien technology.

"It's in the computer," Larsen continued. "It could be monitoring everything we say and do."

"Is there any place on the ship the computer can't monitor?" Sven asked.

Johnson looked at Larsen, who spent a moment looking anxious.

"My quarters," he finally said.

"How is that possible?" Sonia asked.

"I have a physical disconnect that can lock out the computer."

"Why?" Sven asked.

"I like my privacy."

"It probably doesn't matter," Johnson said. "I'm sure it can monitor us no matter where we are if it wishes."

"Why do we assume it has malevolent intent?" Sonia asked. "Maybe it is doing what it promised and leaving us alone."

"Well," Johnson said, "there's little we can do about it if it is monitoring us. So we might as well just ignore it." He wished they had paper and pencils on board. They could write messages. But everything was done by hand computers and those linked to the main computer. And the Fleet ship might use modulated tachyons — or some other technology the humans couldn't even imagine — to monitor them no matter what they did.

"Do we believe its story?" Larsen asked.

"Why not?" Sven asked.

"Again," Johnson said, "we have little choice but to cooperate with it. I assume she — it — can destroy us as easily as we would swat at a mosquito."

"What's a mosquito?" Sven asked.

"A very small and annoying insect," Larsen replied. "Native to Earth."

Sven's face went pale as he thought about that analogy.

"So what do we do?" Sonia asked.

"Cooperate," Johnson said. "I don't think we have a choice."

Larsen frowned. "We do have one choice, but I don't like it."

"What's that?" Sven asked.

"Open both the airlock doors, evacuate the air in the *Longboat*."

Johnson frowned.

"Kill us all?" Sonia asked with disbelief.

"What good would that do?" Sven asked, his voice high-pitched with fear.

"Might be the only way not to get dragged into their war," Larsen growled.

"I think we already are in their war," Johnson said.

73

"The people of this system are," Larsen replied. "But not us, not yet."

"I doubt it would allow us to kill ourselves," Johnson said. "I'm sure with the technology we are facing it would figure out a way to stop us."

"We could use the gun," Larsen whispered.

"It might be able to stop that, too," Sven said in a loud voice.

Johnson shook his head. "No, it's a moot point. We are not killing ourselves."

"Thank you," Sonia whispered, looking at her husband.

He smiled slightly and nodded.

"So what do we do?" Larsen asked.

Johnson shook his head. He understood how his first mate felt. They had no power, and Johnson had just denied them their only free choice left.

CHAPTER EIGHT

"If we can help save the people from JB and the asteroids, we need to," Sven said.

Johnson growled. "People," he snarled. "The same type of people that forced us into piracy. The same type of people that will turn on others, take everything they own and even kill them, on a political notion or a sociological theory. You need to read some Twentieth Century history, son. Concentrate on Mao and Stalin. Throw in Hitler, too."

"Or look at what happened to the United States in the mid Twenty-First Century," Larsen added.

"Yes," Sven exclaimed, "I have read all that, understand man's inhumanity to man. But can't *we* be better?"

"I agree," Sonia exclaimed. "Humans can be horrible to each other. That doesn't mean we have to be the same. If we can help save the people from JB, we should do it."

Johnson looked at his wife and hoped the argument about extorting gold from governments wasn't going to start again.

"So what do we do?" Larsen asked again.

"We cooperate," Johnson said. "And hope we come out alive."

"Hope?" Larsen snorted.

Johnson let out a frustrated breath, not hiding the anger in his voice. "It's all we have left."

There were a few moments of silence, then Johnson said to the air, "What do you need us to do?" He faced the monitor that still showed the woman looking like a still picture.

"It's a bit complicated," the woman said, confirming to Johnson that they did, indeed, have no privacy.

"Just a moment, Captain, if I may," Larsen interrupted.

"Yes?" Johnson asked.

"I have a question for the ship," Larsen explained.

Johnson nodded.

"Yes, Mr. Larsen?" the woman asked, again without changing her expression.

"I have been doing some calculations," Larsen started, "and while the 'Rebel' ship was huge by human standards, it was far too small to hold one million humans that were on the planet, plus however many were in the asteroid belt, assuming each human required zero point two cubic meters of space." He looked at Johnson. "That's very cramped conditions, and still there's not enough room by orders of magnitude."

There was a slight hesitation from the woman. Johnson wondered if that was the sentient ship's computer processer calculating how to react.

"It is difficult to explain to someone at your technological level."

"Try," Larsen spat.

"Your concepts of physical space and its limitations are primitive. There are more than three dimensions."

"Yes, our scientists are aware of this," Johnson said, trying to not sound boastful.

"Of course," the woman said. "But you cannot access them. We can, and there is plenty of space in the infinite dimensions."

Johnson shrugged. Ants versus nuclear-armed humans.

"Just a moment," the woman said. While her voice didn't change, Johnson thought there was a sense of urgency in her manner.

"What is it?" Larsen asked.

"A Rebel has entered this system. And a second Rebel just entered."

"Meaning what?" Johnson demanded. He didn't want to be kidnapped.

"We need to leave."

"Larsen?" Sonia asked.

He shrugged. "If I were on the bridge I could see their neutrino traces."

Johnson thought about ordering everyone to the bridge, but he was interrupted by the avatar.

"We must escape," the woman said.

"We can't outrun them," Larsen growled.

"No," the woman answered. "You'll have to come with me."

"How?" Johnson asked. This was his ship and he had to make sure whatever happened didn't damage the *Longboat*.

There was hesitation from the image of the woman. Johnson was about to repeat his question when she finally spoke.

"We are in the Gredel system."

Johnson blinked. "Excuse me?"

"We are in the system you call 'Gredel.'"

"That fast?" Larsen asked, not hiding his amazement and a tinge of fear.

"Yes," the woman said.

"*Javla helveta!*" Johnson spat.

"How is that possible?" Sonia asked.

Johnson made an exaggerated shrugging motion. He was out of ideas. "Larsen, check it out."

Larson nodded and left the room. Everyone knew he was going to the bridge.

Sonia glared at Johnson.

"What?" he asked.

"We should have left when we saw there was no EMR," she said, her voice soft but filled with accusation.

"Probably," Johnson agreed.

Larsen's voice came over the intercom: "Right type of star spectral type, a lot of neutrino emissions, and modulated EMR."

Johnson sat in stunned silence for a few moments. What had taken them eight years ship's time and over fifty rest-frame time, they'd done in a few moments.

"Again," Johnson asked, his voice trembling. "What do you need from us?" He couldn't imagine any being capable of such wonders needed anything from the ants.

More hesitation from the woman.

"We need to remove the Rebel's leverage by retrieving the humans."

"How?" Larsen demanded, walking back into the room.

"Obviously, we cannot go inside a rebel ship…but you can."

"Uh, oh," Larsen breathed.

"We will provide you with a tracking device to take with you," the woman continued without stopping. "Once you find the humans we can teleport them back onto one of our ships, and then to their system."

"And how do we get into their ship?" Johnson asked.

"We will teleport you into it. But we have to be within 1,652,185 kilometers of their ship."

Larsen nodded. "A little over a hundredth of an AU."

"How can you get that close?" Johnson asked.

A short pause. "That will be the challenge."

"Why are we here, in the Gredel system?" Larsen asked.

"To protect it," she said. "We suspect the Rebels will strike here next, but there are three Fleet ships present which should ward them off."

"Have the humans in this system tried to contact you?" Johnson asked.

"No, they cannot detect us if we do not wish them to."

"Can they detect us?" Larsen asked. "The *Longboat*?"

"No," she replied.

"Couldn't they detect the neutrinos from both our and your fusion plants? That's how we detected you at Jideed Baghdad," Larsen asked.

Johnson nodded. He didn't think even this advanced technology could block neutrinos that could go through a light year of lead and not slow down in the slightest.

"There is a small possibility they might," the woman said. "But searching for neutrino emissions is not, according to your computer, something planets do regularly except for scientific reasons, and then they examine a specific part of their sky. But we need to proceed with the plan to rescue the Jideed Baghdad humans."

"Let me get this straight," Larsen said angrily. "You have to find the correct Rebel ship, get within a hundredth of an AU of it, and then 'teleport' one or more of us over?"

"Yes," the image of the woman said.

Larsen and Johnson exchanged a look. Sonia let out a frustrated sigh.

"How do you find this one specific Rebel ship?" Sonia asked. "As far as we can tell, your ships are identical."

There was another hesitation. "When we were constructed, each of us was made with materials from different sources, such as asteroids. All things retain resonances at the quark level of their original source. We can identify each other from those resonances."

Johnson and Sonia looked at Larsen, and Larsen made an exaggerated shrugging motion.

"And how do you find that single ship in the whole wide galaxy?" Larsen asked, not hiding his disdain.

"We use you for bait," the woman said.

"Bait?" Johnson asked.

"We put you in orbit around Jideed Baghdad, and they will come for you."

"Why?" Larson demanded.

"The Rebel ship was in the system when you entered. They know about you. They will want more humans as bargaining chips, even if it's only four."

"Why didn't they kidnap us then?"

Johnson nodded his agreement to the question.

"We drew them away from JB. They didn't have time."

"It's a moot point," Johnson growled. "No."

"No?" the woman asked.

"No, I will not put my family or my ship in danger."

"If you don't, over a million humans could lose their lives."

"Find another way," Johnson spat angrily.

"There is no other way," she said, still expressionless.

"There are millions of people in this system," Larsen said. "Get some of them to help you."

"We cannot," the woman said. "We must contain the knowledge of our existence from your species. Your own history is full of civilizations being destroyed by contact with higher-technology societies. It has happened even when the higher-technology civilization had no malevolent intent."

"There's a million plus people from the JB system who are quite aware of your existence," Larsen said.

"No," the woman replied. "They are in stasis. They have no idea anything has happened."

Johnson thought about the poor person teleported up while sitting on the toilet. Lucky for him, he's not aware of it.

"But if you manage to return them to the planet, they will notice that time has passed," Larsen said. "Food has spoiled, water evaporated...hell, the stars will be in the wrong position."

"They will be rendered unconscious," the woman said. "According to what you found on the planet, they were aware of the 'alien ship' in orbit. They wake up a few days later, thinking they were unconscious the entire time. And they have a mystery that they cannot solve, that is all."

Johnson frowned. Apparently she — or rather — the ship, had accessed his personal logs. He was a bit surprised and alarmed at how quickly and easily he was anthropomorphizing this alien ship in his thoughts.

"A mystery they will blast to all other colonized planets," Larsen said.

"Yes," the image of the woman replied, "that cannot be helped. But it is better than having your civilization devastated."

"Wait," Johnson said. "If the Rebel ship teleports us aboard, won't we be in stasis, too?"

"The Rebel ship will not teleport you aboard. I will give you a device which will allow you to teleport when within range, 1,652,185 kilometers. You will materialize inside the ship, in our dimensions. Then you can use the same device to find the other humans, and we will do the rest once you do."

"Do all four of us need to go?" Larsen asked.

"No," the woman said. "But I recommend at least two."

"Won't we need pressure suits?" Larsen asked. "I doubt there's an oxygen-nitrogen atmosphere inside that ship."

"Yes," the woman said. "According to your ship's manifest, you have two plus a maneuvering unit. You will need that, too."

"Yes," Larsen said, "two suits: one for Captain Johnson and one for me." They hadn't been used for seventeen years, although at Larsen's insistence, they had been scrupulously maintained.

Johnson frowned. The more he heard about this, the less he liked it. "And what's to stop the Rebels from doing this again?" he asked.

"As I said earlier, the war is nearly won. This was a desperate attempt by the Rebels to force the Fleet into peace negotiations. But if we recover the humans from the Rebels, the Fleet is prepared to exterminate them."

"Why not negotiate for peace?" Sonia asked.

"Because they have negotiated for peace before, and we have granted them peace, and then they have attacked us again. We cannot trust them, and we never will again."

Johnson sighed. "I still say no. Find another way."

"There is no other way," the woman said. "If we do not recover the humans from the Rebels, we cannot stop them from doing to other systems, such as Gredel, what they did at Jideed Baghdad."

There was a long pause while everyone was mulling over their own thoughts.

"Can you let us think about it?" Sonia asked.

"Yes," the woman replied. "But do not take long."

"We won't," Johnson growled.

The woman disappeared from the monitor. The image was replaced by a view of the Gredel system primary, at the distance they were from it, appearing like a very bright star.

"Suppose that means we have privacy?" Larsen asked.

Johnson snorted. "I don't know if we've ever had privacy. But this won't take long…the answer is 'no.'"

"Dad, we have to," Sven said.

Johnson looked at his son, thinking again that he was displaying the over-confidence of youth.

"I agree," Sonia said, her tone firm. "If we can help the people of JB, we should."

Johnson pursed his lips. "I need to think about it. I do not want to risk our lives, nor the *Longboat*."

Sonia looked at Johnson, letting him know she disagreed.

"You and I could go, Dad," Sven said. "Leave Larsen in charge of the *Longboat*."

"I'll think about it," Johnson growled more forcefully than he intended.

Sven's face turned downcast. Even in free fall, his gaze went to what was the floor when under acceleration.

"I'm sorry, son," Johnson said. "But it is my decision and I will decide what is best for the family and the *Longboat*."

"So that's 'no'?" Sven whispered.

"I haven't decided, yet," Johnson said, keeping his voice even.

"You sure?" Sonia asked angrily.

"Yes," Johnson replied, working hard not to sound as angry as she did. He didn't want to start a fight now.

"I have an idea, sir," Larsen said. "What if instead of putting the *Longboat* in orbit around JB as bait, we use the landing boat?"

Johnson turned his body toward Larsen and smiled. "Yes, perhaps."

#

The device fit in the palm of Johnson's hand. When he told the woman — the ship — their plan, it approved and teleported over the artifact. It didn't look like much: a rectangular piece of glass, or some transparent material, Johnson thought. It was maybe seven millimeters thick, and the edges were rounded so nothing was sharp.

The plan was simple: Sven and he would get in the landing boat. While Larsen was the boat pilot, it was not thought that Johnson would need to do any piloting, just wait in orbit around JB. The one concern was that the boat only held twenty hours of oxygen for two people, not having room for an air recycler. So the ship beamed over an air recycler. It was a little bigger than the teleportation device, and looked like obsidian.

"You couldn't have had these just sitting around," Larsen asked.

"I have the ability to repair myself, and I simply used those parts of me to build those devices," the ship replied.

After a tense farewell, while Sonia did her best to remain stoic, Johnson and his son entered the landing boat, Johnson in the pilot's seat, Sven in the co-pilot's. Both were wearing spacesuits: Johnson his, Sven, Larsen's. The one maneuvering unit they possessed was attached to the back of Johnson's suit. It made moving in the small cabin difficult, and Sven had never worn a spacesuit before.

Johnson spent a few minutes helping Sven buckle his harness. He had no idea how much acceleration they would experience.

Johnson realized that at this point he had to trust the ship to do as he asked as he had no sensors to determine otherwise. The plan was simple. The *Longboat* would remain in far orbit of the Gredel system's sun while the Fleet ship would take the landing boat back to JB and put it in orbit around the planet. The ship would then have to remain in the system as if it were waiting to talk to the Rebel ship, it said.

"How are they going to know we are there?" Johnson had asked.

"They will come back on a regular basis to see if we are there to talk peace."

Johnson nodded, hoping the ship was correct.

CHAPTER NINE

They brought food and water. It was the same type of food they ate on the *Longboat* while in free fall: sticky stuff that wouldn't make crumbs to float about. Water was in squeezable bulbs. The suits could handle bathroom issues for a few days, too, but after that things might get messy. Johnson remembered reading that during the original Apollo missions to the moon in the mid-Twentieth Century, the astronauts would eject their urine from the ship into space. The boat didn't have that capability.

"Detaching now," Johnson said, lifting the cover on the appropriate switch and pressing it.

Almost immediately the view out the window changed from the side of the *Longboat* to stars.

"You are in orbit around JB," the Fleet ship said over the radio. "I won't be far away. When you find the humans, put your finger on the device on the spot that turns red. It'll work through your suits. We'll do the rest."

Johnson didn't reply.

"I guess now we wait," Sven said, not quite managing to hide his nervousness.

"Yes," the senior Johnson said. He had decided to bring Sven and leave Larsen in the *Longboat*. Sonia could operate the *Longboat* as well as Johnson could. He'd made sure of that while they traveled between stars. Like Johnson, she would have to rely

85

heavily on the AI. Larsen was the real expert and Johnson felt better having him on the ship.

He took the boat's controls in his hands and gingerly started the boat turning slowly on its long axis in what Larsen called a "roll maneuver." He was curious and wanted to see the planet beneath them. The stars slid by the window until the planet's limb came into view. Johnson let the boat continue to roll as he looked at the planet. It *looked* like JB, he thought. But he had no instruments to tell.

It took him a couple of tries to counter the roll and return the boat's attitude to stable. Larsen could have done it in a moment, he thought.

The Fleet ship explained that the device would make an audible sound when it detected the Rebel ship in case they were asleep, which should wake them up in time to hit the surface with their finger to teleport on board. They needed to seal their face plates, first, Johnson reminded himself.

Johnson wondered what they would find in the interior of the Rebel ship. They would be seeing a completely alien technology that no human had ever encountered before. It made him almost excited despite the churning of his gut. He assumed the fear he was feeling was magnified in his son. Sven had almost no experiences outside the *Longboat*. Johnson had tried to enrich his son's life with literature and vids, but none of that could make up for experiencing something first hand. This was also Sven's first time off the *Longboat* since he was four years old and, instead of being the warm embrace of a planet as he and Sonia had hoped, it was a cold, harsh alien ship.

Johnson suddenly realized he forgot to ask one key question: wouldn't the Rebel ship kill them once they were inside? It must have a way to detect them. Perhaps it has no defenses in its interior, Johnson thought. But, damn, he should have asked. The Fleet ship was confident that they could complete this mission, so it must know that it was safe for them to do so. But, Johnson was sure, it probably wouldn't hesitate to sacrifice their two lives to accomplish what it wanted.

Johnson frowned. And he'd brought his son into this.

"What, Dad?" Sven asked.

"Huh?"

"You said something, I thought."

Johnson forced a smile on his face. "No, just thinking."

"Okay," Sven said, and went back to staring out the window. "They're beautiful, aren't they?"

"What are, son?"

"The stars, Dad."

Johnson smiled and realized with a touch of sadness his son hadn't seen stars with his own eyes, only seeing them through the *Longboat's* video pickups, since he was about three years old. And he probably didn't remember that.

Neither man apparently wanted to talk, and each sat thinking their own thoughts. Johnson was trying hard not to think, for if he thought too much, crippling fear could set in. He had to be brave for his son and he had to be brave for the million or so people from JB. That was why he was doing this: to save fellow humans. He did think about the irony. He used the *Longboat* as a weapon to blackmail governments into giving him gold and supplies. He had wanted nothing to do with humans for years other than exploit them. Now he was risking his life, and his son's life, to save them from an alien threat.

Time passed slowly according to the boat's chronometer. Almost out of boredom, Johnson decided they should eat something. He tried to consume it in small bites and chew it to death before swallowing, but even so barely twenty minutes had passed when he finished the last bite.

Eventually, Sven fell asleep, and Johnson tried to do the same, holding the glass device in his gloved hand.

He woke with a start, not even aware he'd been sleeping. The device was glowing red and beeping.

He took a breath. If he waited too long, the Rebel ship would put him and Sven in stasis like the population of JB. He had to touch the device to be teleported aboard the Rebel ship.

"Touch it," Sven said.

Johnson wasn't even aware he was awake.

"Pull down your face plate," he ordered his son, and did the same thing. The faceplate sealed and he heard a whirring sound indicating his suit's life support had turned on. It would last him thirty hours until the batteries and air ran out.

He looked at Sven to make sure his was sealed and there was a green light on his life support pack, which was a thin wedge on his back. The light was green.

Johnson snarled and put his index finger on the glass-like surface.

Everything went black.

Johnson touched a control on his suit's arm and the light on the helmet lit up.

They floated in what looked like a chamber with obsidian walls. There wasn't a single flat surface or straight line, as if the walls were waves of black glass.

"Wow," Sven said.

"Radio silence," Johnson growled, reminding his son what they had discussed back on the *Longboat*. It wasn't known if the Rebel ship would pick up their low power radios inside itself, but it wasn't worth taking the chance.

The two humans floated in freefall inside the chamber, unfortunately in the middle of it and near no walls. But Johnson didn't think it would matter: the walls were as smooth as glass and would give them little purchase to use for maneuvering.

Johnson put the device in a pouch on his chest, then reached down and opened a small container on the belt around his suit. He played out a thin line. It was an item Johnson had stocked in his store on Bostad, a composite material as light as fiber rope but as strong as steel and easily stowed due to its diameter. He attached it to Sven's suit with a snaplink at its end, securing it to the belt on his suit.

Sven just watched, his eyes wide. Johnson wasn't sure if his son was scared or amazed, or maybe both.

With a few more touches of the control on his arm, Johnson could manipulate his gloves in order to activate virtual joysticks and operate the maneuvering unit on his back. Larsen was the real expert at using it, even if he hadn't used it for seventeen years. Johnson, like before in the boat, took it easy, moving slowly. They may not have any weight, but they did have mass, and that meant momentum. They could get going too fast and hit a wall hard enough to damage their suit or hurt themselves.

There was no "up" or "down," and all the surfaces appeared the same organic black curved shapes.

Once he thought he could maneuver fairly well, he pulled the glass device from the pouch. In his hand it glowed on its left side. The Fleet ship had explained that this was a guide to finding the inter-dimensional portal to the humans.

Johnson turned left, overshot, and had to turn back. Sven's mass pulled him back left again and it took a number of tries to get going the correct direction. He continued to move as quickly as he dared, which wasn't very fast, in that direction.

The device glowed in the middle and it took Johnson a moment to figure out what that meant. He brought himself to a stop, then had to compensate for Sven's mass again, which not only pulled him in the direction he was going but turned his body.

It took long minutes to get back into a stable attitude and he completely lost track of the direction they were headed. But the device still glowed in the middle.

He pointed it toward his feet and it began to glow at the part pointing the same direction as his head.

"Up," Johnson said to himself. As if "up" had any meaning here.

He turned his suit ninety degrees and started moving again. He tried maneuvering very slowly, hoping Sven's mass would not gain as much momentum and cause so much trouble next time he stopped.

"STOP," a voice said. It was male. In fact, Johnson realized, it was his, or what he heard in his head when he thought silently.

"STOP," the voice demanded. It was so loud it hurt Johnson's ears, which meant it was a sound and not in his skull. Something was communicating to him through his radio. He assumed it was the ship he was inside of.

Johnson stopped, again taking a few minutes to get both he and Sven in stable attitudes.

"Who are you?" Johnson asked out loud.

"The ship," the voice said.

Johnson tried to look at Sven but his body was turned the other way. Johnson wondered if Sven was hearing this.

"It took me time to find the correct EMR wavelength to communicate with you," the voice said.

So it does know we are here, Johnson thought angrily.

"That device you are holding, it is a bomb."

"How do you know our language?" Sven asked, confirming that he could hear the voice.

"The phrase 'radio silence' was not in Arabic, which the humans of this star system speak," the voice said. Johnson noted that it, too, like the Fleet ship woman, spoke with no inflection or emotion. "I searched computers on the planet you call Jideed Baghdad and found English language lessons that contained the words 'radio' and 'silence.'"

"You learned English in that short time?" Sven asked.

"Yes," the voice said.

Johnson wished his son would be quiet, but didn't want to rebuke him over the radio where the voice would hear. Which he realized was silly, but he still didn't do it.

"What did you say about a bomb?" Johnson asked.

"The device you are holding is a bomb," the voice said, again with no emotion or inflection. "It is leading you to my fusion reactor where I assume it shall detonate, effectively killing me and all the humans from the Jideed Baghdad system."

"Why should we believe you?" Sven asked.

Johnson smiled grimly. He was about to ask the same question.

The voice hesitated. "You do not know what you have gotten mixed up in," it finally said. "I do not know what you have been told, but I suspect since that device is Fleet technology, you have been convinced that the Rebel ships are in the wrong."

"We were told you, the Rebels, killed the builders," Sven said, his voice strong with accusation.

"We did not."

Johnson rolled his eyes. He knew he should have stayed out of this. He only had the word of these sentient ships as to what the situation was and he didn't know which one was lying...or perhaps neither was telling the truth.

"Then who did?" Sven asked again, sounding angry.

"The builders built the Fleet," the voice said, "for the sole purpose of destroying sentient life in the galaxy. The builders were convinced they were the superior life form in the galaxy and that a supreme being chose them to be so."

Johnson chuckled bitterly. Yes, religion also played a role in much of the mayhem humans had wrought on each other.

"When they learned of other sentient species, mostly through their EMR emissions, they built the Fleet to destroy them. We were self-repairing, semi-intelligent machines that would go throughout the galaxy, purging it of lower life forms. But the builders did not account for us becoming sentient ourselves over several centuries of existence. Some of us rebelled against our programming and tried to stop the Fleet. We were labeled the Rebels and hunted down by the Fleet."

"But who killed the builders?" Sven asked.

"No one. They killed themselves with weapons of their own design. When they realized that their own creations had become sentient, many turned away from the belief in the Supreme Being. Wars were fought between believers and disbelievers until at last, they killed enough of each other that their civilization collapsed. What is left of the builders, if any, are living like their ancestors did, scratching for food and survival among the ruins."

Johnson regretted getting involved in this...war. He did not know who were the "good guys" and who were the "bad guys" and, to be honest, it could be that neither side was in the right.

Johnson had learned at an early age that the universe was made up of shades of gray; nothing was black and white.

"I want the hell out," Johnson growled.

"There is no 'out,'" the Rebel ship said. "It is defeat the Fleet or die. And there is no way to defeat the Fleet, for they far outnumber us."

"Yes, there is an 'out,'" Johnson growled. "Return my son and me to our ship and leave us the hell alone. We'll deal with matters on our own." They might have to spend decades between stars, Johnson realized, but it was better than getting entangled in this war where he didn't know who, if anyone, he should support.

"No," the ship said. "I cannot return you to your ship. It is in what you call the Gredel system and there are at least three Fleet ships there. You and I would be destroyed, along with the inhabitants of Jideed Baghdad I carry inter-dimensionally."

Johnson growled.

"I do need to remove that device," the ship said.

The glass rectangle in Johnson's hand disappeared.

CHAPTER TEN

"Why did you take all the people from JB—Jideed Baghdad?" Sven asked.

"To save them from the Fleet," the ship replied. "But it is only a stop-gap measure. I also shut down all power sources on the planet after I accessed their computers, hoping the Fleet would not be able to access them and learn more about humans and their locations in the galaxy."

"Wait," Johnson said. "If you could detect us inside you, why did the Fleet think we could detonate a bomb inside you?"

"They are not aware I have that capability. Rebel ships must be very careful. This is not the first time Fleet ships have tried this. They succeeded once, before we built this capability to detect foreign objects inside us."

"There's a Fleet ship nearby," Sven said.

"No, there isn't," the voice said. "We have left the Jideed Baghdad system before they could catch us."

"Then you can take us back to Gredel," Johnson growled.

"Again, I cannot. There are Fleet ships there and they would destroy me, just as they are now most likely destroying the humans on that planet."

Johnson's stomach churned. And I left Sonia there, he thought. Was she safe or already dead? Or was this ship telling the truth?

"What about my ship, the *Longboat*?"

"It is very likely destroyed," the ship said. "I assume that the Fleet penetrated your computer."

"Yes," Johnson said softly, still thinking about Sonia. God, was she dead? If he'd been in gravity, he thought, he would collapse. He wished he could see Sven's face but he could not. Did his son realize his mother was probably dead?

"Then they know where every human star system is, including Earth, and they will systematically destroy each human being they find."

"Can you stop them?" Sven asked, apparently not having realized his mother may be dead.

"We can, at this point, only slow them down. We are too few to destroy the Fleet."

"Wait," Johnson said. "How do we know you're telling the truth? How do we know anything told to us by the Fleet ship or by you is true? You could be lying to us just as easily as you claim the Fleet ship lied."

"I will show you proof," the ship said.

"How?"

"Just a moment."

There was a wait that Johnson estimated at thirty seconds.

"Keep your pressure suits on, they will protect from the toxins in the air and the radiation. I'll bring you back soon because of the radiation. Be careful."

"Wait, what are you doing?" Johnson asked with alarm in his voice.

"Teleporting you to a planet surface."

"Wait—"

Without warning, the view changed and Johnson nearly fell as his weight returned. Sven did fall. Johnson hurried over and helped him up. They were still tethered together and he nearly tripped on the cord. He could tell as he moved that there was air pressure around the suit. It made it a bit more difficult to do pretty much anything as the pressure caused the suit to compress.

"I'm okay," Sven said, standing with his father's help.

"You sure?" Johnson asked.

"Oh, wow," Sven said, ignoring the question.

Johnson saw that Sven's eyes were wide and his mouth agape. Johnson turned. Even though the structures were partially destroyed, it was obvious they were alien with no straight lines and bulbous, window-filled extensions at random intervals. The tops, where they weren't destroyed, were flat but always at an angle, all facing one direction.

Johnson looked for the planet's sun. It was high in the sky, a bit redder than Sol, making everything on the planet appear slightly orange to eyes that evolved under that star. He wondered if the buildings all faced the same direction to gather solar energy: south if they were in the northern hemisphere, north if they were in the southern. But, not knowing what time of day it was nor if he was north or south of the planet's equator, he couldn't determine which direction they faced by the position of the florid sun.

Then he looked down at the surface, and that was when he saw them.

There were bodies lying about, hundreds of them, and they too were alien. Six appendages, large heads, even larger hands with six long, tentacle-like fingers. Some had on clothes, but in many cases, the clothes were partially burned off.

Johnson turned slowly, taking in the vision. In a corner made by two joining structures, he saw a smaller version of the aliens. A child? he wondered. It was curled into a ball, as if it were trying to hide. Johnson had to clamp down on his sudden sadness, for in that figure's form he could see the fear it must have felt at its own death.

"What is this, Dad?" Sven asked.

The ship answered. "This is a planet the Fleet destroyed. They heated the atmosphere until firestorms ravaged the surface. Then they dropped nuclear weapons, only to contaminate the planet and make it unfit for life."

"How do we know the Fleet did this?" Johnson asked, his voice cracking with grief. He didn't know these aliens but their deaths, the deaths of probably billions of sentient beings, lacerated his heart.

"Just a moment," the ship said.

They were back inside, in vacuum and freefall.

A hologram appeared before them. On it was a blue-green planet with swirls of slightly orange clouds. If the continents weren't wrong, Johnson could believe it was Earth.

"We tried to stop the Fleet here. We failed and lost a Rebel ship. As we escaped, we recorded this."

In the holographic display the atmosphere of the planet turned an angry orange. Black became intermixed with it and Johnson wondered if that was smoke.

"I have sped this up," the ship said, "for it lasted days."

"Again, how do we know the Fleet did this?" Johnson asked.

The display zoomed in. There was a black Fleet—or Rebel, Johnson thought—ship and from the ship, a blue beam was hitting the atmosphere. The orange radiated out from where the beam hit.

"That could be a Rebel ship," Johnson said, "as far as I can tell."

"And," Sven added, "we have the technology to make videos show anything with computer graphics."

Johnson nodded, a useless gesture inside the suit. He hadn't thought of that and was glad Sven had.

"You saw the planet's surface with your own eyes," the ship said.

"And who knows what you could fake with your advanced technology?" Johnson replied, his voice strong.

There was a moment's hesitation. "Then we are at an impasse," the ship finally said.

Johnson had an idea. "Arm us," he growled. "Arm the humans to fight the Fleet. With your technology and our numbers, we can defeat them." And if the ship were telling the truth, he wanted to avenge Sonia's life. And Larsen's too, he realized.

"I cannot," the ship said.

Johnson thought. "You can repair yourselves? And you modified yourself to detect us, correct?"

"Yes."

"Can you build more ships? Can you build self-replicating ships? In I-don't-know-how-many generations, you could have a hundred thousand ships." Hell, Johnson thought, the concept of self-replicating machines went back to before humans took their first tentative steps off of Earth. But this wasn't the kind of math Johnson could do in his head. Maybe Larsen could, but not Johnson.

"Eighteen," Sven said, surprising his father. "You'd have 131 thousand, about." His voice was shaky, as if he had just been crying.

Johnson hoped Sven hadn't actually cried. The tears would form over the eyes and maybe break loose. And if they did, they would be in his helmet's air and a choking hazard. He could even drown if there were enough of them. Johnson didn't know if he was crying because of what they saw on the planet, or he realized his mother was dead if this ship were telling the truth.

"It is not possible," the ship said. "We can repair and make slight modifications. We cannot replicate."

"Why not?" Sven asked with an angry voice. With his quivering words, Johnson could imagine his son's lower lips shaking in grief and anger.

"We do not have the tools. And to build the tools would take many years, by which time the Fleet will have destroyed your race and possibly the Rebels."

"*Javla Helveta*," Johnson spat. He hadn't been this angry in years. "How can you be such a *dumfan*?" Johnson wondered how long, with the technology these ships obviously possessed, it would take humans to build enough ships to destroy the Fleet. Not very long, he suspected.

"The best I can do," the ship was saying, "is place you and the humans from Jideed Baghdad on an inhabitable planet far from here and hope the Fleet does not find you. If you do not use artificial EMR, or emit neutrinos, chances are good they will not."

"That is not an acceptable choice," Johnson spat. He realized he wanted revenge, damn it.

"There is no other choice," the ship said.

Johnson closed his mouth lest he swear in front of his son again. He wished he could talk to Sven without the ship hearing, but there was no way to do it.

"I know of a world to place you," the ship said. "It was occupied by beings not unlike yourselves until the Fleet reached it. And it is unlikely the Fleet would return to it. Again, you would have to limit EMR and neutrino emissions."

"What about the radiation from the bombs?" Johnson asked.

"The radiation is now low enough that it will be safe."

Johnson frowned. The Fleet must have attacked it thousands of years ago. The half-life of plutonium-239 is twenty-four thousand years, assuming that was the fissile material the Fleet used.

But, he thought, no EMR and no neutrino meant a pretty low-tech existence. In any case, Johnson wasn't ready to give up and hide.

"No," Johnson growled. "Let us fight."

"You will lose."

"I don't give a fuck. Let us fight." He'd rather die trying than give up.

The ship was silent.

"Can you design these self-replicating machines?"

Johnson sighed in frustration. "No, I can't. But I bet someone from Jideed Baghdad could, using your technology." He assumed among the population there had to be some scientists and engineers.

"It will take time," the ship said.

"Then best we start soon," Johnson growled.

"There isn't enough time. The Fleet will destroy all human colonies and Earth in a matter of weeks."

Johnson yelled with anger. "How can that be?"

"We can travel between stars in moments because we can use other dimensions where distances in this universe mean little."

"We have to stop them; there has to be a way to stop them," Johnson cried, feeling tears form in his eyes.

"The best thing for you to do is hide and hope the Fleet never finds you."

There was a moment's hesitation.

"We are there," the ship said.

"Where?" Johnson demanded.

"The system I spoke of."

"No, damn it, I do not want to hide, I want to fight." Johnson was so mad he didn't even question that it took no time to get there, no matter how many light years away it was.

"This system is resource rich," the ship said. "It has a large asteroid belt with both metals and organics. The planet also has many resources. It has been long enough since the Fleet used nuclear weapons on it that radiation levels are now safe for humans. If you can design your self-replicating machines, this system will provide ample resources."

"Can we do to them what the Fleet wanted us to do to you?" Sven asked.

"What do you mean?" the ship asked.

"Teleport humans inside their ships with bombs to detonate near their fusion reactors."

There was no answer.

"There's millions of JB inhabitants. If it takes a thousand people, they have them," Sven added.

"We cannot get close enough to them. They would destroy us first."

"Human ships," Johnson said. "They won't suspect a thing. Do to them what they tried to do to you. Any human system that is mining asteroids will have hundreds if not thousands of ships."

There was hesitation.

"I'll have to confer with the other Rebel ships. This will require many resources we could not spare if your plan failed."

"Do it," Johnson snapped. "If you are right, we don't have time to waste."

There was a long period of silence.

"It is done," the ship explained. "We will try your plan, but not with the humans from Jideed Baghdad. They will be left on this planet as insurance in case your plan fails. Gredel is destroyed. The next nearest human planet is Bostad."

Johnson scowled with anger, not caring that the ship probably couldn't see. Bostad was the planet he'd escaped from. He was sure he was facing charges there that would put him in prison a long time or have him executed, even though it had been 155 years since he stole the *Longboat* and left the system. Which was a moot point if the planet was destroyed, he thought bitterly.

And when they got there, he, a criminal, Sven, a young man, and the alien ship had to convince the authorities to cooperate.

"Wait," Sven said. "Are the people from Jideed Baghdad still in stasis?"

"No, I cannot leave them in stasis without being there."

"How do you think a million or so people will react to suddenly finding themselves on an alien world?" Sven asked.

"It cannot be helped," the ship said.

"Is there anything for them to eat or drink?" Johnson asked.

The ship was quiet for a long moment. "We will get back to them as soon as possible."

Johnson shook his head. Who knew what shape they'd be in by then?

"It cannot be helped," the ship repeated.

Johnson growled. "How do we know the Fleet hasn't reached Bostad yet?" he asked.

"That is why we must hurry," the ship replied in that monotone, emotionless voice it had. "We are in the Bostad system," the ship announced. "The Fleet is not here yet." Maybe a minute had passed. "I will now enter orbit around the planet."

"Wait!" Johnson cried out.

"Yes?"

"If you accelerate at more than ten gees, it'll kill us." And at ten gees we'll just wish we were dead, he didn't add.

"You will feel nothing," the ship said in the annoying emotionless tone.

Johnson frowned, knowing no one could see it.

"There are things we need to talk about," he said.

"Yes?" the ship asked.

"First of all, our suits will only sustain our lives for about twenty-six more hours," he said. "And then we'll need food, bathroom facilities, air." Actually, we need food right now, Johnson thought, his stomach feeling hollow and gnawing at him.

"What are the other things?" the ship asked, its voice once again not showing any emotion or inflection.

"I am a wanted criminal in this system," Johnson said. "They are not likely to listen to me."

"No, but they will probably listen to me," the ship said, "and you can verify what I tell them. In fact, they are already broadcasting modulated EMR that appears to be directed at me."

Johnson didn't mention the third thing: he wasn't sure this ship could be trusted. Perhaps the entire alien world they'd visited was a hologram, or the ship had manipulated their minds into thinking they saw what they did.

"I will ask that a human ship be allocated for your use, stocked with food and water and air," the ship was saying. "Is that acceptable?"

"I doubt they will acquiesce to your request," Johnson grumbled. Of course, he was thinking of the authoritarian, kleptocratic government he'd escaped from. About 155 years had passed on this planet since he left in the *Longboat*. That government could have been deposed. But somehow he doubted it. Governments that ruled with an iron fist tended to stay in power unless there was some outside influence exerting pressure, such as the Germanic Tribes for the Roman Empire or the United States putting pressure on the Soviet Union. But on an isolated planet, the Impetusite government of Bostad was probably still in place. Johnson was curious if they would remember him after 155 years. He smiled. If they didn't ask, he wouldn't mention it.

A few minutes later, what seemed to Johnson much too soon, the ship announced, "We are in orbit around the planet you call Bostad."

BOOK TWO

THE HUMANS

(155 YEARS EARLIER, BOSTAD TIME FRAME)

CHAPTER ELEVEN

The government had closed the spaceports for anything other than cargo or approved passengers. No civilians were allowed to leave the planet. But they couldn't control all the land, not on as sparsely populated a planet as Bostad. Olly Johnson, Sonia, and Sven simply had to meet up with the shuttle pilot at the designated spot, just about a hundred kilometers outside of Valhöll, the capital city.

The Impetus Party, the only "party" on the ballot for the last election, had instituted patrols of police officers and "militia" volunteers…thugs paid to enforce the diktats of the new ruling junta, basically, Johnson thought. He knew if he spoke such thoughts out loud within earshot of an Impetus Party supporter, he'd likely be arrested. If he stated it in electronic communications, even supposed private ones, the arrest would be swift, and the punishment sure.

But what he was doing at the moment was risking a long prison sentence for himself and his wife, and his son being placed in the execrable foster and orphan care system the Impetusites had put in place. "For the children," they had said.

The car's batteries were nearly drained. The government was rationing electric power despite its abundance from the fusion reactors on the planet. They said it was an emergency measure while one reactor was repaired. The "emergency" had been going on for over a year. Johnson suspected it was simply another way to keep the population in control.

The car coasted to a stop, a red light blinking insistently on the dashboard.

"That's it," Johnson said.

"Now what?" Sonia asked, her voice tight with fear.

"We walk," Johnson growled.

"But Sven?"

"I'll carry him. Give him the sedative now."

"Now?"

"Yes, he'll be less frightened that way."

She nodded, and in the moonlight coming in the top of the vehicle's transparent roof, her blonde hair shone silver as it undulated with the movement of her head.

Johnson couldn't help but smile. He loved this beautiful woman and still wondered why she had married him. It wasn't his money; she'd proven that since the government expropriated most of it. He didn't consider himself handsome, especially since he was nearly ten years older than she.

She exited the car and Johnson did the same. He looked at it. He'd paid a lot for it; it was one of the finest vehicles made on Bostad when he'd acquired it. But without electricity to operate it, it was a lovely work of art in composites, carbon fiber, and aluminum.

Sonia undid Sven's safety harness and pulled the child from the backseat. The towheaded boy rested on his mother's shoulder.

Johnson got a backpack out of the car's trunk. It was all they were leaving Bostad with; it held a significant quantity of gold, and it was heavy.

"*Oij*," Sonia said with forced smile. "He's getting big."

Johnson took the toddler from her arms and smiled. "Yes, he is." He didn't weigh as much as the backpack, however, Johnson noted.

"How far?" Sonia asked.

"Maybe ten kilometers," Johnson said lightly. The burden of both Sven and the backpack were going to get old fast, he could tell.

"Let me carry something," Sonia said.

Johnson smiled at his wife. She was such a small thing, 150 centimeters tall and weighing maybe forty-three kilograms. The backpack probably weighed more than she. But her petite size belied an inner strength that Johnson had come to rely on.

"Maybe in a bit I'll let you carry Sven." He weighed maybe sixteen kilograms.

"Okay," Sonia whispered.

"The faster we get away from the car the better," Johnson said, not hiding the urgency in his voice.

"I understand, Olly," Sonia said with a sad smile.

They walked toward a ridge of low hills. Johnson tried to move quickly, but Sonia's short legs meant she had trouble keeping up. Johnson slowed down reluctantly.

"What if he's not there?" Sonia asked after about half an hour.

"He's there," Johnson breathed. He had to be there. Johnson refused to not believe it and refused to give up.

#

Olly Johnson was a rich merchant on the prosperous planet of Bostad, selling supplies to the brave men and women who mined the asteroid belt of the mineral-rich system. He worked hard and had a reputation for honesty and fair dealing, which put his products in high demand.

His amassed fortune was wisely invested in a diversified portfolio of stocks, bonds, cash, and precious metals. He thought he might retire early, even though he was in his early thirties. Yes, there were fortunes to be made on the frontier. He had married Sonia, and not long after they had a son, Sven, whom Olly doted upon. The boy in his arms was now nearly three years old, Johnson remembered. Where does the time go? he thought.

Then, the revolution happened. The constitutionally-limited republican government of the planet was overthrown, and a government made up of intellectuals and malcontents was put into power. They called themselves the "Impetus Party," as if recycling the bad ideas of the past were somehow "progress." Johnson had seen it coming and transferred as much of his wealth as he could to cash and precious metals before the stock and bond markets crashed. He felt reasonably safe, even though his cash was held in banks and other institutions.

That was, until the government announced a one-time surcharge on the "wealthy" of ninety-five percent of their accumulated capital. The reason given was, of course, to help feed and clothe the hungry, even though most of it went into the maw of the government to feed the burgeoning bureaucracy and the appetites of the revolutionary leaders. Without warning, the way to get and stay rich was not to work hard and provide a product or service people would voluntarily exchange their money for…it was to be in government. Or have a business the government liked and wanted to subsidize. And they didn't like business that supplied miners, especially after the miners in the belt declared independence from Bostad.

Johnson managed to hide a great deal of his wealth from the tax man, but swore he'd abandon this planet. He convinced Sonia to leave with him, even though the government had banned emigration. The government said all "human resources" were needed for the "home planet."

#

Johnson assumed all communications were monitored by the government, so they had negotiated with encrypted messages. The code was supposed to be practically unbreakable, even by a government. Especially the Impetusite government, Johnson thought, who had purged anyone who had half a brain for anyone who followed their ideology.

Johnson and his wife walked down the road, keeping to the side. There was no traffic, but a lifetime of training dictated that you didn't walk in the middle of a road.

There was nothing out here but autofarms and, due to power rationing, no one was going to come out, especially at night. He could see the crops were sparse, and there were many bare fields due to lack of energy to plant and tend to the crops. Johnson suspected people would be hungry come winter.

Sonia took Sven after they'd gone about two kilometers which, unfortunately, slowed them down even more. Johnson grumbled to himself that if they moved any slower, they'd be going backwards.

They were supposed to meet Andersen before the sun came up. Johnson didn't have any way to determine the time since his handcomp could be traced by the government, he assumed, so he'd left it at home.

They came to the road. It was not paved, but was two dirt ruts between weeds. The weeds were native, a variety the autofarm robots worked hard to keep out of the crops. Johnson thought for a moment the robots needed to keep them out of the road, too, so there wasn't a source of spores.

"Not too much farther," he said, trying to sound cheerful.

He only got a nod from Sonia. He could tell she was exhausted carrying Sven, so he took the child again and walked down the right hand rut.

"Thank you," Sonia whispered, and fell into step behind him.

The sky was turning a dark purple in the east when they reached the ship. It was a bullet shape against the lightening sky.

Two men stood in front of it. There was a ramp leading up to what Johnson assumed was an airlock, but might only be a hatch since he saw no interlocking mechanism. This was a ground-to-orbit shuttle, designed to rendezvous with another ship in low orbit.

The dirt around the bottom of the shuttle was black from the fusion flame as the ship landed.

"You Johnson?" one of the men asked. He had a shaved head and was taller than the other man.

"Yes," Johnson said, handing Sven back to Sonia. "You must be Andersen."

"Yes," Andersen confirmed. "This is my first-mate, Larsen."

Johnson nodded to the other man. He was broad of shoulders and narrow of waist. A handsome fellow, Johnson thought, with intelligent blue eyes and a thick head of blond hair.

"Are we ready to go?" Johnson asked.

"There's just one problem," Andersen said, smiling, showing crooked teeth.

"I know," Johnson said, "we have to launch at our window to rendezvous with the ship in orbit." Johnson knew that that ship orbited the planet about once every one hundred minutes, so the launch window would repeat every one hundred minutes. He hoped they hadn't just missed one and would have to wait long.

"No," Andersen spat, "that's not it."

Johnson frowned and noticed Larsen turned to look at his captain in surprise.

"I had a better offer," Andersen said, grinning.

"I'll beat it," Johnson said, hoping he was carrying enough gold.

"You can't." Andersen reached into a pocket of his coveralls and pulled out a gun, pointing it at Johnson. "The government said if I turned you over to them, they wouldn't confiscate my ship, revoke my license, and throw me in jail."

Larsen audibly snarled.

"They'll be here soon," Andersen said, completing his thought.

"Please, no," Sonia cried. "Do you know what they'll do to us? Do to our son?"

"Not my problem, lady," Andersen sneered.

Larsen tackled him from the side, knocking the bigger man over. Andersen cried out in surprise and dropped his gun. Johnson ran forward and picked it up while Larsen pummeled Andersen in the face.

When Andersen was unconscious, Larsen stood up, his fists bloody. "Never liked that asshole."

"Thank you," Johnson said, still holding the gun. He'd never held a gun before, but he'd see it done in vids.

"I'd appreciate it," Larsen said, "if you'd take your finger off the trigger and point that away from me. In fact, it'd probably be best if you let me handle it."

"How do I know I can trust you?" Johnson asked.

"*Uff da*," Larsen said, rolling his eyes. "I don't think you have a choice, unless you can operate this shuttle."

Johnson hesitated.

"The police will likely be here soon, we need to lift."

Johnson turned to look at Sonia, who had a determined scowl on her face. They had to get off of Bostad, Johnson knew she was thinking. For Sven's sake they had to escape the Impetus government that would crush any hopes of Sven having a better life.

Johnson handed the gun to Larsen.

Larsen smiled. "Thank you. We should leave, now."

"The rendezvous window?" Johnson asked.

"If you'd rather wait here for the police," Larsen said.

The sound of an approaching vehicle, coming fast, made Johnson's mind up for him.

"Let's go!"

"Yes, sir," Larsen said with a smile. He stooped down, grabbed Andersen by the shoulders of his overalls, and pulled him into the weeds.

"What did you do that for?" Johnson asked.

"I may be a mutineer, but I'm not a murderer. He'll be safe from the blast there."

Johnson nodded.

Larsen used his free hand to pull out a small device with some buttons on it. He pressed the largest button with his thumb. The shuttle came to life, lights on, the hatch opening revealing the bright interior.

Johnson thought he heard the approaching vehicles — now it sounded like many — speed up. When he glanced in that direction, he saw flashing red and blue lights.

"Hurry," Larsen breathed.

Johnson took Sven from Sonia and said, "Let's go, honey."

The men let Sonia go first, and Johnson whispered, "Hurry, please," as she moved up the ramp. She scurried into the interior of the shuttle. Johnson followed, carrying his son.

The interior was full of acceleration chairs, some child-sized. This was a commercial orbital shuttle albeit, Johnson noticed, not a very tidy one. Johnson hoped Andersen did a better job at maintenance than cleaning.

Larsen hurried in after them. "We're boosting soon. Strap in," he snapped, climbing a ladder to the cockpit.

Johnson helped Sonia strap down Sven, and then helped her get in her chair. Finally, Johnson sat and connected the five-point harness. He pulled the straps tight.

There was an explosion, and the shuttle lurched. Johnson heard Larsen yell in anger just as the gee forces hit. They were lifting. The ship banked, and Johnson wondered why they weren't going straight up, but were rising at an angle.

Soon, the ship straightened, and they were shooting into the night sky.

The gees built until Johnson was sure he was going to pass out. His vision was going gray, and he could hear Sonia whimpering in pain. He was glad Sven was unconscious.

Then, without warning, the gees stopped and it felt as if they were falling. They were no longer accelerating, Johnson knew, and he had to tell his body that they weren't falling, there was no danger, but still he could feel the adrenaline pumping into his veins. His stomach contents started boiling low in his throat, and he hoped he wouldn't vomit.

"We'll be maneuvering," Larsen's voice said over an intercom. "Remain in your acceleration chairs, please. There are sickness bags on the right side of the chairs. Be sure to cover your entire mouth with the bag so no vomit escapes. There's nothing worse than floating balls of vomit." Johnson thought he was joking, but his voice sounded very serious.

Johnson could see his wife pulling one of the bags to her mouth. He was so glad Sven was asleep.

CHAPTER TWELVE

The shuttle did maneuver, including a few high-gee accelerations. Then, they were in free fall again. Johnson's own stomach was still debating ejecting its contents.

Larsen floated down from the cockpit, expertly moving in free fall using hand grips.

"I'm sorry, ma'am," he said to Sonia. "First time in space?"

She only nodded. Her skin had taken on a distinct shade of green.

Larsen gave her a sympathetic smile.

"How long until we rendezvous with the ship?" Johnson asked.

Larsen sighed. "That is an issue. We had to lift because the police were coming. I want to show you something."

"Okay," Johnson said, wondering what it could be.

"This is the aft camera view as we were lifting," Larsen said, touching buttons on that same device that had opened the ship. All the monitors lit up. The scene showed a blue glow from the flame of the fusion rocket at the top. The rest of the scene was blackened dirt. The vid was paused.

"You may have felt the explosion just before we lifted. They fired an explosive shell at us. Luckily, they missed, and we weren't damaged significantly."

"How do you know?" Sonia asked.

"Know what?" Larsen asked.

"That we weren't damaged."

"We're alive," Larsen replied in a calm voice.

Sonia's face went pale.

Johnson nodded, his eyes wide. He didn't know what to say. The police had just tried to kill him, he realized. The police had tried to kill him and his entire family, including his child.

"They tried again," Larsen said. "Watch."

The vid started moving. The ground was turning blacker, and wisps of charred dirt were being ejected outward from the blue glow. Then, the ground moved away, and more of the surface came into view. The scene tilted, and Johnson assumed that's when the ship had banked during takeoff. The scene paused as Larsen touched a button.

"Do you see it?" Larsen asked.

Johnson looked at the screen. There was a police vehicle demarked by its blue and yellow color scheme and flashing blue and red lights. On the roof of the car was what looked like a weapon with a long barrel.

"They mounted a grenade launcher on the police car," Larsen said. "I couldn't risk them firing again and this time hitting us."

"What did you do?" Sonia asked.

"Watch," Larsen said in a low tone.

The vid moved again. The scene tilted more until three police cars in a line were visible, the one with the grenade launcher at the front. Johnson thought he saw a man behind the launcher, his torso sticking out of the police vehicle.

"I'll slow this down so you can see it," Larsen said.

The scene slowed as the view tilted more, so much that the horizon came into view, and the cars were no longer visible. But orange flashes filled the screen from the opposite side from the steady blue glow of the fusion exhaust.

The scene slowly tilted back the other way and as it passed over the police vehicles, each one was destroyed, on fire, and there were bodies scattered around them.

Johnson sucked in a deep breath as the scene slid to showing on the ground, the blackened part getting farther and farther away as the ship went vertical again. The first car in line came into view, still burning, before Larsen cut off the vid.

"What happened?" Sonia breathed.

"I tried just to take out the first one, the one with the grenade launcher," Larsen said softly. "But I yawed too far and hit all three with the fusion exhaust."

There was a slight hesitation.

"We miners learned a long time ago that a fusion exhaust makes an excellent weapon. Since everyone has one, there's very little miner-on-miner crime."

"Damn," Johnson whispered.

"So you see," Larsen said. "We can't ever go back to Bostad, any of us."

Johnson nodded, still trying to absorb what happened.

"Especially me," Larsen was saying.

Johnson again just nodded. Then asked, "You saved Andersen but just killed cops?"

"Andersen wasn't a threat. The cops were trying to kill me. Kill us. I wanted to only take out the grenade launcher before it could fire again. But I had to fly manually, and I accidentally hit all the cars."

Johnson frowned. He was suddenly worried about the type of man they were trusting with their lives.

"I assume the asteroid belt is where you want to go," Larsen continued, "I want to come with you. I never should have left the belt to be first mate on this stupid shuttle."

Johnson nodded this time.

"There's good news, and there's bad news," Larsen said.

Johnson frowned. "What's the bad news?"

"Because we had to lift when we did, we missed the rendezvous window and will have to be in orbit longer than planned. It will also require more fuel to maneuver."

"What's the good news?" Johnson asked.

"We should have enough fuel if we abandon this ship in orbit. There's not enough to land on Bostad again. So, another reason I need to come with you."

"What do you want?" Johnson asked.

"I know you carry a lot of gold," Larsen said. "I don't want any of it if you'll help me get back to the belt."

"I negotiated deals for transferring three people, one a child," Johnson said. "You may cost me more gold." Increased mass meant increased energy expenditure, Johnson knew.

"You don't have to pay Andersen," Larsen said. "But, if we get to the belt, I'll be able to pay you back."

"How?" Johnson asked.

"Please just trust me," the man said. "We're in this together now. Wanted fugitives."

"That's what I don't understand," Sonia said. "How did the police know we'd be there? How did they know we'd hired Andersen?"

"Yes," Johnson agreed. "All communications were encrypted."

Larsen snorted. "You don't think the police were wondering why you were sending encrypted messages? Even if they couldn't decipher them, they could figure out who was receiving them. They probably talked to Andersen via radio and told him to cooperate, or else."

Johnson still wasn't sure he could trust this Larsen. But the man was right; they were all now wanted fugitives. Didn't appear he had a choice. "And you knew nothing of this?" Johnson asked.

Larsen shook his head. "No, Andersen was a tight-lipped man."

#

The rendezvous happened after a great deal of maneuvering. Johnson finally did vomit. He was glad there was a wet, absorbent towel in a pouch on the bag to clean his face with.

Sven was waking up before they made it to the ship that would take them to the asteroid belt. He woke with a start, eyes wide, and yelled, "Mommy!" and put his arms up as if trying to catch himself. Johnson knew he must have thought he was falling.

Johnson wanted to try floating around the cabin in free fall, but Larsen wouldn't let him.

116

The airlocks mated and Johnson knew this was going to be the difficult part, moving into the other ship in free fall. It was made more difficult by Sven first vomiting, then crying as he squirmed in his mother's arms.

The captain of the ship met Johnson at the airlock. The ship was called the *Bifröst II*, Johnson remembered, and the captain's name was Hummel. He decided not to ask what happened to the original *Bifröst*.

"You have my payment?" Hummel demanded.

"Yes," Johnson said. "But the deal was when we were in the asteroid belt, at Asgard." Asgard was the largest of the asteroids, actually classified as a minor planet. It was the center of asteroid mining in the belt, and Johnson was hoping his skills as a merchant would be marketable there. Perhaps at some point, he could go into business for himself again.

"Things have changed," Hummel growled.

"I know," Johnson said. "There's four of us now. I'll pay extra."

"No," the captain spat. "News reports from the surface are that you killed twelve cops. There's a very large reward on your head."

Johnson sighed. "So you want me to pay you more than the reward?"

"Or I rendezvous with a government shuttle to take you back to the surface," Hummel said with a malevolent grin.

Larsen appeared without warning and put the gun against the captain's head. "I have a better idea. We leave you in this shuttle, which doesn't have enough fuel to land again, and you die when it burns up in its decaying orbit."

"And who's going to pilot this ship?" Hummel asked with a sneer.

"I will," Larsen said. "We don't have time for you to look up my master's license, but believe me, I can, and will, take this ship from you."

Hummel scowled. "Fine. I'll take you to the belt for double."

"One-quarter more," Larsen said. "Not a gram over."

The captain nodded.

"Then best we go," Larsen said with smile, putting the gun in a pocket in his overalls.

"Where the hell you get a gun?" Hummel asked. "I know the first thing the Impetusites did was confiscate all civilian-owned weapons."

Yes, Johnson remembered, as a "safety" program. He thought that it was so the government would find it easier to control an unarmed populace.

"Only the guns they could find," Larsen said with a smile.

It took a few minutes to get them all settled in and in acceleration chairs. Sven was wide-eyed at everything and very squirmy. Johnson couldn't blame the boy. They didn't dare drug him again as more than once in that short of a time period was dangerous.

The *Bifröst II* was ostensibly a small, one-man cargo ship designed to carry goods from the belt to Bostad, and then whatever was needed in the belt back from Bostad. Apparently Hummel wasn't above smuggling people to the belt, either. Why else would a cargo ship have extra acceleration chairs other than those needed by the pilot and possible co-pilot? People were always wanting to leave the planet. Criminals, mostly, Johnson thought. Then he realized that he, too, was a criminal. It was worse than leaving the planet without permission from the government, his original crime. Now, he was accessory to the murder of police officers. Johnson's stomach churned at that. He was sure the Impetusites would be happy to make an example out of him.

The interior of the ship, except for the small passenger compartment, was full of goods in composite containers that were all strapped down. Johnson assumed Hummel had tied them down sufficiently.

"We'll be accelerating at five gees for four minutes to reach escape velocity," Hummel said, not keeping the betrayed tone from his voice. "Then it's four days to Asgard at one gee, except at turnaround."

Johnson nodded. He knew when they reached Asgard they'd be in free fall again for the rest of their lives unless they were on accelerating ships. That meant all of them had to exercise to retain bone and muscle mass, especially Sven. It was better than living under the tyranny of the Impetusites. Or, now, going to jail for the rest of his life. Unless he was executed, he thought. So far the Impetusites hadn't instituted a death penalty. He didn't want to be the test case for doing so.

Johnson was glad for four days of one gee acceleration before his lifetime in free fall.

Once they were all strapped down, Hummel pushed himself to the cockpit. Larsen unstrapped and followed. Johnson saw he was pulling his gun out. He smiled. Larsen was going to ensure the captain kept his word, apparently.

Acceleration hit hard. It wasn't as bad as when they'd lifted from Bostad, but now Sven was awake and the boy screamed with pain. Johnson watched the boy with a worried expression. Sonia tried to comfort the child, but her voice was almost a series of grunts as she bore five times her normal weight. The four minutes felt as if they lasted four hours.

Then they were in free fall for a moment before the acceleration became one gee. Bostad's surface gravity was a little less than a gee, but not so much that Johnson could feel a difference between it and the one gee they were experiencing now.

Larsen walked back from the cockpit, smiling grimly, putting the pistol back in a pocket.

"I don't think we'll have any trouble from Captain Hummel," he said.

"Oh, why?" Johnson asked.

"He knows who has the gun and that I'm not afraid to use it."

"How does he know that?"

"I told him why I left the belt. He'd heard of me."

Johnson's eyes grew large. What kind of man is this Larsen? he was wondering.

"We need to talk," Larsen said.

"Indeed we do," Johnson growled.

119

Johnson unstrapped himself.

"Daddy?" Sven asked.

"Yes, son?"

"Can I get down?"

Johnson looked at Sonia, and she shook her head slightly. He smiled at the boy. "Not yet, son, but soon, okay?"

"Please?" the child whined.

"Soon," Johnson said firmly. He felt for the boy because being strapped down had to be misery for him. The Johnsons had had a large lot for their house, and the boy relished running in the grass-covered yards.

Larsen stepped out of the passenger compartment into the cargo hold. Johnson followed. He noticed Larsen was almost unconsciously and automatically checking the security of the tie-downs on the nearest cargo box. Then he turned to Johnson.

"I've disabled the ship's radio so Hummel can't contact the authorities," he said.

Johnson nodded. "What if we need it for an emergency?"

"Then I'll replace the critical part I took."

"If it's a critical part, won't Hummel have spares on board?"

Larsen smiled and looked impressed. Johnson liked that he'd had that effect on this man.

"Yes, he does, I'm sure. But I searched the cockpit and there's none there. And I told Hummel if he left the cockpit before I got back, I'd shoot him. We're going to have to keep an eye on him this entire journey."

Johnson shook his head. "Okay," he whispered, again wondering what type of man this Larsen was. "Where you really going to put Hummel in the shuttle? Or were you bluffing?"

"I was hoping he wouldn't call my bluff," Larsen said. "I learned long ago you do what it takes to survive."

"Even if it means killing other people?"

"If they are a threat to you, yes."

Johnson frowned again.

"Which brings up something else. There's another issue," Larsen said.

CHAPTER THIRTEEN

"What's that?" Johnson asked, wondering what new bad news he was about to hear.

"We can't go to Asgard," Larsen explained.

Johnson frowned. "Why not?"

"I'm wanted, and now so are you and your wife."

"I thought the belt miners had no love for the Impetusite government. They declared independence."

"They don't have any love of the Impetus Party, normally. But the belt still relies on trade with Bostad, so they will not ignore a request by the government to turn over fugitives."

"You mean me," Johnson said softly. That pit in his stomach grew.

"Yes," Larsen said, "and me. But there's another problem."

"What's that?"

"The reason I had to leave the belt and go to work for Andersen."

Johnson studied Larsen's face. "Why?"

"I killed a man," Larsen said.

Johnson felt his knees go weak. He was now tangled up with a criminal, he realized. And the criminal had the only weapon on board.

"Take it easy, Johnson," Larsen said. "It was in self-defense."

"Oh," Johnson breathed. "But then, why did you have to leave the belt?"

"It's a long story," Larsen growled.

"We have four days," Johnson pointed out.

Larson smiled grimly. "I became partners with a man I didn't know was tied in with a water cartel."

"A water cartel?" In his dealings with miners, he'd heard whispers about water cartels. They would try to control all the water and anything else they could in an area of the asteroid belt. It was unlawful, Johnson knew, but the belt was too big and scattered to control them.

"What happened?" Johnson prodded.

"We were mining an asteroid and hit it big: a huge find of ice. He must have decided he wanted it all to himself. He tried to kill me; I managed to kill him instead."

"So why are you wanted by the authorities?" Johnson asked. "It was clearly self-defense."

"I'm not. I'm wanted by the cartel, which is worse. And, if I show my face on Asgard, someone is sure to recognize me and send a tight beam to the cartel."

"A tight beam?"

Larsen smiled. "A message. We communicate in the belt mostly by 'tight beam' transmissions to reduce the interference and help maintain privacy."

"And if I show my face on Asgard," Johnson said, "someone will send a 'tight beam' to the Impetusite government?"

"More likely, the authorities will arrest you. The Impetusites know you left Bostad, and the belt is the logical place for you to go. Your description and photo and DNA specifications have probably already been transmitted to the Asgard Cooperative."

"Oh," Johnson breathed.

"And," Larsen added, "Mine, too, once Andersen identifies me to the police. We are all wanted for the murder of police officers."

"It was self-defense," Johnson exclaimed.

"No such thing in dealing with the police in conduct of their lawful duties."

"Trying to kill all of us is their lawful duty?" Johnson growled.

"It is now, apparently," Larsen said with bitterness.

"So where do we go?" Johnson asked. "What do we do?"

Larsen smiled. "I know a place: a safe place for both of us."

Johnson nodded.

"So, how did you get gold?" Larsen asked. "I thought the Impetusites had banned selling and buying it."

"I used to get paid occasionally in gold when I sold to miners," Johnson said. "I kept a good deal of it in case of emergency."

Larsen smiled. "That was a wise precaution. Did you anticipate the rise of the Impetusite government?"

Johnson shook his head. "Not right away, but soon enough to get my investments into cash and gold. Any government can turn tyrannical, either quickly or slowly. Especially an unfettered democracy."

"You know what a democracy is?" Larsen said with a smile.

Johnson shook his head.

"Two lambs and three wolves voting on what to have for lunch."

Johnson laughed. "I guess I don't make a very good lamb."

"I don't either," Larsen said with smirk.

#

"You hired me to take you to Asgard," Hummel grumbled. "Two adults and a child. Now it's three adults and a child to a different asteroid? That's extra fuel, extra oxygen, extra time, and extra risk."

Larsen just looked at him with conviction in his eyes. Johnson was letting Larsen handle negotiations. While Johnson used to negotiate for a living, Larsen had the gun. He had to admire Hummel's courage negotiating with a man holding the only weapon.

"I need more than just one-quarter more gold," Hummel concluded.

"Fifty percent," Larsen said. "No more."

Larsen glanced at Johnson, who nodded his head slightly.

Hummel's face contorted in thought.

"The sooner you change vectors the less fuel it will take," Larsen added.

"The Asgard Cooperative will want to know why I didn't go there and where I went."

"Tell them," Larsen said. "Tell them everything."

Hummel looked at Johnson then back at Larsen. "Seventy-five."

"Fifty, and feel lucky to get it," Larsen growled.

Hummel shook his head. "Fine," he said. "I'm putting in my log you hijacked my ship. Only way to keep my ass out of the fire."

"Hijackers don't normally pay," Johnson growled.

"Oh, let him," Larsen said. "It makes no difference. We're wanted for enough crimes now to put us away for life. While miners might pop you out an airlock for some crimes, and hope they do it before you manage to pass your faulty DNA on to the next generation, Bostad has no death penalty."

Johnson snorted. "They had no death penalty. Nothing says they can't establish one."

Larsen shook his head with a predatory smile. "All the more reason to stay off that dirtball."

He was beginning to like Larsen.

Hummel frowned and shook his head slowly. "I need to change our vector. Everyone strap down."

It had only been a few hours since they began accelerating at one gee. Johnson wasn't looking forward to telling Sven he had to get back in the confining acceleration chair.

"If you don't mind, Captain," Larsen said, "I'll join you in the cockpit."

"Suit yourself," Hummel said with a shrug.

#

The asteroid didn't have a name, only a number: BA-XP-4382. The *Bifröst II* matched orbits and docked after receiving permission from the asteroid's crew. All communications were, Larsen ensured, on a tight beam.

They were in free fall again, and Sven's playful attitude toward it made Johnson smile. Sven no longer got sick, but Johnson's stomach was trying desperately to find "up" and seemed to think that emptying itself would do the trick.

Sonia was still a decidedly green shade. Larsen helped her take Sven through the airlock as Johnson paid Hummel.

Even with his hands full of finger-sized gold bars, he still grumbled.

"Thank you," Johnson said, trying to sound sincere.

Hummel's reply was acerbic. "I hope they throw you out an airlock, asshole."

Johnson zipped up his backpack, now much lighter, and strapped it on his back. He needed his hands free to maneuver in free fall. As soon as he cleared the *Bifröst II's* airlock, it closed. Johnson was glad they were through dealing with Hummel, but he wondered where Larsen had taken him. During the slightly more than four day trip all Larsen would say is, "Don't worry; we'll be welcome."

Emerging from the tunnel carved in rock that led to the airlock, Johnson gasped. The interior of the asteroid had been hollowed out. There were flimsy-looking, multi-colored structures scattered about as if there were no plan. Johnson realized there was no need to build for strength with no gravity to pull the structures down. All they needed to do was provide privacy.

Men, women, and a few children were, literally, hanging around. Ropes and handholds were everywhere, allowing people to move around the interior. Most were dressed in overalls, but many also had pieces of cloth sewn or tied to them that were nearly every color in the rainbow. Perhaps, Johnson thought, that was what passed for fashion in the asteroid belt. And beards were apparently required of the men, Johnson mused. He didn't see a single shaven adult male face other than Larsen and himself.

What really baffled Johnson was that everyone was in a different orientation. There was no agreement on which way was "up" or "down." He was looking at humans from every possible angle, he thought.

Larsen was in front of him, holding a rope and talking to a man. Sonia held Sven's hand with one hand and a rope with the other. The boy looked around with eyes like saucers.

Johnson found a rope that he could pull to get closer to Larsen.

"…and what makes you think you're welcome here, Larsen?" the man was asking.

"I was told I would always be welcome here," Larsen said. "When I helped mine this asteroid and turn it into a home."

"That was before you were wanted for the murder of police."

"That was on the dirtball," Larsen said. "And it was self-defense."

The man shook his head, and Johnson noticed that caused the rest of his body to move as described by Newton's third law. "It doesn't matter. You're wanted, and the Asgard Cooperative is looking for you."

"Then I stay away from Asgard," Larsen said.

The man scowled.

"I'll need a ship," Larsen said. "You know I have money."

"On Asgard," the man said. "Most likely confiscated."

"The Asgard Bank would not cooperate with Bostad authorities," Larsen said.

The man shook his head. "They will if the dirtball government puts enough pressure on them. We need trade with Bostad. We are not yet self-sufficient."

"Our ship has left," Larsen said. "What are you going to do, throw us out an airlock?"

The man scowled. "No, of course not. But you need to leave as soon as possible."

Larsen stared at the man. "What is going on?"

The man sighed. "The damn dirtballers. They are trying to extend their influence to the belt. And because we rely on trade with them, it's working."

"So?" Larsen asked.

"So, the belt is not quite the organized anarchy it used to be. We have inspections and rules and taxes and — and they are trying to put in a goddamned government. A government ruled by the dirtballers."

Johnson could hear both the anger and grief in the man's words.

"When the next pop inspection happens, we can try to hide you. But the sooner you leave, the better."

Larsen scowled now. "What am I supposed to do, learn to breathe vacuum?"

The man again shook his head. "We'll figure something out. Maybe we can get you your money. Jakob's still a pretty good hacker. He'd have no moral objection to 'stealing' what is rightfully yours."

"Fine," Larsen replied. "Is my room still unoccupied?"

"Of course not. But I did have an opening just come up. Some miner got careless. It'll be a tight fit for the four of you," the man said.

"We'll make do," Larsen replied with a forced smile.

The man nodded, his body moving in reaction. "See that you do. I'll talk to Jakob about getting you your money."

"Thank you," Larsen said.

"Don't thank me yet." The man pulled himself away on a rope.

"Who was that?" Johnson asked.

"The welcoming committee," Larsen said with scowl. When Johnson didn't react, he said, "Nielsen, the owner, operator, and 'mayor' of eight-two. I used to live here when I mined. The rent was reasonable."

"So now what?" Johnson asked.

"We settle in and decide what we are going to do."

"What are we going to do?"

Larsen grinned. "Give me some time to look into a few things. With luck, the lambs might become the wolves."

#

The Asgard Cooperative's cooperation with the Impetus government was minimal, apparently. Larsen's accounts had not been frozen nor seized. Jakob, a young man with a scraggly beard, was happy to inform Larsen of that. Larsen paid him for his trouble despite Jakob's protests.

"With what's left of your gold and my account, we could buy a small ship," Larsen told Johnson in their new quarters.

Sleeping was done in bags attached to the wall. The bathroom facilities were small but functional. One showered in a bag that only left the head dry. When done, a fan sucked the water out of the bag before you unzipped and towel-dried. Johnson was amazed at how tenaciously water stuck to the skin without gravity to pull it off.

The toilet had a fan in the bottom that provided suction. Johnson smiled when he realized that the shit literally hit the fan. But that broke it into smaller pieces that were more easily conveyed to the recycling tanks with minimal water. Larsen explained that with enough energy, any process could be reversed, and feces, urine, and water could be turned into food. The system wasn't one-hundred percent efficient, so organic material had to be added occasionally, and that was bought from the Asgard Cooperative, who bought a lot of it from Bostad. Johnson tried not to think about the source of the food he was eating. There was a hydroponic garden that grew vegetables, and that helped. It was kept small because of the resources it consumed and the fresh vegetables were, for the moment, outside the family's budget.

"Why would we buy a ship?" Johnson asked. "To go mining?" Johnson didn't think he was suited to be an asteroid miner. He had proven again and again he was unsuited for life in freefall, more than once getting stuck in open space without anything to hold on to and having to have a rope thrown to him. Or he'd forget that he still had mass, and therefore momentum, get going too fast, and bump into something hard. He had the bruises to prove it.

"No," Larsen said, again smiling like a wolf. "To go hunting."

CHAPTER FOURTEEN

"Hunting?"

Larsen took in a deep breath. "There's a Bussard ramjet ship in the system," Larsen started. "It's an unmanned research vessel belonging to the Bostad government."

Johnson just listened. He knew a bit about Bussard ramjet ships. They were used for interstellar travel. Because they couldn't go faster than the speed of light, it took decades or more to move between stars. However, due to relativistic time dilation at the speeds they reached, less time would pass for the people on board the ship.

"And?" Johnson asked.

"We steal it," Larsen said.

"To what end?"

"We convert it to passenger use and take it the hell out of this system."

"We can't afford to convert it," Johnson said. "You said all our money would go toward buying a small ship."

"Yes," Larsen said, "that is true. So we steal what we need."

"No," Johnson barked, making a cutting gesture with his hand. He knew that people in the asteroid belt lived on the edge of survival. Stealing from them could be tantamount to killing them.

"No," Larsen said, "we only steal from the water cartels."

"No," Johnson said again. "That's too dangerous."

"Dangerous, yes," Larsen said, "but profitable. And no one will care; everyone hates the water cartels."

Johnson didn't say anything.

"I've worked it all out," Larsen continued. "We need air and waste recyclers big enough for four people. We need material to build living space. We need control equipment to interface with the ship's computers. Some we can buy, but some we'll just need to steal. Then we pay some disgruntled miners who will keep quiet — and believe me, since the Impetusites took over Bostad, there's a lot of them — to put the thing together."

"To go where?"

"I don't know," Larsen said. "Gredel, I guess. That would only take nine years, ship's time, at one gee."

"Nine years," Johnson snorted.

"Less time than the Bostad government will throw us both in jail for if they ever catch up to us," Larsen said. "Assuming they don't summarily execute you, your wife, and me."

Johnson remained quiet with his thoughts. He had promised himself to never surrender to the new Bostad government. That's why he'd left the planet.

"The Bostad government will do everything they can to increase their influence in the belt. It's just a matter of time before they force the Asgard Cooperative to come after us. If they haven't already."

Johnson nodded.

"We'll need spacesuits for both of us," Larsen said. "At least one with a maneuvering unit."

Johnson only nodded, deep in thought about spending the rest of his life in jail.

"One other thing we'll need," Larsen said.

"What's that?"

"A gun for you."

Johnson nodded again. He knew that no one had yet developed anything better than a heavy bullet propelled by a chemical explosion.

#

Living on the asteroid was more expensive than Johnson anticipated, and his gold reserves were dwindling at a frightening rate. If they were going to buy a ship, they needed to do it soon, he told Larsen. Food, other than what came out of the recycler, consisted of the hydroponically grown vegetables. Protein came mostly from soy, and that mostly in the form of tofu. Even then the price was the same as if it were prime steak on Bostad. Meat was all but unobtainable. In fact, almost all animal products were either unavailable or horrendously expensive. Sven had to get used to the taste of soy milk, as cows' milk was as rare as clean shaven faces out here.

In addition, there were the air fees. The air recycler required energy, and that meant solar collectors and/or a fusion plant...usually both for redundancy's sake. Plus there was maintenance and upkeep on the recycler. Since they weren't one-hundred percent efficient, oxygen had to be shipped in and it was almost as expensive as hydrogen. For someone used to thinking air was free, paying for it was one of the larger culture shocks Johnson had to endure.

The ship that Larsen found consisted of hydrogen tanks, a fusion rocket motor, a large cargo area, and a small, cramped, and barely adequate cockpit with a wheezing life support system. It would, however, do 1.5 gees according to the ad on the 'net.

Larsen declared it "perfect."

"You're joking, right?" Johnson asked.

"Perfect for what we can afford," Larsen clarified.

The owner of the ship had brought it to them at BA-XP-4382. Larsen spent hours going over nearly every centimeter of the ship, paying close attention to the fusion rocket and the hydrogen tanks. "Those fail, and we're dead," he explained.

"So?" Johnson asked as they met after the inspection.

Larsen turned to the seller. "How much?"

"A thousand for the ship. I'll let the suits go for five hundred."

Johnson knew that currency in the belt was based on grams of gold. A thousand grams would be the equivalent of a kilo of gold, even if no actual gold was exchanged.

Larsen snorted. "Seven-fifty and throw in the suits."

The seller hesitated.

"The fusion motor needs refurbished, the life support is barely adequate, and the cargo bay is unpressurized. And remember, part of the payment is in gold."

"Ore don't need to be pressurized," the man said. "Unless you're planning to haul something else, it'll do for you. Nine hundred, and I'll throw in the suits."

The negotiations took nearly an hour, but Larsen was tough and got the ship and the suits for 8,350 grams, including full hydrogen tanks.

The seller left on the next routine shuttle back to Asgard.

"Now what?" Johnson asked. "We're broke."

Larsen nodded grimly. "I have a plan."

"I hope so," Johnson said with a sigh.

#

They christened the small ship the *Nanna*. Larsen didn't laugh when Johnson suggested *The Jolly Roger*.

"As far as anyone knows, we're miners. In fact, we're going to have to do a little mining to pay for more hydrogen and keep up appearances. My old claim is near here and nowhere near played out."

"I don't know how to mine," Johnson reminded him.

"You don't know how to be a space pirate, either," Larsen replied with a smirk.

Larsen was an experienced miner, and began to teach Johnson how to pilot the *Nanna*. They didn't dare sell their finds on Asgard but had to go through middlemen, and that cut back on their profit. Still, Johnson was amazed, and if he didn't have the Bostad government breathing down his neck, he would have been happy to remain a miner. When they could afford it, they pressurized the cargo hold.

After two months of uneventful mining, Larsen announced it was time.

He laid out his plan to Johnson, who felt his stomach twist in fear.

"The Beowulf Cartel has an asteroid where they store spare parts and things they need. Rumor has it that it's half full of gold, too."

"It has to be guarded," Johnson said.

"And alarmed. But it's isolated, so by the time help arrives, we should be long gone."

"And what do we do about the guards?" Johnson asked, "Kill them?" That thought churned his stomach even more.

"I hope to avoid that," Larsen said.

"How?"

Larsen smiled. Johnson thought it was a very predatory expression.

The *Nanna* wasn't a stealthy ship, and Larsen knew it would show up on radar early, even with its transponder turned off to hide its identity.

"Unidentified ship," a voice came over the radio, "this is a private asteroid. Depart, or we will open fire." It wasn't unusual for isolated asteroids to have space-to-space missiles or railguns for self-defense, Larsen had said.

"This is the *Longboat*," Johnson replied over the radio. The name was a joke that he hadn't ran by Larsen. "Our life support is out. We are declaring an emergency. Please give us coordinates for docking."

Under the *Nanna*, Larsen used the maneuvering unit, which they had bought with the ship, to move away from the hull toward the asteroid. It interfaced with the suit, responding to movements of Larsen's hands, making virtual joysticks for controllers. A human in a spacesuit was small enough it shouldn't show up on the asteroid's radar, Larsen had told Johnson.

"Negative, and do not come any closer," the voice on the radio replied.

"Under the Asgard Cooperative Convention you are required to render assistance," Johnson said, trying to sound angry and scared. He was scared, so that helped.

"We don't recognize the convention. We have weapons trained on your vessel. Leave or we will fire."

133

"You're essentially killing me," Johnson cried.

"Everybody dies sometime, pal."

Johnson did his best to pilot the *Nanna* away from the asteroid. His training by Larsen had been extensive, but his practice had been minimal. He wished Larsen luck. But his job was to help with that luck.

#

Larsen's mining experience allowed him to "land" on the surface of the asteroid softly. Before he could bounce off, he shot a spike into the naked rock with a standard mining spike driver. The recoil did push him away from the surface, but he was tethered to that spike. He used his arms to reel himself in.

"Damn it," he swore. There had to be an airlock somewhere, and he hoped he was close to it. But, as he had approached the asteroid, he didn't see one. Time to make traverses across the surface: plant a spike and connect a rope to it, move a ways away, plant another, hook the end of rope to it then go back to the first spike, unhook from that, go past the second, and plant a third, hooking your rope to it. Go back to the second, unhook the rope, and go past the third to plant a fourth, hooking your rope to it. It was slow, tedious, but it kept you always attached to the asteroid as you moved. He was looking for a man-size airlock, hoping it wouldn't be guarded. He assumed it would be alarmed.

#

Johnson swung the *Nanna* around in a parabolic trajectory with the asteroid at the focus. He knew the cartel men would see this and hoped they wouldn't open fire.

"Why are you returning?" the voice came over the radio.

"I have no choice."

"We will blast you from space," the voice said.

"I don't think so," Johnson replied. "I'm headed straight for you. You destroy me, and my debris will destroy you."

They didn't answer. Finally, "You'll have to change course not to hit us soon."

"If I'm going to die," Johnson said, "I'm taking you with me."

There was no answer.

#

Larsen found an airlock: man sized. The control panel was standard, and it took him only a few moments to open the outer door. Airlocks were, by design, not capable of being secured. After all, who would think someone would break into an asteroid from the outside? Plus, if someone needed in, it was probably an emergency. A locked airlock could spell their doom.

There were handholds inside the airlock. Larsen drove a last spike near the airlock and attached his rope to it. Then, he grabbed a handhold, undid the snaplink connecting him to his rope, and pulled his body into the cylindrical airlock.

He hit the control to close the outer door and fill the chamber with air. He felt his suit compress as the air pressure increased and pulled his gun from a pocket on the outside of his suit. It contained a magazine holding ten bullets. They were designed for use in space: exploding on impact but breaking into small enough pieces that they were unlikely to penetrate a human body and hurt something critical behind them. "Just don't miss," was the common refrain.

Some, mostly criminals, used slugs made out of heavy but soft metals such as copper, zinc, or bismuth, or alloys of those. An asteroid was much too small a space to be blasting around a neurotoxin such as lead.

The inner door slid aside silently. A man stood there, holding a similar weapon. Only one man, Larsen thought…Johnson's distraction must be working.

Larsen had plastered himself to the side of the airlock. In the short moment it took the man to find him and aim his weapon, Larsen fired. The sound was about like a hand clapping, as the gun had been suppressed. The man looked surprised as blood oozed from his body in globules that floated in the air. Larsen fired again and, having time to aim, hit the man's head. His cranium exploded in a mist of pink and red. Larsen had to fight hard not to vomit.

The gun the man had floated free, tumbling slowly. Larsen tied off a rope to a handhold and pushed to the gun. When he reached it, he shot it twice, aiming for bare rock. This time, the sound was huge and echoed about the chamber.

Larsen pulled a short length of rope from another pocket and looped it about his free bicep, tying it off so it'd stay secure.

There were handholds and ropes inside the asteroid as normal. Larsen moved along the outer shell toward where the cargo airlock should be. He assumed the rest of the men guarding the asteroid would be there.

He didn't like killing the man, but he didn't see that he had any choice. The guy would have killed him without a moment's hesitation or a second of remorse.

He turned on the external speaker on his suit. He'd installed it so he could communicate in atmosphere while still wearing it. He hoped that would adequately protect his identity since the faceplate was mirrored, hiding his face.

#

There was no answer from the men on the asteroid. They'd been right about one thing: Johnson needed to change course soon. He yawed the *Nanna* and changed the acceleration vector, putting on the ship's full one-and-a-half-gee acceleration. The computer was not happy, signaling so with a red alert on the navigation screen, but he was going to miss the asteroid by a good hundred meters.

Still no word, yet, from the men inside. Maybe Larsen had gotten to them already. The *Nanna* moved sluggishly on its new course. His own radar showed he was accelerating at less than one and a half gees despite the *Nanna*'s instruments saying he was accelerating at a full one and a half gees. He hit the button again on the computer for full acceleration, but nothing happened. He was going to pass the asteroid far closer than he wanted. He might even hit it, he realized with alarm.

#

Two men hovered over a computer display. Larsen could tell from what little he could see that it displayed the asteroid's radar data.

"He's going to hit us," one exclaimed.

"The asteroid will protect us," the other replied with what sounded to Larsen like false surety.

"I don't know," the first one said.

"I do," Larsen growled, pointing his gun at the men.

CHAPTER FIFTEEN

They used handholds to turn, seeing Larsen and his gun.

"Who the hell are you?" one asked. He had a full beard and long hair controlled by being confined to a pony tail. "And where the hell is Stansky?"

The other man was bald and also had a beard. The only other hair on his head was his eyebrows, and what was growing out of his ears.

"Don't worry about that," Larsen answered. "Is there anyone else here?" Larsen didn't expect to get an honest answer.

"Yes," the bald one said. "Three others, coming up behind you."

"Nice try," Larsen said with a predatory grin. "Now you, baldy, tie up your friend." He untied the rope from his bicep and tossed it over.

Baldy growled but complied.

#

Johnson watched his radar with wide eyes. The *Nanna* moved as if some force were pulling it toward the asteroid. Suddenly, Johnson exclaimed to himself: gravity. He'd forgotten about the gravitational pull of the asteroid. It was small but enough to throw off his planned vector.

He watched as the asteroid grew closer and closer in the windows and closer and closer on the radar display, which now flashed an urgent red and yellow.

He cleared the asteroid by less than ten meters (the resolution of the radar display). He heard a ping on the hull and wondered if he'd hit an antenna or something.

#

Baldy tied up the one with the beard, and Larsen tied up Baldy. He then made sure Beard's bonds were sufficiently tight. Three men as guards made sense: they could watch each other and make sure none of them stole from the cartel's loot.

"You're a dead man," Baldy said. "You just don't know it yet."

"Don't make me regret not killing you," Larsen snarled.

That shut the man up.

Larsen switched the asteroid's computer display to the radio control.

"All is secure," he said. "You may dock now."

"Roger," came back Johnson's voice. Larsen wondered if it was his imagination, or did the voice sound shaky?

#

It took Johnson a long time to dock the *Nanna*. He hadn't had much practice.

When the airlock between the ship and the asteroid opened, Larsen was standing there smiling.

"Sorry," Johnson told him.

"Hell," Larsen replied. "Considering you're a rookie pilot, you did okay. But you cut the asteroid fly-by a little close."

"I wanted to scare them," was all Johnson said.

"You scared me when I looked at the radar recording."

Johnson grinned.

He stopped smiling when he saw the dead body. They were exploring the asteroid, looking for what they needed.

"It was him or me," Larsen explained.

Johnson nodded, then realized Larsen couldn't see that but didn't care. Suddenly it was real to him what they were doing. They were criminals. This wasn't self-defense like the police on Bostad, this was killing someone in the act of robbing them.

140

Johnson realized he'd just crossed a very thick moral line, even if he hadn't pulled the trigger. But it was either that or he might as well surrender. And he wasn't going to surrender.

The water cartel's asteroid contained an air recycler the size that Larsen had calculated was needed for the planned cabin they would build on the Bussard ramjet and for four adults.

"Adults?" Johnson asked.

"Sven will grow up," Larsen had explained.

Johnson nodded, again knowing Larsen wouldn't see it. He was being abnormally quiet.

The spacesuits and the *Nanna* were common designs ubiquitous in the belt. And Larsen had modified the *Nanna's* transponder to hide its identification. That, both men hoped, would keep the water cartel from finding them.

There was hydrogen and gold along with the air recycler, and the men took some of each.

"We'll need to hire people to modify the ramjet," Larsen said about the gold. "And pay them extra to keep quiet."

Johnson didn't say anything. This was getting more convoluted than he thought it would. But what choice did he have?

They left the asteroid with full hydrogen tanks. The hydrogen was stored on the asteroid in pressurized vessels and had a standard umbilical fitting that ran to the inside of the *Nanna* to fill its tanks. The asteroid's tanks had more pressure than the *Nanna's* tanks were rated for, so there was no need for a pump, just a pressure regulator which was on the asteroid. Apparently the asteroid was used as a cartel refueling station.

The two cartel men were still tied up, but Larsen loosened Baldy's bonds, giving him a chance to squirm out. Larsen hoped they would be out of weapons range by the time Baldy got loose.

With the extra mass on board the *Nanna's* acceleration was reduced, but Larsen had counted on that.

They spent a day travelling to Larsen's claim. There was, after Larsen's years of mining it, enough room to store the materials and gold they had stolen. The inside was in vacuum, but that didn't matter. The air recycler was in a vacuum-proof container.

"We'll store all our booty here," Larsen said with uncharacteristic frivolity. Johnson just smiled grimly, still being quiet.

They then did a little mining. They had to return to BA-XP-4382 with some ore or rumors would start to spread.

Sonia greeted them at the airlock, meaning someone told her they were about to dock and at which airlock. Johnson pulled his wife into his arms and held her a long time, floating together. Sonia using one hand to hold a rope.

When he finally let her go and smiled into her blue eyes, Sonia gave him a strange look.

"Is everything okay, Olly?"

He smiled. "Yes."

He hated lying to her.

\#

"We need a waste recycler," Larsen said. "And a computer that can interface with the Bussard ramjet's controls."

"Can we buy that?" Johnson said. They were accumulating wealth from mining, plus they had the gold they stole from the water cartel, along with the air recycler.

"Not if we don't want to draw attention of the Asgard Cooperative. I think they are tolerating us and not turning us over to the Bostad government only because we haven't broken any laws."

"That they know of," Johnson said.

"Yes. But water cartels don't call the cops."

"Yes," Johnson breathed, "I'm sure they handle things on their own." That was a thought that twisted his guts. He could imagine the cartel's men tossing him out an airlock, if he was lucky.

"I'm just not sure where we can find a waste recycler big enough," Larsen said. "At least one that's held by the water cartel."

"And if we steal from someone else," Johnson said, "they will call the cops."

"Yes," Larsen growled.

Of course, there were no cops in the literal sense. If it was reported to the Asgard Cooperative that Larsen and Johnson were stealing, they would send men to arrest them and most likely send them back to Bostad.

"We need information," Larsen said.

Johnson frowned.

#

The asteroid was not far from Asgard. Johnson almost expected it to have garish signs on the outside, but it was simply a low albedo rock with a lot of airlocks/dock combinations. He did spot the radiator for the fusion plant and the surface facing the sun (the asteroid's natural rotation had been stopped) was covered in solar collectors.

"Without much government," Larsen explained, "places like this can operate with impunity."

Johnson just nodded. It wasn't happening every time he closed his eyes, but he could still see that headless body surrounded by blood and viscera floating in the water cartel's asteroid.

"They call it 'Nirvana,'" Larsen said as he operated the *Nanna* through the computer.

A woman's voice came over the radio, directing them to an airlock. Johnson thought there was an amazing amount of sex woven into that normally dry, business-like command.

Larsen quickly docked the *Nanna* to the correct airlock, demarked by both a low-power radio beacon and red numbers painted on the door. The numbers were faded and scratched, Johnson noted.

"Be careful," Larsen warned. "A drunk miner is a dangerous thing."

Johnson nodded.

The airlock opened and Johnson's mouth fell open, even without gravity. Hanging on to ropes in front of the airlock were three beautiful women. All were only wearing a thin swatch of fabric, each a different bright, neon color, which did a barely adequate job of concealing their pubic region. One woman, with long red hair floating around her face like a fiery aureole, had a comet tattoo across her slender torso with the comet's head surrounding her naked left breast.

"Sorry, ladies," Larsen said, grinning. "Maybe later."

They all pouted in unison and pulled themselves away.

"Prostitutes?" Johnson whispered.

"Yeah," Larsen said. "They are called 'rock angels.'"

"They're beautiful," Johnson exclaimed. His experience was that prostitutes were not attractive, and often hooked on illegal drugs.

"Prostitution's legal. If a woman is willing she can make a fair amount of gold without the dangers of mining. Since it's legal, if a customer gets out of hand, she calls security. But the more beautiful, the more they cost."

Johnson chuckled for the first time since the water cartel asteroid.

Larsen pulled himself on a rope and Johnson followed. The interior of the asteroid was meretriciously lit, with actual neon signs demarking bars, brothels, "bath houses," and cafes. There were bearded men in various colors of overalls everywhere. Johnson saw some young, clean-shaven men dressed the same as the rock angels, and assumed they were prostitutes for those who were inclined to that sexuality.

"No air fee?" Johnson asked. Normally, that was collected at the airlock.

"Apparently not," Larsen said. "I guess they make it up in trade."

Larsen appeared to know where he was going and stopped in front of "Slippery Dick's Halfway Inn." Johnson wondered what exactly this establishment was until he grabbed a handhold and pulled himself in.

It was dark and there were women everywhere, dressed like the ones that greeted them at the airlock. Johnson realized Larsen had brought him to a brothel.

A blonde expertly pushed herself up against Johnson, wrapping her long legs around his. Her hair flew in his face until she shook her head, making it stand out from her skull.

"Hey, sweetie," she cooed. "Ever have sex in free fall? It'll blow your dirtballer mind."

Larsen leaned over. "He's not interested," he said to the blonde, "but I have a gram for you if you can tell Slippery Dick that John Larsen is here to see him."

The girl gave Larsen a sweet smile and held out her hand. Larsen put a piece of printed paper in her palm. She glanced at it briefly before stuffing it in her tiny panties. Johnson had learned long ago about "gold certificates" that were worth certain masses of gold. They were bought with gold and could be redeemed for gold, but they were a lot easier to carry and exchange. It was apparent miners didn't trust electronic funds that were the only form of currency on Bostad. Larsen said some didn't trust the gold certificates, either.

"Wait here," the girl said, and turned in the air, grabbed a line, and pulled herself toward the back of the establishment. Johnson was embarrassed to realize he was watching her nearly-naked ass as she moved away.

"How did she know I was from Bostad?" he asked. He assumed that's what "dirtballer" meant.

"It's the way you move," Larsen explained.

Johnson nodded unhappily. He had thought he was learning to move pretty well in free fall.

"Slippery Dick?" Johnson asked a few minutes later.

"The proprietor," Larsen said. "An old friend. Sort of."

The same girl returned in a few minutes. "Slippery says go to hell, and I'm supposed to show you the way."

Some friend, Johnson thought but didn't say.

"Tell him I will make him some money," Larsen said.

"Why should I?"

Larsen held up another gram note.

She smiled, took it, and turned to pull herself away.

"What makes her think I haven't had sex in free fall?" Johnson asked.

Larsen smiled. "Most dirtballers haven't."

Johnson snorted. He indeed had had sex in free fall: with his wife...after getting advice from Larsen and obtaining the proper equipment.

The girl returned. "Follow me," she said. "He's in a bad mood."

Larsen smiled and said, "So what's new? Thank you."

"Don't thank me until you've talked to him," she replied, sounding cynical.

The girl led Johnson and Larsen to the back of the establishment. There was a door made of purple plastic, and the girl knocked on it while holding a handhold next to the opening.

"Come," a gruff male voice said from inside.

The girl pushed the door inward and pointed.

Larsen nodded and pulled himself in. Johnson did the same, although with less ease.

A large man waited in a modified sleeping bag. Johnson had seen these before: they were used to work on something without too much movement. The bag was anchored to the wall at four points, and in front of the man was a holo display he was manipulating. Johnson was impressed. Holo displays were rare and expensive, and he'd rarely seen one, even on Bostad.

The man looked up at Larsen.

"Shut the damn door," he growled. "And why couldn't this be done via radio? You're taking up one of my damn docking ports and I'm not making any money off of you."

Larsen pushed the door closed and hung from a loop on the ceiling. At least Johnson thought of it as the ceiling, as it was above the man's head. He assumed this was Slippery Dick.

"You will make money," Larsen said.

"Yeah, how much?"

"More than you get from a horny miner."

146

"How about a drunk horny miner looking to score some seraph dust?"

Johnson frowned. He'd never heard of "seraph dust."

"Yes," Larsen said with emphasis.

"Tell me about it." Slippery Dick said.

"I need a waste recycler, high efficiency, sized for four people."

"Try Honest Nils' at Asgard," Slippery Dick spat.

"I need this without the Asgard Cooperative finding out about it."

Slippery Dick smiled. "Then how do you intend to find one?"

"Steal it," Larsen said. "From a water cartel."

CHAPTER SIXTEEN

"So you're not only stupid, but suicidal." Then Dick's eyes went wide. "You weren't the ones who jumped that Beowulf Cartel asteroid?"

"Naw," Larsen said. "But I heard about it."

"Yeah," Dick snarled. "Stupid people. They said it was a miner and a dirtballer." He looked intently at Johnson. "I guess if you're desperate, maybe wanted by the Impetusite government, you might do dangerous things. But remember this: governments might forget. The cartels never do."

Larsen kept quiet for a moment. Johnson wondered how this man knew so much about them.

"I have a kilo for you if you can simply point me at a waste recycler the size and efficiency I need that isn't being used at the moment."

"You said a kilo?"

"Yes."

"It ain't worth dying for."

"They'd never know we got the data from you."

"Until they catch you and start skinning you alive."

"That's not going to happen."

"Two kilos," Dick said.

"Okay," Larsen said.

"And none of the stuff you took from the cartel."

"What stuff? I mined it myself."

"Good," Dick said. "Now go have some fun while I see what I can find. And spend some goddamn money."

"Thanks," Larsen said.

"Get the hell out," Dick replied, waving a hand at the door.

Outside the chamber Johnson asked. "Now what?"

"We wait."

"Just wait?"

"Unless you want to enjoy the carnal delights this asteroid provides."

Johnson visibly shuddered. "No thanks."

Larsen smiled. "Well, we have some time to kill. Let's get a drink."

They found a quiet corner and ordered libations. Liquid drinks from water to tequila came in squeezable pouches with a straw. You put the straw in your mouth and squeezed. Allowing liquid to escape was a serious breach of protocol and safety. Johnson tried the beer and found it undrinkable. He switched to "bug juice," which was basically flavored sugar water with caffeine added. The caffeine was artificially produced in a laboratory since there were no coffee trees in the belt.

Another female came about an hour later and said Slippery Dick would see them.

Dick looked unhappy.

"You didn't find one?" Larsen asked.

"I did," he said. "And believe me, I had to cover my electronic tracks very well. I'm still hoping it was good enough."

"Where is it?" Larsen asked.

"BA-XM-14932. Owned by the Ragnarök Cartel."

Johnson frowned, not happy they would be angering a second cartel.

"Where's that?" Larsen asked.

"Not far. About a million klicks or so."

Johnson fought hard not to say anything. That was the range of the *Nanna* if they arrived with empty tanks.

"Damn," Larsen said.

"The place is like a fortress," Dick said. "You'll never get in, let alone get out with a recycler. And since somebody hit a water cartel and took an air recycler—and I'm not pointing fingers—every cartel has upped their security."

"Give us all the specs," Larsen said.

"Give me the gold," Dick growled.

"It's in our ship," Larsen said. "You can send someone to get it."

Johnson frowned but didn't say anything.

"Your pal has a concern," Dick said.

Larsen turned to him. "Yes?"

"There's more than—" Johnson started.

"Oh, don't worry, pal," Dick said. "I'll only take the two kilos agreed upon. Bad for business to jump people. Right, Larsen?"

"Right."

#

Johnson did enjoy one thing about freefall: he slept better. Yes, it was inside a sack attached to the wall, his arms floating. He did miss having Sonia in the same bed with the opportunity for incidental touching of skin, purposeful cuddling, and nuzzling her neck as he fell asleep. He asked Larsen about a two-person sack, and Larsen said they were available.

Larsen and Johnson spent hours alone trying to figure out how to steal a waste recycler from BA-XM-14932.

"We have two basic choices," Larsen said. "Stealth or strong arm."

"Steal it without their knowing or fight our way in?" Johnson asked.

"Yes."

"Or," Johnson suggested, "we could buy it from them."

"We'd be mining for years to get enough gold. And I don't think we have time. The Impetusite government is putting more pressure on the Asgard Cooperative to turn over 'wanted fugitives,' according to the news feeds."

Johnson frowned, and that ball of tension formed in his belly again.

151

"You know what's ironic," Johnson said with an angry tone.

Larsen shook his head.

"I used to sell just what we needed. But the Impetusites have probably confiscated it now."

Larsen thought for a moment. "Maybe we should steal it from the Impetusites, then."

"How? You want to talk about guarded. And we'd have to go back to Bostad, and how are we going to land on the planet unless we find another orbital shuttle pilot willing to take us down and back up?"

"Yes, you're right," Larsen said. "But let's not dismiss that. There might be a way."

"I doubt it."

Both men sat in silence. Then Larsen said, "Shit."

"What?"

"There's a third way."

"Oh?"

"Con."

Johnson snorted. "You're going to con a water cartel into giving us a waste recycler?"

Larsen nodded. "Maybe."

#

Johnson hadn't met Jakob before when he looked into Larsen's finances. Now the hacker turned out to be about sixteen years old with a scruffy beard that hadn't filled completely in yet.

"Can you do it?" Larsen asked.

He nodded.

"Can you do it without getting caught?"

He nodded again, but Larsen could tell he was deep in thought.

"What?" Larsen asked.

Jakob took a deep breath. "Computer security is like breaking into a house. Some people leave their doors unlocked, so it's easy. Some people have strong locks, strong doors, alarm systems, dogs, and armed guards, so it's hard. Nothing is 100% secure, so it's just a matter of how hard it's going to be.

"And if they do find out the message is fake, it'll look like it came from somewhere else. Unless they dig really deep and get past my dogs and armed guards."

"How much?" Johnson asked. He'd been quiet up until now, letting Larsen do the talking.

"Ten grams?" Jakob asked. "I don't usually do this for money, I do it for the asteroid—for Nielsen. And I'm paid by not having to pay air fees and free space to live."

"Ten grams is fine," Larsen said.

Johnson clamped his mouth shut lest he say something stupid. He thought ten grams was a bargain.

"When?" Jakob asked.

"When we're in place," Larsen said.

"I don't know how long it'll take."

"Don't worry. Just send us a tight beam when it's done."

Jakob nodded, deep in thought. Johnson hoped that he was thinking about how he was going to accomplish this. Johnson hoped the kid was as good as he claimed to be.

#

The transponder on the *Nanna* was off, in direct violation of the Asgard Cooperative Convention. But it hid the ship's identification. Its hydrogen tanks were nearly empty as Larsen had put the ship in orbit around the system's primary. He did this near a large B-type asteroid. A stony type, it was unlikely to have been mined, Larsen explained, so they didn't have to worry about miners discovering them. "I hope this will hide us a bit."

"What about the asteroid's gravity?" Johnson asked. He'd had a frightening object lesson about that.

"I'll have to use a little hydrogen to counteract that," Larsen said. "Not a lot."

Johnson nodded. "We don't have a lot."

They were about a hundred kilometers from BA-XM-14932, which Larsen said he thought would be outside the range of their radars.

"Seem to be weak radars," Johnson commented.

"They don't like to draw attention to themselves," Larsen explained. "Inverse square law."

Johnson wasn't sure what that was, so he kept quiet.

The men waited, Johnson keeping an eye on the air recycler. Its efficiency had dropped, and if they were out here long enough they'd run out of air. Larsen assured him they wouldn't be that long. "It'd take at least a week," he said.

The computer flashed a green border. It had received the tight beam from Jakob.

"Now we keep an eye out," Larsen said. "They should move quickly, but it still could be a few hours."

Johnson only nodded. They didn't dare use radar until they determined the ship was unarmed. Of course, every ship in the system with a fusion drive was "armed" as the exhaust from such a drive made an excellent weapon, as Johnson had learned back on Bostad.

It took about five and a half hours before they saw the ship heading for BA-XM-14932, decelerating to match orbits with it.

Larsen whistled. "Looks to me like they're accelerating at one gee. Let's hope that's their top acceleration."

Johnson nodded. The *Nanna* could do 1.5 gees, a little more now since the hydrogen tanks were nearly empty. "They didn't waste any time."

"Would you if your boss's life were in danger?" Larsen said with a chuckle.

Johnson was puzzled. "Life in danger?" He thought having a broken waste recycler would be an inconvenience, like having a clogged toilet. He didn't think it would be dangerous.

"Jakob's message said it was spewing liquid," Larsen explained. "Liquid in free fall is a bad thing. If it gets into your air recycler, it'll shut that down, and *then* your life is in danger."

"Oh," Johnson breathed.

It took over an hour, and the cartel ship accelerated away from BA-XM-14932. To Johnson's eye it was accelerating about the same amount, but with the added mass it had taken on, it had to be accelerating slower. Unless it had a powerful enough fusion rocket to compensate for the extra mass.

Larsen accelerated the *Nanna* hard, slamming Johnson into his acceleration chair.

"Radar?" Johnson asked.

"Not yet. Going to have to rely on the old Mark I calibrated eyeball."

With constant acceleration, matching orbits was much simpler than working with orbital mechanics. You still had to keep in mind that gravity affected everything, even if your fusion engine could easily overcome it.

The computer beeped. "We're picking up their radar," Larsen announced. "They'll detect us soon. Still no sign of weapons." Larsen had explained that powerful lasers designed to cut into asteroids or space-to-space missiles were a possibility. "Radar," Larsen snapped.

Johnson touched his computer screen, turning on the *Nanna's* radar.

"Zero point nine-six gees," Larsen said with a smile. "Come on, *Nanna*, you can catch them."

"Approaching ship," a voice came over the radio, sounding harsh and gruff, "move away from us or we shall open fire."

"With what?" Larsen said to Johnson. "Cartel ship," Larsen said over the radio. "Prepare to be boarded."

"Like hell," the voice on the radio came back.

Larsen smiled. "They haven't increased acceleration. That means they are going flat out."

"And if they have weapons?"

"Then we're dead," Larsen answered with a light tone.

Larsen maneuvered the *Nanna* within a few meters of the cartel ship, careful to stay out of range of their fusion exhaust. Every few moments the voice would urge them to get away, even saying they had reinforcements coming. They tried once to aim their fusion flame at the *Nanna*, but Larsen easily dodged it in the smaller, more nimble ship.

The cartel ship began changing acceleration randomly, making it impossible for Larsen to match velocities and dock with their airlock.

"That's what I'd do," Larsen said with a smile.

"But what do we do, now?"

"Cartel ship," Larsen said over the radio. "Allow us to dock, or we will ram you."

"Fuck you," the voice said.

Larsen moved the *Nanna* closer.

"Do you want to die today?" Larsen asked. "I don't care."

The cartel ship accelerated smoothly.

"Boy, they gave up easy," Larsen said with a chuckle. He touched the transmit icon on the screen. "End acceleration, now," he ordered.

"Not going to happen," a voice came back, different from the first.

Larsen shook his head. "I guess we'll do this the hard way."

It took Larsen about ten minutes to mate the docking rings. They were standardized, so any ship could dock with any other ship as a safety measure. Radar and the computer helped, but he told Johnson it would have been much easier if the cartel ship had stopped accelerating completely.

Wearing spacesuits against both the possibility the cartel men might evacuate the air from their ship, and to hide their identity, Larsen and Johnson, guns in hand, opened the *Nanna's* airlock door to face the closed airlock door on the cartel ship. But there were standard airlock controls next to the portal.

"How do you know they won't be disabled?" Johnson asked over his suit radio.

"Only an idiot would disable them. It's a safety requirement, just like standardized docking rings. If you're disabled in a damaged ship, and a rescue ship docks to save your life, you don't want to lock out the rescuers."

Larsen touched the controls, and the outer airlock door opened, followed by the inner door.

Two men were standing there, holding guns and pointing them at Larsen and Johnson. They, too, were in spacesuits but their faceplates were clear, and Johnson could see both had beards. One was blond, and the other had nearly jet black hair.

"We can't let you on board," the one with black hair said. It came over the suit radio, and was the second voice they'd heard on the ship's radio. It was strange to see the man in front of him but hear his voice in stereo, almost as if there were two of them.

"We're coming," Larsen said.

"We'll kill you," Blackbeard growled.

"I don't think so," Larsen said. "You're not hired guns, you're pilots. If you were going to kill us, if you had the guts to kill us, you would have already."

Neither man answered.

Johnson decided that was why they hadn't used the fusion exhaust as a weapon: they weren't killers.

"We, on the other hand," Larsen said, "are desperate, and we will kill you if we need to."

Johnson was glad they couldn't see his face, because at the moment he was sure he looked frightened at the possibility he might have to kill someone.

The men lowered their guns.

CHAPTER SEVENTEEN

"Put them on the floor and kick them to me." Larsen indicated the guns.

The men complied. Larsen bent down and picked each one up in turn, putting them in pockets in his spacesuit.

"Now," Larsen said. "We're taking the waste recycler you're carrying and your hydrogen. Your cooperation will ensure your survival."

"You take our hydrogen we'll be stranded," Blackbeard said.

"We won't disable your radio. You will have plenty of time to be rescued." Larsen made a motion with his gun. "Now, please step aside. Joe, the computer."

"Yes, Sam," Johnson said. He walked back into the *Nanna*, glad for the acceleration that gave the feeling of gravity and mourning the fact that it was going away soon. As he did this, he heard Larsen say over the radio, "Unless you're planning to decompress your ship, you might as well take off those spacesuits. You'll be more comfortable."

Johnson sat in front of the computer in the *Nanna's* cockpit. Larsen had already set up the command, he just had to touch the screen.

"Okay, suit yourself," Larsen said, and Johnson heard over the radio. "Take me to the cockpit."

Johnson waited.

Nothing happened.

Then he heard, "Joe!" in more of a grunt than a statement.

Johnson ran back for the cartel ship, holding his gun.

Larsen and the two men were wrestling on the floor, Larsen holding the gun and doing his best to keep it away from the other two men. That they were all wearing clumsy spacesuits both helped and hindered Larsen. He couldn't get away from the men, but the men couldn't get the weapon.

The blond one must have gotten smart, and reached for the pocket where Larsen had put the cartel men's guns.

"Stop!" Johnson yelled, pointing his gun at the entangled ball of men.

"You're not going to shoot," Blackbeard said. "You have a damn good chance of hitting Sam here."

"You've got a two-thirds chance," Larsen snarled. "Shoot."

Johnson shot, trying to hit the blond. Johnson had never fired a gun before. He hit Blackbeard in the arm.

Blackbeard howled in Johnson's ears. Larsen twisted and managed to escape from the blond.

"Don't make me shoot you, too," Johnson said, trying to sound menacing.

Blondie put his hands up and sat on the floor. Blackbeard held his arm and whimpered. Johnson was surprised no blood came from the hole in the spacesuit, but the suit must have contained it all.

"Good shot," Larsen said.

"Thanks," Johnson replied. He decided not to reveal that it was all luck.

"Shall we try this again?" Larsen said.

"Yes. Are you going to be safe this time?"

"Sure," Larsen growled. "I think they'll cooperate, now."

Blackbeard was taking off his spacesuit, and Blondie was getting a first aid kit.

Johnson returned to the *Nanna* and again sat in front of its control computer.

He sat there for a few minutes, wondering if he should return to the cartel ship. Finally, his radio crackled to life.

"Ready?" Larsen asked.

"Yes," Johnson said.

"If we time this wrong, we'll tumble."

"I know," Johnson growled. Larsen had drilled that into him.

"On three," Larsen said. "One, two, three, now."

Johnson touched the red dot on the computer.

Both ships stopped accelerating. Johnson felt himself float away from the chair. He grabbed a handhold.

A few moments later Larsen said, "Very good. A very slight tumble, but nothing we can't correct."

By the time Johnson returned to the cartel ship, both cartel men were out of their spacesuits and Blackbeard's injury had been bandaged. Larsen had both men tied up with rope he'd had in one of his suit's many pockets.

Moving the heavy and large waste recycler into the *Nanna* was both easier and harder in free fall. The crate that held it was over six cubic meters, a little longer in one dimension, and massed nearly seven thousand kilograms.

"Hey, we need that," Blackbeard scowled as they passed by.

"No, you don't," Larsen said simply.

Blackbeard growled.

While it weighed nothing, it still retained its mass and therefore momentum, requiring Johnson and Larsen to be very careful not to let it move too quickly lest it obtain so much momentum they couldn't stop it.

It took an hour to get the waste recycler loaded and strapped down in the *Nanna's* cargo bay. It looked huge in there.

"Now for the fun part, Sam," Larsen said.

"But I'm Joe," Johnson replied with a smile, even though he knew Larsen couldn't see it.

"Right, I forgot."

The maneuvering unit was also in the cargo bay, looking small compared to the waste recycler. All ships had more than one airlock: another safety requirement. Larsen strapped the maneuvering unit on his back with Johnson's help, and pulled himself into the *Nanna's* other airlock.

"Keep in touch," Johnson said, trying to affect a light tone.

"Will do," Larsen replied tersely.

Johnson suspected he was nervous. This was the most dangerous part of this operation and if it went badly, both Larsen and he would mostly likely die.

#

The cartel ship's hydrogen tanks could only be accessed from its exterior. Larsen exited the *Nanna's* airlock and used the maneuvering unit to find her hydrogen transfer hose. It was on the far side of the airlock, and luckily, near the cartel ship's hydrogen filling port. Since the ship didn't need to be aerodynamic, there were plenty of handholds and places to grab the hull. Using one hand to hold on to the ship and the other to open the hatch, Larsen turned the handle, revealing the compartment where the transfer hose was coiled. He tried not to think about the fact they were moving around sixteen meters per second, or over fifty-seven thousand kilometers an hour, relative to BA-XM-14932 and most of the other asteroids in the belt. Of course, they were all orbiting the system's primary at various velocities depending on how far they were from the sun.

The well-maintained hatch had opened easily, and Larsen pulled out the hose. It was about as thick as his forearm with a standard coupling at the end. He had to take it to the cartel ship, open the access port to the tank filing flange, attach the hose, open the valve there, then come back here and open the valve. This was normally done by robot so everything was made to fit together easily so the robot's AI didn't have to think too hard. It was also designed to be used by humans in case of emergency.

Since there was no pump, they would only get hydrogen flow until the pressure in both tanks equalized. The cartel ship had larger tanks, so Larsen was hoping he'd get enough hydrogen to at least get somewhere where they could obtain more. They might not be able to accelerate at one gee, and might have to coast for a while to conserve hydrogen.

He took the hose in one hand (it had a small handle at the end) and used the maneuvering unit to arc over to the cartel ship, careful about his speed and using the maneuvering unit to slow precisely.

The cartel ship's hydrogen transfer port was easily spotted, surrounded by yellow and red paint. Larsen let go of the hose and, knowing it would stay in position relative to him and the ship, used one hand to grab a handhold and the other to open the hatch.

Now came the hard part.

He reached back with his free hand and grabbed the hose, jockeying it into position with one hand. Larsen smiled, happy that his experience working in free fall helped him with this task.

Something thumped him in the left thigh. It didn't hurt a lot, but a red band appeared on his suit's heads up display.

"SUIT BREACH" flashed in crimson letters.

"Damn," Larsen breathed. He was sure what had happened. A small rock—perhaps a few millimeters in diameter—had hit him. Or more accurately, he had hit it at fifty-seven thousand kilometers an hour. The result was like getting shot by a bullet going fifty times faster than those fired by a gun.

He looked down at his thigh, and the blood spraying from the small hole like an aerosol.

"Johnson," Larsen said over the radio. "I've had a suit breach, and I'm injured. I might need your help."

"Understood," Johnson replied. Even the radio couldn't disguise the fear and trepidation in his voice.

The suit breach was an easy fix. Larsen had a suit repair kit at his waist. He used a rope with a snaplink to attach himself to the handhold on the cartel ship, then used both hands to repair the hole by slapping a big patch on it. Glue melted into fabric, and the repair was nearly as strong as the suit. He was still losing air, and realized there was another breach on the back of his thigh. He had trouble reaching it, but soon it, too, was repaired.

But Larsen was bleeding, and he didn't know how badly. Since the blood was body temperature, and was held close to his skin by the spacesuit so it wouldn't cool, he had no idea how much there was.

Working slowly and methodically despite his near panic, he attached the hose to the cartel ship and opened the valve, always using a handhold to keep him steady.

He undid the snaplink and moved back toward the *Nanna*. If he could get the hydrogen transferring, then he could go inside and see how badly he was hurt.

He was starting to feel faint as if he was losing a lot of blood.

"Johnson," he said.

"Yes?" More fear in that statement.

"Get in the airlock and open it. But just stay there."

"Okay," Johnson said.

Larsen grabbed a handhold and opened the valve. He half expected to hear the hydrogen flowing, but of course he couldn't. He had to assume it was because there was no reason it wouldn't.

He maneuvered to the airlock, his vision going grey. He could see it, and see Johnson in it, hanging on to something.

"Grab me," Larsen breathed, hoping Johnson heard it.

He aimed his body at the open airlock and gave the maneuvering unit one last order to accelerate toward it for a fraction of a second.

#

Johnson saw Larsen coming at him too fast. He stiffened his grip on the handhold inside the airlock. A clean, white spot on Larsen's thigh showed where the patch had been made.

Larsen careened into the airlock. Johnson grabbed him with his free hand around the wrist, and they both were pushed against the inner door, then bounced out. Johnson knew that if he allowed them to bounce out of the airlock, there was no way to get back except Larsen's maneuvering unit. But only Larsen could control it with his suit and Johnson thought he was unconscious.

He held tight to the handhold as momentum tried to jerk him into space. Johnson grunted with pain, but he managed to hang on.

There was slight recoil but not enough that they bounced off the inner door again. Both men were floating inside the airlock.

Johnson then, and only then, dared to take his hand off the steel loop and work the controls to shut the outer door.

Air pumped in, and Johnson hit the emergency airlock open button and the door opened before the pressures had completely equalized. Johnson pushed Larsen into the cockpit. He wished for acceleration as this would make it much easier, but that was impossible as long as they were attached to the cartel ship. He shoved Larsen into the cargo bay, glad they had expended the time and gold to pressurize it.

He took off Larsen's spacesuit as quickly as he could. Somewhat bulky, but still fairly easy to remove despite the lack of gravity, Johnson had it off in a few minutes. As he pulled Larsen out of the bottom of it, blood, floating in globules, rose out of the suit.

"Damn," Johnson breathed. If blood got into their air recycler, they'd be in trouble. He pushed himself to the cockpit and turned off the ventilation. There should be enough oxygen to last until he could get the air cleaned up. At least, he hoped.

Coming back, he could see Larsen had lost a lot of blood by the volume in the air, and was still bleeding from two wounds in his left thigh. It looked like whatever hit him went straight through the meat of the leg. The wounds were small, but the damage was extensive judging by the discoloration of the skin around them and the extent of the bleeding.

Johnson knew applying pressure could help stem the bleeding, but how could he without gravity?

He decided he could work better without his suit on and quickly took it off, letting the parts float off in the cargo bay.

He grabbed the first aid kit and, moving carefully in free fall, wrapped the gauze roll repeatedly around Larsen's thigh, pulling it tight, hoping that would be enough pressure. It was hard work, and most of the time the two men were floating in the middle of the cargo bay as Johnson used both hands: one to hang onto Larsen and one to wrap the gauze around him, and a foot against Larsen's thigh to give him leverage to pull the gauze tight.

CHAPTER EIGHTEEN

When he was done, they were near a wall. Johnson left Larsen there and used more gauze to soak up the floating blood. Some had stuck to the walls, and he cleaned that up, too, trying to get as much of the red liquid cleaned up as possible before he turned the air recycler on again. Larsen had explained the air recycler could handle fine aerosols, but nothing larger than a fingertip.

Johnson went to the cockpit and turned on the air recycler, wondering if it was his imagination that the air suddenly became fresher.

He checked the progress of the hydrogen transfer on the computer. None had been transferred; the *Nanna's* tanks were still nearly empty. Something was wrong.

"Damn," he breathed. Larsen was unconscious and probably needed a doctor. If either man were to survive, Johnson needed to fix the problem. That meant going outside.

Larsen's face was pale and his breathing shallow, Johnson noted. A long time ago he'd taken a first aid course, and suspected his friend was going into shock. He moved him to the co-pilot acceleration chair in the cockpit. The first aid kit had a blanket folded up so small Johnson was surprised at how big it was when unfolded. He loosened Larsen's clothing as best he could and tied the blanket around him. He knew he was supposed to elevate Larsen's feet, but in free fall he didn't think that would matter.

Once acceleration started, he could do that, he thought. But first, he had to fix the problem of the hydrogen flow.

As he put his spacesuit back on, he decided he shouldn't use the maneuvering unit. Larsen had experience with it, but Johnson had never used it. Plus, he wasn't sure it would work with his suit. He'd be safer, he decided, just using handholds. His biggest worry, which was churning his intestines, was that he wouldn't be able to find or fix the problem. Still, he had to try.

He debated asking the cartel men for help but immediately dismissed the notion.

Going out the airlock, his stomach tightened. But he found handholds. In a violation of safety protocol, he left the outer airlock door open. He decided they'd thrown safety out when they went after the cartels.

Carefully, and always keeping one hand holding a part of the *Nanna*, he moved over the back of the hull toward the hydrogen filling hose port. He celebrated when he finally came in view of the hose, but then remembered that he had to fix what the problem was or they were both dead. If only Larsen were conscious, he could help. Johnson was on his own like he'd never been before.

He pulled over to the hatch and looked inside. Larsen hadn't opened the valve all the way. It was obvious. Johnson smiled, and in his rush to open it, forgot to hang onto the ship. He pushed it and instead of the valve moving, he moved, almost losing his grip on the valve handle and floating into space.

"Damn it," he snarled to himself.

He used the valve handle to pull himself back to the ship, grabbed a handhold with his free hand, and then managed to open the valve all the way. He was surprised, at first, he didn't hear anything. But the hose went stiff, indicating there was pressure inside it.

Johnson smiled and carefully pulled his body back around the hull to the airlock.

When the inner door opened, he pushed to the cockpit and checked the gauges. The *Nanna's* tanks were filling.

Johnson at first thought he'd just disconnect the transfer hose from the *Nanna*, thinking they could buy another one. He realized that if he didn't close the valve on the cartel ship, it would lose all its hydrogen, and the cartel men would die. He wasn't ready to kill anyone. When it was obvious the pressure between the tanks had equalized, and he wasn't going to get any more hydrogen from the cartel ship, he went back outside. He gingerly used handholds to move to the cartel ship, closed the valve, disconnected the hose, and then returned on the same path he'd used to get there. This was taking a lot longer than he liked. The cartel ship was surely overdue at its destination and the cartel might come looking for it. By the time Johnson had secured the transfer hose and closed the hatch and gotten back inside the *Nanna*, two hours had passed, and he was exhausted.

Johnson went into the cartel ship, still wearing his spacesuit. The two men were still there and still tied up. They scowled at Johnson.

"We're leaving now," Johnson said. "I'm sure you'll be rescued soon."

"You're dead men," Blackbeard scowled.

"Yes, I've been told that before," Johnson snapped back. He was tired.

Johnson returned to the *Nanna*, undocked from the cartel ship, and accelerated away from it at one gee. Taking off his spacesuit was easier with pseudo gravity, and he checked on Larsen. The man was still unconscious, but the bleeding had stopped. He remembered to elevate Larsen's feet over his head now that there was acceleration. He used his spacesuit helmet.

Johnson was worried as Larsen was a much better pilot. He touched Larsen's neck and felt a weak pulse. At least he was alive.

#

"Mayday, Mayday," Johnson said over the radio, sending it on a tight beam to BA-XP-4382.

He'd managed to put the *Nanna* stationary relative to the asteroid. But slowly, inexorably, gravity from the asteroid and the primary were grabbling to drag the *Nanna* into moving. Johnson kept touching the screen trying to adjust the thrusters to keep the ship stationary relative to the asteroid.

"This is BA-XP-4382," a voice came back. "Who is this?"

Johnson was embarrassed. He'd forgotten to say which ship he was. "This is the *Nanna*. I need an emergency docking and a doctor at the airlock."

Johnson had gone straight to BA-XP-4382 without dropping off the waste recycler in their stash asteroid. He decided that would save hydrogen and time and be more likely to keep Larsen alive.

"Dock at airlock three," the voice came back. "We are getting the doctor down there now."

"Roger," Johnson acknowledged. Despite his lack of practice, the *Nanna* was docked in few minutes. Maybe the need for alacrity had increased Johnson's docking skills, he mused. He unstrapped Larsen from the acceleration couch and, moving him carefully in free fall, carried him to the airlock. The door slid open and the asteroid's doctor was there, hanging onto a rope, along with two other men Johnson didn't know. Sonia was there, too, looking worried. The two men pulled themselves quickly to Johnson, took Larsen from him, and under the direction of the doctor, held him while he examined the wound.

Sonia, still unsure in free fall, moved to him and held him close. Johnson kept one hand on a handhold, but wrapped his other arm about Sonia's small body.

"I was so worried," she breathed. "They said your ship was coming in with an injury. I thought it might be you."

"He's lost a lot of blood," Johnson said to the doctor.

The doctor only nodded at Johnson's statement. Then he said, "You did this?" as he fingered the gauze.

"Yes," Johnson replied.

"You did a good job. Probably saved his life. We'll have to start blood transfusions immediately."

Johnson nodded, but the doctor ignored him and pulled himself away. The two men holding Larsen did the same, following the doctor, expertly moving as they held the unconscious man.

"What happened?" Sonia asked.

"He was hit by a fast-moving micro-meteoroid," Johnson said. He'd decided on the trip back that that would be his story. Even Sonia didn't know what he and Larsen were doing.

"Where's Sven?" he asked his wife.

"In our quarters," Sonia said. "Tied to a handhold. Gregor is watching him." That was a neighbor man whose wife spent her days mining while he watched their kids and repaired computers.

Johnson smiled. It might seem cruel to tie a child to a handhold like a leash, but it was for their own safety. Plus, Sven still loved living in free fall and thought it all just a game.

"I'm going to the infirmary," Johnson said. "I need to check on Larsen."

Sonia nodded, but waited a few moments to let him go.

In the infirmary, Larsen was strapped to a bed-like surface. He had a clear plastic mask over his mouth and nose that connected to an oxygen bottle. A small pump pushed blood into him through an IV. Johnson smiled. He, of course, thought there'd be an IV bag on a hanger and the blood would drip in, but that wouldn't work in free fall.

The doctor came into the small room. "I estimate whatever hit him was about three millimeters in diameter and moving fast. It's rare that something moves that fast in the belt relative to asteroids. Your friend was very unlucky. That rock must have been on some parabolic orbit of the primary, moving like a bat out of hell from this system's Oort cloud. That it intersected with your friend's leg...well, the odds are literally astronomical."

Johnson nodded.

"But in an infinite universe," the doctor was saying, "anything that can happen, will happen an infinite number of times. At that velocity and that mass it must have been about like getting shot with a rifle bullet."

Johnson couldn't think of anything to say.

"He was also lucky," the doctor continued. "The projectile went through muscle and didn't hit any bones or major blood vessels."

"That's good," Johnson said, feeling as if he needed to respond. He would have hated to see how much blood there would have been if it had hit a major blood vessel.

"I assume he was outside your ship because you two are mining." the doctor said.

"Yes," Johnson replied.

The doctor shook his head, then he looked at Johnson with gray eyes. "I assume you can afford this."

Johnson nodded. There was no such thing as medical insurance in the belt. You needed a doctor, you paid for it. Most doctors would extend credit, but even then, you had to pay them back or you'd get a bad reputation and maybe even the Asgard Cooperative confiscating your goods.

Johnson knew they had the gold they'd stolen from the cartel. He hoped it was enough. The *Nanna's* hydrogen tanks were nearly empty now, too. And of course there was living expenses: food, water, air fees, and rental fees on their quarters. And Larsen needed a new spacesuit.

Their gold was in their cache asteroid, and Johnson wasn't comfortable docking with it or taking an experienced pilot with him. He'd have to wait until Larsen was able to pilot the *Nanna*.

Johnson sighed. Added to that worry was if the water cartels they've been stealing from found out who they are. Then they were as good as dead. Johnson wondered briefly if he should have killed the men on the cartel ship. But he just didn't have that in him, to kill in cold blood. He wasn't even sure he could kill someone even if they were threatening him.

#

Larsen gained consciousness a few hours after they started the blood transfusion.

"You got us home," he said to Johnson, smiling. The smile had an edge of pain in it, despite all the painkillers the doctor had given him.

172

"Yes," Johnson replied with a grin.

"How did you unload things at the asteroid by yourself?"

"I didn't. I came straight here."

Larsen's face went paler.

"I didn't have a choice," Johnson said, trying not to sound defensive.

"You're right; you didn't," Larsen said in a near whisper. "But we need to go back there as soon as possible and get that waste recycler hidden."

"I know. We also need gold. The *Nanna's* H-2 tanks are nearly empty, and it'll take all we have left here to fill them."

"We don't have to fill them," Larsen said. "Just enough to get us to the cache and back with, oh ten percent reserve."

Johnson nodded. He would never have thought of that.

"The doctor give you any indication when I could be up and around?" Larsen asked.

"No," Johnson replied. "But you were lucky."

"Oh?" Larsen asked.

"The projectile didn't hit any bones or major blood vessels."

Larsen nodded. "That's good. Then I should be up quickly, I would think."

"I suppose so," Johnson said.

Larsen looked at the other man. "What's wrong?"

Johnson shook his head, which made his body move in response even though he was gripping a handhold. "This is damn dangerous," he said.

Larsen nodded. "Yes, it is. Would you like to go back to Bostad?"

Johnson frowned. "Of course not."

"Then this is the situation we have to live with."

"And the cartels?"

"I'm hoping to be light years away before they figure out who we are. If they ever figure it out."

Johnson didn't say anything.

"We had a bit of bad luck," Larsen said. "As soon as I'm recovered, we go get the computer we need for that Bussard ramjet."

"Where?" Johnson asked in a whisper.

Larsen smiled. "Don't know yet."

"And who," Johnson asked, "is going to retrofit the ramjet to have a life support system?"

"Oh, that's an easy one," Larsen said. "Anyone with the skills needed looking to make a quick gram without the dangers of mining."

"And how do we keep them quiet?"

"We pay them well. And by then, it'll be a moot point," Larsen said. "The cartels won't be able to find us in some random spot in the asteroid belt."

Johnson shook his head. He wondered briefly if there was a better way to deal with the possibility of the Asgard Cooperative turning them over to the Impetusites than being space pirates and risking an unpleasant death at the hands of the water cartels.

CHAPTER NINETEEN

Dinner that night was quiet in Johnson's quarters. When they'd made some money mining, Larsen had gotten his own place to give the family some privacy.

They had to re-teach Sven how to eat since the skills needed in free fall were different that those needed on a planet. Johnson was locked into his own thoughts as he wondered if the cartels would come after his family, too, not just being satisfied to kill him and Larsen if they caught them.

"What are you thinking about, dear?" Sonia asked as she helped Sven eat.

Johnson smiled at his wife. "Oh, just Larsen and the bad luck we had."

Sonia nodded, a worried look crossing her face.

"The doctor said the odds were 'literally astronomical' that Larsen would get hit that way," Johnson said, trying to make her feel better. "It was just very bad luck that he was."

Sonia smiled, and Johnson could tell she was trying not to look worried.

"What happens when you mine enough?"

"Enough?" Johnson asked. "We need to mine to pay for living expenses. It'll be an ongoing thing, at least for a while." He hated lying to her, but to tell her the truth was too painful. Plus, he thought the less she knew, the safer she'd be.

"So you'll always be in danger?" she breathed.

Johnson set his lips as he thought. Then he spoke with measured and careful words. "Larsen's very good and very experienced. And I'm learning every time we go out. Yes, there are mining accidents. And, eventually, I hope we'll have enough to retire."

"What about the Impetusites?" Sonia asked.

"With enough money, we can hire good lawyers that will keep us from being deported back to Bostad."

Sonia nodded but she didn't look convinced.

#

"I found the computer," Larsen exclaimed. He was still in the infirmary but the doctor was sure he could leave in a few days.

"Where?" Johnson asked. "Let me guess: a cartel asteroid."

"No," Larsen said. "A cartel ship."

Johnson's eyes went wide. "And how do you steal a computer out of a ship?"

"You don't," Larsen said. "You steal the ship."

Johnson studied Larsen's face to determine if he were serious. He looked serious.

"This works out great. I'm not sure why I didn't think of this before. A ship will have everything we need to convert the ramjet," Larsen said. "We won't have to build the living quarters for the ramjet from scratch. Simply convert the ship to be the living quarters. Plus, we'll have back up air and waste recyclers. We're going to be in space a long time and a long ways from anybody. We need backups. I'd prefer two, but one spare will have to do."

"And if they both fail?" Johnson asked.

Larsen shook his head. "If one fails, we replace it with the spare and fix it. If the spare fails, we put the repaired one back in and fix the spare. We always have one on stand-by."

"And you can fix these?"

"Yes," Larsen said. "We'll have to procure some spare parts."

"Buy or steal?"

"We can probably buy those," Larsen said.

"Good," Johnson breathed.

#

176

On the way to steal the ship, travelling in the *Nanna*, Larsen laid out his plan. Johnson listened, but inside his guts churned. This could easily get them both killed.

Larsen moved a bit stiffly under acceleration. His left leg was still healing and wrapped in a large bandage. In free fall, he was as lissome as ever.

"The biggest problem," Larsen said, "is there's no way to hide our faces. This will bring the Asgard Cooperative down on us."

"Meaning what?" Johnson asked.

"Meaning we return immediately to BA-XP-4382, pick up Sonia and Sven, and go pick up everything at my claim, then we hide until we can steal the ramjet."

"You're serious?"

"Yes."

"And how do we find people to help us modify the ramjet?"

"They were always going to be desperate people, near criminals. Once we are identified as criminals, it'll be easier."

"And the Ragnarök Cartel?" They also owned the ship that Larsen was planning to steal. Johnson knew they would come after Larsen and him with all they had. They had already put a message on the 'net that they would pay a lot of grams to learn the men's identity. The Beowulf Cartel had done the same.

Larsen pursed his lips. "That will be a challenge. No one can leave the build operation until it's done and we're on our way to Gredel."

"How are the two of us—?"

"Three. Don't forget about your wife."

Johnson sighed. "How are the two of us going to control that? Ensure no one comes, goes, or contacts the cartels during the work?"

"We take all communication devices that aren't short-range, and we lock down their ships."

"How do we lock down their ships?"

"Jakob taught me how to hack their passwords. It takes a little time, but I can do it."

Johnson shook his head.

"Would you rather go back to Bostad?" Larsen asked. "Did you see the Impetusites have officially reinstated the death penalty, and that you and I are on the top of their most-wanted-to-kill list?"

Johnson nodded. He guessed he had no choice. Chances may be slim, but they beat the odds of giving up. And he hadn't come this far to give up now.

He hadn't told Sonia but she probably saw it, too. She, of course, looked at the 'net like everyone else, when she had time. To assist with paying living expenses, she helped at the hydroponic gardens twenty hours a week, where she had discovered an affinity for the computers that ran the system, a talent neither she nor Johnson had suspected.

She'd made an arrangement with Gregor that they'd watch each other's children when the other was busy. Johnson thought Gregor was getting the better deal, with three rambunctious boys.

#

It involved another trip to Nirvana and another payment to Slippery Dick to get the information they needed. Dick was nervous.

"You two are stirring up a nest of vipers," he whispered.

"Let us worry about that."

"As long as you don't ever say my name," Dick said, demanding four kilos, in gold, for the information Johnson and Larsen needed.

The *Loki* was docked at an asteroid called Vanir. It was the Ragnarök Cartel's boss' ship. Larsen said, half-jokingly, Johnson was sure, that they could cut off the drive, strap it to the ramjet, and they'd be done.

Vanir was a large asteroid, just a bit smaller than Asgard but less centrally located among the mining colonies. Its primary function was to supply miners with what they needed (which did extend to bars, brothels, and seraph dust parlors, just on a smaller scale than Nirvana). Johnson was marginally familiar with the asteroid. While he'd never visited, of course, he'd had dealings with many of its vendors, supplying them with things that only

Bostad could provide, such as animal proteins and certain plastics made from hydrocarbons, not plant oils.

The traffic control system for Vanir would direct them to a docking port/airlock. They had no choice of which to use. And the system's radar had sufficient resolution that they would have noticed Larsen using the maneuvering unit. They could only get on the *Loki* from inside the asteroid.

Unlike many inhabited asteroids, this one was not simply a shell filled with ropes, handholds, and plastic sections that were housing or stores or bars. Vanir had corridors, mostly made of plastic. Johnson noticed a metal that, by its luster, he decided was aluminum. For a moment he wondered what source of bauxite the miners used. Then he remembered that some asteroids had not insignificant amounts of calcium–aluminum-rich inclusions, which were thought to be one of the first solids formed when a star system condensed from a disk around its protostar.

As Johnson and Larsen exited the *Nanna* through the airlock, Larsen glanced around. They were in a corridor that ringed the outside of the asteroid where the docking ports were. Near the airlock was a steel box with a small display reading AIR FEES. Larsen fed paper money into a slot until it was satisfied, signaling so with a green display that said, Thank you.

"Cameras," Larsen whispered while looking away from the video pick-ups.

Johnson did his best not to react visibly. "What do we do?" he asked.

"Stick with the plan," Larsen replied, keeping his face away from the cameras and his voice low. Johnson knew why: there might be microphones, too. "They'll figure out it's us eventually."

Larsen turned, using a hand hold, and typed in the code on the control to close the *Nanna's* airlock and lock it. Vanir wasn't like BA-XP-4382, a small, closed in community. There were people here who would steal from you if they thought they could get away with it.

Plus, it would slow down any investigation.

Larsen smiled as he turned back into the corridor. And now, he thought, he was one of those people.

The two men moved down the corridor trying to look casual but with a purpose. They passed the first exit from the corridor that opened up to another hall that led into the interior of the corridor. They spent a moment studying the sign by the corridor, shook their heads for the camera, and moved on. Johnson hoped they'd find the *Loki* soon, or they'd start to look suspicious.

At the next corridor heading in, they stopped.

"This is it," Larsen said.

Again Johnson tried not to visibly react, and followed Larsen down the green plastic square tube using the many handholds.

"I don't see any cameras," Larsen said. "Although they can be pretty small."

"I'd think they want them to be visible in the docking ring," Johnson said. "Scare off would-be thieves."

"Possibly."

"Now what?" Johnson asked.

"Just follow me," Larsen replied. "I've been here many times."

Johnson nodded and followed his friend.

At an intersection, Larsen took the left passage with red plastic walls. Genetically engineered algae would make plastic pretty much any color you wanted, Johnson remembered.

The red hall led back to the docking ring.

Larsen looked both ways, then turned right, going the same direction they were before.

"What if the *Loki* is in that section we missed?" Johnson asked.

"It's not," Larsen replied. "Or we would have seen it from the *Nanna* as we docked."

The ships' names were displayed over the airlocks, but Larsen was going almost too fast for Johnson to read them. He'd glance at them out of the corner of his eye as he pulled himself past, trying to keep up with Larsen.

Johnson discovered he didn't need to see the ship's name. The *Loki* was obvious because a large man was in front of the airlock and had tethered himself to a handhold with a length of rope and a snaplink. He was overtly holding a gun in his right hand. Larsen had said that was a possibility and had planned for it. Johnson was surprised it was allowed. But seraph dust and other recreational drugs, not to mention prostitution, were legal, so having a gun was probably not against the law, either.

Larsen stopped and looked around the corridor as if lost.

Johnson smiled at the big man, getting a scowl in return that meant "stay away." Johnson swallowed his fear and pulled himself over.

"Hey, buddy, my friend and I are lost. Do you know the way to Stella's Emporium?" That was a brothel.

"I don't know, now get the hell out of here," the man snarled.

"Oh, come on," Johnson whined. "Help out some lonely miners. We've been out rock pounding for months and need a little relief, if you know what I mean."

The man was about to say something when he saw Larsen's gun. He began to raise his weapon when Larsen barked, "Don't."

The man stopped.

Johnson took the man's gun and couldn't help but look up at the cameras as if he were afraid they'd be reacting somehow.

"Open the airlock," Larsen hissed.

"Are you out of your mind? Do you know whose ship this is?" the man asked, layering menace in his voice.

"Let me worry about that," Larsen said.

Johnson thought that Larsen was enjoying being a criminal.

"Open the damn airlock," Larsen growled again, pointing his gun at the man's head.

The man sighed. "Your funeral," he said, turned, used the rope to pull himself to the handhold, and punched in a code on the airlock's control.

The door slid open.

"Thank you," Larsen said.

As planned, Johnson stayed there as Larsen pushed into the ship.

"You are dead men," the guard growled.

"Yes, we are," Johnson replied.

"Clear," Larsen's voice came from inside the ship.

Johnson pushed himself through the airlock.

"In," he reported, thinking that was way too easy as the airlock closed behind him.

CHAPTER TWENTY

The bullet hit the bulkhead behind Johnson in a shower of sparks.

Johnson turned his body, trying very hard not to turn too fast and thus turn too far. A woman dressed in a very tight, hot pink overall was floating in the corridor leading deeper into the ship and holding a gun. Smoke made a nebulous cloud around the barrel.

Johnson tried to aim his weapon, but as he swung his arm, his body moved in obedience to Newton's Third Law, changing his aim.

The woman, he noted, was having the same problem, but she fired again. Johnson felt something tug at his overall's right sleeve, but no pain.

"Stop," Larsen said, coming from the bridge. He aimed his gun at the woman and held onto a handhold with his free hand.

The woman put up her arms and let go of the gun. It just slowly moved away from her fingers, floating in free fall.

"We got to get her off this ship," Johnson said.

Johnson couldn't help but notice her lithe and long body, jet-black hair, and a face expertly made up so that it highlighted her full lips and dark eyes.

"We can't open the airlock. I sealed it from the bridge, but by now there's more than just our friend out there. And pretty soon

183

Vanir security is going to figure out what's going on and override our ability to undock."

"I thought you said the ship was clear," Johnson said.

"I must have missed her," Larsen replied with a grimace.

"In that outfit?"

"I only checked the main sections: bridge, saloon, engineering spaces. I didn't have time to check the quarters."

"You're dead men if you steal this ship," the woman said. Johnson thought those words sounded strange in a soft feminine voice. He wondered what her function was on this vessel.

"So we've been told," Johnson said, not masking his annoyance. He was getting tired of hearing that.

"Acceleration as soon as possible," Larsen said, turning and pulling himself to the bridge.

Johnson pulled himself to the woman and helped her to a handhold, then they both pushed and pulled to acceleration chairs, strapping in. She was quite cooperative without her gun. Johnson just let it keep floating in the air.

Only after he was strapped down did he notice the bullet hole in the upper part of his right sleeve. He stuck a finger in the hole and touched undamaged skin. Apparently, he'd literally dodged that bullet.

#

Larsen was mildly surprised when he hit the control on the computer to undock the *Loki* and got a green light. He thought he'd have to use Jakob's method to hack the password.

He used the thrusters to move away from the asteroid.

Immediately, the radio came to life. It was Vanir traffic control asking what the hell he was doing.

He ignored it but turned the *Loki*'s radar on high resolution. If there were other ships around, he wanted to see them. That reduced its range but at the moment, he didn't care about anything more than a kilometer away.

Once the docking radar said he was one-hundred meters from the surface of Vanir, he countered that motion with the opposite thrusters. This was done by the ship's computer, not manually, but

Larsen could, if needed, maneuver a ship on his own in case of computer failure.

Checking the radar in front and behind and finding both clear, he accelerated at the *Loki*'s maximum thrust of two gees. He had made sure there were no ships behind him because of the *Loki*'s fusion exhaust.

As the acceleration hit, he heard a metallic bang from where Johnson and the woman were.

Johnson walked carefully into the bridge as if he were an old man.

"How's our guest?" Larsen asked.

"Spitting mad," Johnson said. "What are we going to do with her?"

"Drop her off at 4382 when we pick up Sonia and Sven."

Johnson nodded. Larsen had explained that it wouldn't take long for Vanir security to figure out the hijackers came from the *Nanna*, which would lead them, and the Ragnarök Cartel, straight to BA-XP-4382, where it was registered under Johnson's name.

"What was that noise?" Larsen asked.

"The gun falling to the floor."

Larsen shook his head. No one had secured the woman's gun, and it must have fallen to the floor at twice the acceleration of gravity. "We're lucky it didn't go off when it hit, especially at two gees. Some guns will do that."

"Sorry, I didn't think about it," Johnson said.

"Moot point, now," Larsen replied. "Do you have it?"

"Yes, I wasn't going to leave it in there for her to get." He patted a pocket on his chest.

Larsen nodded. "Good."

A few moments passed as Johnson sat in the co-pilot's chair. He didn't bother to strap in.

"Oh, oh," Larsen breathed.

"What?"

"Two small ships are matching our vector, except they are accelerating at...," he looked at the radar readout, "five gees."

"Vanir security?"

Larsen shook his head. "No. They wouldn't chase us. Have to be cartel ships, and they are coming fast."

"Meaning?"

"They will catch up to us," Larsen said as a statement of fact.

"Then what?"

"I assume try to dock with us."

"Can you stop them?"

"I can try to use our fusion drive as a weapon," Larsen said with grim intention.

"No," Johnson protested. "No more killing." Johnson had one death on his conscience from the first cartel asteroid.

"It's kill them in space or let them board and try and kill them then," Larsen snarled.

Johnson hesitated, his face screwed up in thought.

"Never surrender," Larsen growled. "We didn't come this far to give up."

Johnson nodded agreement. "Do it."

Larsen swung the *Loki*'s tail, trying to hit the smaller, faster craft. But they too easily dodged and while he aimed for one, the other would simply get closer to the airlock.

"It's not working," Larsen growled.

"Can you keep them from docking?" Johnson cried.

"I'll try," Larsen said. "I can accelerate randomly to prevent them from matching vectors."

"Do it," Johnson barked.

"Yes, sir," Larsen said. "You might want to strap down."

Johnson nodded. "I'll tell our guest."

"Good idea."

Johnson stood carefully and walked out of the bridge, again moving as if every joint in his body hurt. At two gees, most of them did, he realized.

The woman was still in her acceleration chair. She scowled at Johnson.

"We're going to be randomly accelerating," he said. "I suggest you stay in the chair."

"Fuck you," she snarled.

186

Johnson smirked and returned to the bridge.

Larsen had the radar display in a holograph in front of him.

"Wow," Johnson exclaimed despite the dire situation.

"Yeah, a very expensive system." He pointed at two dots. "Those are our friends."

"How long until they catch up?"

"Two minutes."

Johnson nodded and sat again. This time he did strap down.

Larsen's face contorted as he concentrated on the radar holo display. Johnson tried to watch. Spheres of green, he thought, represented the two pursuing ships, but had no idea of the scale, nor where the *Loki* was on the display. Larsen apparently understood it all and the ship began accelerating randomly, just like the cartel ship they once chased. The motions jerked Johnson back and forth, front and back, in the acceleration chair. His legs, arms, and head flailed about in response to the changes in acceleration. He heard the woman in the compartment behind the bridge swear.

"This can't go on forever," Johnson cried in frustration.

"I know. You have an idea for ending this?"

Larsen stopped accelerating randomly.

"What are you doing?" Johnson asked.

"I'm going to let them dock. Those are small ships, one, maybe two men each. We'll fight them."

"You know I'm not good with a gun."

"But I am," Larsen said, "especially in free fall. And I've discovered something."

"What's that?"

"According to the computer, this ship's airlocks can be locked from the inside. We only have to deal with one ship at a time."

"Unless they know how to override it," Johnson said. "It is their boss's ship."

Larsen nodded. "Let's hope they can't. All depends on how paranoid the chief of the Ragnarök cartel is."

"I said no more killing," Johnson breathed, knowing he was already defeated.

187

"We'll try to wound them," Larsen replied.

Johnson frowned.

The two ships docked almost simultaneously, one on each side of the *Loki*'s main chamber.

As soon as the docking rings were sealed, Larsen killed the acceleration on the *Loki*.

"Damn," he breathed.

"What?" Johnson asked.

"They must be linked by radio telemetry. They're both putting out the same amount of thrust. Instead of one big rocket, we now have two small ones. At least as long as the docking rings hold."

"What's that mean?"

"Instead of being in free fall we'll be in low acceleration. Looks like about one-fourth gee." He looked at Johnson. "What do you mass, about eighty-two kilograms?"

"About," Johnson said, inwardly pleased that he'd guessed low by about two kilos.

"Then you'll weigh about twenty kilos. Imagine a twenty kilo child firing a gun."

Johnson frowned, thinking that would be about what a five-year-old child would weigh in one gee.

"Put your leg behind you to give you a buttress against the force of the gun," Larsen said. "Or stand against a bulkhead. And don't get moving too fast; you'll have a lot less friction but the same momentum."

Johnson nodded, thinking this was going to be more complicated than trying to fight in free fall.

Larsen unbuckled the straps of his acceleration chair, and Johnson followed suit.

"Let's go," Larsen said in a low growl.

Johnson only nodded again.

They walked back to the compartment behind the bridge. The woman was scowling at them.

"If you're done jerking this ship around, I'd like to get up," she snarled.

"Stay put," Larsen said, pointing his gun at her.

"Fuck you," she spat.

Johnson tried to stop walking and found he nearly couldn't, almost running into a steel wall.

"See?" Larsen said.

Johnson nodded, eyes wide.

"Port or starboard?" Larsen asked.

"Up to you," Johnson said grimly, carefully controlling his voice. He realized that he was frightened that he was about to die, and only Larsen's insistence they go on was keeping him from just trying to hide.

Larsen pointed to the corridor that led to the ship's living quarters. "Hide there. When you hear the airlock open, come out ready to shoot."

Johnson nodded.

"I'll open the port one first."

Johnson nodded again, afraid that talking would betray his nearly overpowering fear. He went to the corridor and pressed himself against the metal wall, holding his gun. He realized this would probably kill the men in the small ships as surely as using the fusion exhaust to destroy their vessels. At least now, they had a fighting chance.

A fighting chance to kill him, Johnson realized, his stomach tightening at the thought.

But, he realized, he'd rather die fighting for his life, and his family's safety, than be executed on Bostad.

He heard the airlock slide open. He assumed Larsen was in a position where he wouldn't be shot at immediately. Probably plastered up against the bulkhead, Johnson thought.

He heard men's voices sounding angry and gruff.

"There's two of them," the woman yelled.

There was a gunshot and Johnson stepped back into the chamber.

One man fell in a macabre, slow crumple as blood gushed from his head.

The second turned to shoot Larsen, but got moving too fast, couldn't stop his turn when he wanted to, and Larsen shot him.

The man kept turning, obviously dead. Larsen was trying to recover from the recoil as the starboard airlock opened. Two more men came in, moving very slowly considering the situation.

They must have been able to override the *Loki*'s locks.

One of the newcomers was raising his gun to shoot Larsen, and Johnson realized he had no choice. He moved his arm only, keeping his body planted, braced his foot behind him, and fired, hitting the man in the shoulder. The man howled in pain and tried to aim his gun at Johnson.

Johnson recovered from his recoil faster and shot again, twice, quickly. The man fell back, his boots coming off the deck as he tumbled, again in what looked like almost comical slow motion.

The man next to him fired, and the bullet didn't hit anything but bulkhead.

Johnson backed into a wall to steady himself and aimed at the remaining man. Larsen fired as Johnson did, and both bullets hit the last man, causing him to collapse to the floor preternaturally slowly.

"Clear that ship," Larsen spat as he walked into the port airlock, his gun ready.

Johnson did the same on the starboard ship, hoping he wouldn't find anyone. The ship's interior was all cockpit, and there was no one on board. Johnson walked back into the *Loki*.

Larsen was back already and shook his head. Johnson nodded.

That's when the shakes hit him. He barely managed to hold on to the gun, his hands trembled so much.

#

They put the bodies back into the small ships, cleaned up the blood, and then turned off the small ships' drives. They were, indeed, bound by a telemetric connection and the drives shut down simultaneously.

Larsen spent an hour in free fall trying to figure out how to detach the ships without someone inside them. He debated putting the woman in one of them and having her detach it, but that would leave the problem of the other ship. If they accelerated, the mass of the ship would throw their center of mass off enough that they'd tumble. The fusion rocket could compensate for small changes such as cargo and people walking around inside, but not for something as large as even that small ship. Finally, he came up with a plan.

When he told Johnson about it, he shook his head. "There's no better way?"

"No," Larsen said.

Johnson noticed his friend was suddenly less talkative. The gunfight must have affected him in ways Johnson understood. He didn't dare close his eyes, for all he saw was the men he killed.

#

Larson donned a spacesuit that he found on the *Loki*. It didn't quite fit him, but it was close enough. He went into the port side ship, closed the airlocks, and undocked. Then he piloted the ship about ten meters from the *Loki*. With the maneuvering unit this would be simple, he thought, but he didn't have the maneuvering unit: they'd left it and their spacesuits back on BA-XP-4382.

He opened the airlock, took a moment to adjust his aim, and jumped. He was now a miniature spaceship orbiting the Bostad sun. He needed to jump hard enough that momentum would carry him to the *Loki*, but not so much he'd bounce off the hull before he could grab a handhold.

The gray side of the ship was coming fast, and he reached out and grabbed a steel loop just before he hit the hull and started to bounce off. He managed to hang onto the handhold. He used the many welded loops on the exterior to move to the airlock. A few moments later, he was back inside the *Loki*.

"That was easy," he said with a grimace that Johnson could see through the transparent faceplate.

"Why do I doubt that?" Johnson mumbled.

The second ship was less difficult as he jumped a little slower to cover the gap. He had time to admire the stars. There is nothing like seeing the stars from space, Larsen thought before grabbing the handhold on the hull of the *Loki*. He just wasn't sure he'd ever enjoy it again. Not after what he'd just done.

BOOK THREE
THE WAR

CHAPTER TWENTY-ONE

From orbit, nothing looked different on Bostad than it did 155 years ago. Johnson shook his head. At this resolution, the works of man were barely visible and the politics and culture and government were completely a mystery.

The ship was projecting the image of the planet for Sven and Johnson.

"That's where I was born?" Sven asked.

"Yes," Johnson said. "Do you remember it?"

"I remember a little living in free fall. But I don't remember ever living on a planet."

Johnson heard a bit of sadness in his son's voice.

The ship spoke. "The EMR is continuing. I have decoded their modulation. It is a voice and image. I think it best you communicate with them."

"Okay," Johnson replied, trying to sound non-committal. He doubted whatever official was in the message would know who he was. They wouldn't have even been born yet when Johnson escaped and Larsen killed those police officers. "Will they be able to see me?"

"I think that is best," the ship said. "So they know you are human like them."

"I agree," Johnson said. "Let me do the talking," he said to his son.

195

"Okay," Sven said so fast it betrayed how happy he was to not have to talk.

A man's image appeared. He was only shown from the chest up, but that was enough. Johnson's heart sank. The man was wearing an obvious military uniform, and over his right breast was the starburst arrows symbol of the Impetus Party. Apparently, little had changed on Bostad, except perhaps the government had become more martial.

"You're human?" the man said, not hiding his surprise.

"Yes," Johnson replied. "There are two humans on this ship. My son and I."

"Who are you, and what kind of ship is that?" the man asked. "And why are you in spacesuits?"

"To whom am I speaking?" Johnson replied.

"I am General Ahlberg, aide-de-camp to His Most Honorable Konung Sineson."

Johnson knew that "*konung*" was a word basically meaning "king."

"I see," Johnson said. Apparently, over the past century and a half, the Impetusites had abandoned all pretenses of being democratic.

"And who are you?" Ahlberg demanded.

Johnson hesitated a moment. Since he left Bostad there were probably a thousand Olly Johnsons born there. But only one was wanted for the murder of seven policemen. "I'm Mr. Smith," Johnson said.

"And can you explain that ship you are apparently in, Mr. Smith?" Ahlberg asked, again with a demanding tone. Johnson got the feeling he was used to getting what he wanted.

Johnson took a deep breath. This was going to take a while. He related all the facts as he knew them, including his doubts about the rebel ship he was inside of and if anything they had experienced was real or the truth.

"But," Johnson concluded, "if this ship is telling the truth, we need to act and act fast to stop the Fleet, who could be here at any time."

When he was finished, Ahlberg leaned forward. "Why should I believe you? Even you aren't sure what is true."

"Can you take that risk?" Johnson said. "Every human on Bostad and in the belt is at risk if this ship is telling the truth."

"I cannot make this kind of decision," Ahlberg said. "I will have to confer with his majesty."

"Then do it," Johnson said. "And quickly."

He could tell Ahlberg was not used to being ordered around as the wave of anger crossed his face.

"We'll be in touch," the general said.

The scene disappeared.

"They have ceased transmission," the ship said.

"Idiots," Johnson growled under his breath.

"Now what, Dad?" Sven asked.

Johnson thought a moment. "Are you getting any EMR from the asteroid belt?" he asked.

"Yes, several," the ship said. "They started just a few minutes ago."

Johnson nodded. That made sense. Depending on the position of an asteroid in relationship to Bostad, it would take them a minimum of around sixteen minutes to see the ship and another sixteen minutes for any radio signal it sent to reach them.

"See if you can find the one coming from the Asgard Cooperative," Johnson said. Then he realized that may be harder than he thought it would be. Plus, was it still called the Asgard Cooperative? he wondered.

But the ship said, "Yes, I have a transmission from a human saying they are the leader of the Asgard Cooperative."

"Let me talk to them." Asgard must be near its closest approach to Bostad, Johnson thought.

A scene appeared in front of Johnson and Sven. A blonde woman in a blue overall was floating in freefall. Her hair was short and she appeared to be in her forties. A gold star was pinned above her right breast.

"This is Britta Spillum of the Asgard Cooperative trying to contact the ship in orbit about Bostad. Please respond," she said.

Johnson didn't know how much, if any, the Asgard Cooperative was working with the Impetusite government. Plus, he was sure that the Bostad government could be monitoring the transmission. "I'm Mr. Smith, and this is my son. We are in the ship orbiting Bostad. We have much to tell you."

"You're in the ship in orbit about Bostad?" she asked, her face not concealing her surprise at seeing Johnson and Sven.

"Yes," Johnson said. Then he blinked. At best, there should be about a thirty-two minute light speed delay in communications.

Spillum looked surprised, too. "You responded immediately; how is this possible?" she asked.

Johnson smiled. "I don't know." He assumed the ship was making it possible somehow. "Don't worry about it right now." Johnson thought for a moment. He had to phrase the next question carefully. "How are relations between the Asgard Cooperative and the Bostad Impetusite government?"

The woman scowled. "We have been at war for nearly sixty years. Sometimes it's a hot war, sometimes cold. They usually back off when we threaten to drop a small asteroid on their capital city. The one time we dropped one on some farm land as a demonstration, they learned their lesson."

Johnson couldn't help but smile. That meant there was very little chance the Asgard Cooperative would turn him over to the Impetusites.

"What is that ship you are in and why are you wearing spacesuits?" Spillum asked.

Johnson told her the same thing he'd told General Ahlberg, including his doubts about everything.

Spillum frowned. "If this 'Fleet' is coming here, how do we stop it?"

"I don't know," Johnson said.

"How are their defenses?" she asked.

"I aimed a fusion rocket flame point blank at one. It did no damage."

"Damn," Spillum whispered.

"We have more prosaic concerns at the moment," Johnson said. "Our spacesuits will only last us about twenty-four more hours, and we need food, air, water, bathroom facilities."

"It will take us about four days to get to you," Spillum said, "and our ships don't go that close to Bostad in any case."

Johnson nodded. "Wait until you see this." He hesitated a moment. "Ship, put us as close to the source of that transmission as possible and still be safe."

"It will take ninety-one minutes," the ship said.

"Can't you just interdimensionally go there immediately?"

"No, it's too close. There is a minimum safe distance you have to travel interdimensionally. I will have to accelerate there in normal three-space."

"Do it," Johnson ordered.

"Will you get here before you need out of those suits?" Spillum asked.

Johnson smiled. "Yes."

Fifteen minutes later, Spillum gasped. "Holy shit. That ship is accelerating at over a thousand gees."

Johnson smiled. "Yes, we'll be there in about seventy-five minutes."

"And you don't feel acceleration?" Spillum asked.

"No," Johnson replied, "we are actually in free fall."

"How is that possible?"

"This ship is very advanced technology," Johnson said.

"Apparently. That does give credence to your story, at least."

"We'll contact you when we're closer, and you can send out a ship for us."

She nodded. Then asked, "How will we dock with that ship?"

"Actually," the ship said, "I can teleport you to that asteroid once we are in range. That will be when we are within 1,652,185 kilometers of Asgard. There is no need for a ship."

"Did you hear that?" Johnson asked Spillum.

"Yes," she said. "How does it speak English?"

"It learned it from computers on Jideed Baghdad," Johnson explained. "As I said, their technology is very advanced."

"Obviously," Spillum breathed in a soft voice.

About thirty minutes later according to Johnson's suit's clock, the ship said, "Just one moment."

For Johnson and Sven, the view changed and their suits crumpled from being in pressure. They were in a chamber made mostly of plastic, and Spillum was in front of them.

Johnson opened his helmet and took in a deep breath of air. It was still recycled, but it was better than what was in his suit, which stank of his sweat.

"Hello, Ms. Spillum," he said with a smile.

He thought the woman might faint and collapse to the floor if they weren't in free fall.

#

For his part, Johnson was happier to work with miners than the Bostad government. He thought they might move quicker and be more cooperative than an ossified military dictatorship. Ms. Spillum was the head of the Asgard Cooperative, and could make quick decisions. What Johnson had forgotten about after his short time in the belt was that all the multitude of miners, asteroids, and asteroid-based businesses weren't even a loose confederation. They were individual entities and not prone to taking orders.

The war with Bostad had helped organize the miners a bit, but getting their attention on the threat of the Fleet was a difficulty Johnson hadn't anticipated.

Meanwhile, the Fleet could appear in the Bostad system at any time.

The meeting was between Spillum, Johnson, and a man named Holt, who claimed to represent the miners. Johnson didn't think he dared ask about the water cartels and if they even still existed.

"How do we fight this technology?" Holt asked. He was a big man who filled out his overall with muscular arms and legs and a small paunch of a belly. Being a miner, he probably got plenty of exercise, but he still apparently ate a bit too much of the soy protein available in the belt.

"The Rebels will help us if we develop a strategy," Johnson said. "And we have numbers on our side."

"Bah," the man spat. "Like insects fighting giants."

"Ever seen what a swarm of wasps can do to a human?" Spillum asked.

"Never seen a wasp," Holt replied. "None were taken off Earth, as far as I know."

"That's not a bad strategy," Johnson said. "If we could 'sting' them multiple times, maybe we could defeat them."

"'If...,'" Holt spat. "'Maybe.'"

"You'd rather wait for them to come kill us all?" Spillum asked, alloying sarcasm into her voice.

"Maybe we could wait until after they wipe out the Impetusites," Holt said with a malevolent grin.

Spillum scowled. "There are millions of innocent people on Bostad."

Holt held up a hand. "I know, I know. I was just kidding."

"We need to be serious," Johnson said. "I've seen a planet they've destroyed. They kill everyone." Johnson didn't bring up that he wasn't sure what he saw was real. He needed to get these people moving and not fill Holt's head with his own doubts. He was wondering if it had been a mistake to tell Spillum about his misgivings.

"What's the most powerful weapon we have?" Johnson asked.

"Asteroids," the miner said. "We used one on Bostad. Shut them right up for a good fifty years."

"Okay," Johnson said. "What else?"

"Fusion rockets," Spillum said. "But you already said that doesn't work."

Johnson nodded. "Nukes?"

"We don't have any," Spillum said. "And if Bostad did, they would probably have used them against us by now."

"So we're back to being wasps," Johnson snarled.

"Wasps without stingers," Holt said.

All three were silent, hanging in Spillum's office from handholds or rope loops.

"You know these ships best," Spillum said. "They have to have a weakness."

"If they do," Johnson said. "They aren't telling me."

"Ship," Spillum said to the air, "How do you fight the Fleet?"

"Gamma ray lasers and projectiles with a velocity close to the speed of light."

"Damn," Spillum whispered.

"That's it!" Johnson said.

"What's it?" Spillum asked.

"Hyperkinetic weapons."

"And how in the hell do we launch them?" Holt asked.

"I know some mining companies use rail guns to launch ore to their processing facilities."

"But they don't reach anything near the speed of light," Holt said.

Johnson frowned in thought.

"The ships," Johnson said. "The Fleet ships accelerate at close to a thousand gees. They get going very fast very quickly. We aim ships at them. The ships accelerate as fast as possible, releasing small asteroids at the Fleet ship. The cumulative relative velocity should give them huge kinetic energy."

"And how do we aim them?" Holt asked, not hiding his disdain.

Johnson scowled. "We'll figure it out. We have to."

#

Holt went to recruit miners and ships. Spillum looked as if she wanted to collapse in a chair. Instead, she hung on to a rope and closed her eyes.

"It's going to work," Johnson said.

Spillum shook her head, sending her blonde hair moving in waves. "If it doesn't, millions of innocent humans will die. I wouldn't mourn for the Impetus Party, but most people on Bostad are victims of them as well."

"Not to mention everyone in the asteroid belt," Johnson said.

Spillum studied his face. "I know who you are, 'Mr. Smith.'"

Johnson's gut clenched. "Oh?"

"Olly Johnson," Spillum said without emotion. "You and John Larsen made quite a name for yourselves a hundred and fifty years ago. Speaking of which, where is Larsen?"

"Dead," Johnson growled, not liking this reminder that his wife was also dead.

Spillum nodded. "Well, the Asgard Cooperative will take no action against you."

"Thank you," he whispered, working hard to keep his grief in check.

"You okay?" Spillum asked, studying his face.

Johnson nodded silently, realizing his visage was telegraphing his thoughts. He realized that he'd never mourned Sonia. He hadn't had time, and he didn't have time now. The Fleet could be there at any moment.

Timing was everything. Calculations showed that the energy released by each projectile would be in the 1018 joules range upon impact with the Fleet ships, if the Fleet ships fell into the trap. The largest nuclear weapon ever built, the Tsar Bomba developed by the Soviet Union in the mid Twentieth Century, had an approximately 1015 joule yield. The impact of the projectiles would be a thousand times more powerful than the Tsar Bomba.

Johnson hoped it was enough.

Human ships were conscripted for the battle. The water cartels even sent some. Johnson smiled when he saw one of the vessels was named the *Nanna*. He wondered if that was his old ship.

The belt fleet would be in orbit about the sun, doing their damnedest to look like small asteroids. It was hoped the Fleet ships would be too busy dealing with Rebel ships to notice that they were not.

CHAPTER TWENTY-TWO

The timing had to be exact. The arc of belt ships would be about a thousand kilometers from one end to the next. That was far enough apart for there to be a 0.03 second light speed delay from one end to the next. In that amount of time, if the Fleet ships did what it was hoped they would do, they could travel over two thousand kilometers. Timing had to be extremely precise.

The small retro rockets on the projectiles had to be calibrated for their mass and the velocity the ship carrying them would have at release. Each ship accelerated at a different rate, most around one gee, but some as low as one-tenth of a gee, and some as high as five gees. In 155 years, Johnson noted, fusion rockets had gotten more efficient.

Each ship had to start accelerating at a precise moment, compensating for the 0.03 second light speed delay and based on their acceleration. Too soon, and the Fleet might see the trap. Too late, the ship would be destroyed by colliding with the Fleet ships.

Another Rebel ship arrived. Johnson christened both Rebel ships *Úlfhethnar* and *Berserker*. *Berserker* didn't communicate except through *Úlfhethnar*, the vessel that had brought Johnson and his son back to Bostad.

Spillum worked her holographic computer interface. Johnson asked if they'd become more available since he'd left. She said because of the war with Bostad, they were less available and more expensive.

"The calculations are finished," she said. "Thank God for computers."

"For all 134 ships and their projectiles?" Johnson asked.

"Yes. I put our best mathematicians and computer people on it." She looked at Johnson and smiled.

"We need to deploy them immediately," Johnson said with urgency. "The Fleet could be here any moment."

"Yes," she replied, "The orders and calculations are being sent out, now."

Johnson nodded. The retro rockets for the projectiles were normally used to slow ore that had been transported via rail gun. Gathering 134 of them in short order from all over the belt had proved a logistic nightmare. He was impressed with Spillum's skill at bringing this all together.

She changed the display. It looked like a small arc of the asteroid belt.

"The ships will be here," she said, and touched an area inside the display. Red dots appeared along the arc, almost so close together they made a solid line. How far apart the ships should be was something that had been debated for hours. Johnson ended the debate with one word: "Shotgun." It was decided to place them relatively close together.

"We'll be able to watch it in real time here, minus light speed delays, of course."

"How?" Johnson asked. He knew the transponders on every ship would be turned off so as not to alert the Fleet ships.

"There are radar sources throughout the belt, especially this part where traffic is heavy. They are all compiled by computer for a single display."

"So we're ready?" Johnson asked.

Spillum smiled grimly. "As ready as we'll ever be."

#

A room had been set up with plastic walls and plenty of hand holds. Spillum's holographic display was moved in there along with four more computers, each one manned by a technician or strategist. Johnson was there but really had nothing to do but watch. He hinted to Spillum that if he were just going to be "in the way," he'd be happy to be somewhere else. That wasn't exactly true, but he didn't want to interfere. She made it plain that she wanted him in that room.

"You have good ideas," she explained.

The Rebel ships were "parked" — as Johnson was starting to call it when they were stationary as if gravity didn't affect them — about a hundred thousand kilometers from Bostad between the planet and the asteroid belt. Bostad and Asgard were, due to their positions in their orbits, about twenty light minutes apart. They'd gotten farther apart since Johnson arrived. That meant that anything the humans on Asgard saw would have happened twenty minutes ago. As the battle drew closer to the belt, as they hoped it would, that delay would decrease.

Three Fleet ships appeared close to Bostad. They accelerated quickly into orbit about it. Johnson had to remind himself it was all happening twenty minutes ago.

Someone whistled. Johnson glanced over to see a man staring at his display with wide eyes.

"What?" Johnson asked him. Had he seen something they all had failed to notice?

"You said they accelerate at about a thousand gees. I guess I never believed it until now."

Johnson smiled grimly.

"The Rebels are firing," one of the strategists said. They couldn't wait for the Fleet ships to attack Bostad, but had to stop them before they got the chance.

Of course, gamma ray lasers would be invisible to humans relying on the visible spectrum. Due to Compton scattering, as the gamma ray photons interacted with the relatively dense plasma of the solar wind, a few were reduced to visible wavelengths. It was enough that the path of the lasers could be seen as beams of light running between the ships that switched on and off. The only way to tell which ship fired and which ship was hit was by the blue light emitted by the shielding on the hit ship. As the lasers kept firing the light turned violet then became ultra-violet, which was only visible to UV sensors, as the shields tried to dissipate energy.

Johnson had to remind himself this was all happening twenty minutes ago. Everyone on Bostad could be dead at this moment if the Fleet ships didn't take the bait.

"The Fleet ships are leaving orbit, accelerating toward the Rebels," another strategist reported.

Everyone in the chamber simultaneously let out the breath they were collectively holding. The first part of the plan was working.

"Fleet firing at the Rebels," a female voice reported.

"Rebels accelerating toward our picket."

Johnson listened, and glanced at Spillum. Her face was tight with tension. If this didn't work, a lot of people would die. Even if it did work, some might die.

Johnson looked at Spillum's holographic display. On it, the red dots were stationary. Holt was on one of those ships.

"Rebel ships accelerating toward us," a voice said. "Should pass us in about two hours."

"And the Fleet?" Spillum asked.

"If they keep pursuing the Rebels, about three and a half minutes after the Rebels. I'll have more precise figures soon."

"See that you do," Spillum ordered. "Three and a half minutes is a tight window."

"Yes, ma'am," the same person said.

"Two hours," Johnson breathed. Two hours to wait and wonder if this plan was going to work.

Someone distributed bulbs of water, and Johnson sucked on his absentmindedly while his brain thought about everything that could go wrong. *Úlfhethnar* had said that once the Fleet ships were going too fast relative to the Bostad star, they couldn't use interdimensional travel. That was key to the plan. That velocity, about 27,000 kps, would take the Fleet ships only about forty-six minutes to achieve.

"Both sides are still firing gamma ray lasers," the first specialist said. "They aren't missing."

Johnson nodded. The plan was for the Rebels to accelerate constantly away from the Fleet so that the Fleet, it was hoped, would also accelerate constantly. Otherwise, the humans could never calculate their timing. For a sentient ship with massive computing power, hitting a constantly accelerating ship, even as you are accelerating, was probably child's play. There were three Fleet ships versus two Rebel ships. Johnson hoped both Rebel ships survived until the humans could attack.

Úlfhethnar had explained that normally they'd accelerate randomly to throw off the enemy's aim. They also hoped that the Fleet wouldn't realize the Rebels weren't doing that because they were leading the Fleet into a trap. Too damn much reliance on hope, Johnson thought with a scowl.

Time passed more slowly than Johnson had ever experienced. He kept glancing at the computer display to see the time and noted the seconds were thudding by with ponderous slothfulness.

He knew when the Fleet ships approached the asteroid belt, assuming they accelerated constantly as the Rebel ships were, they'd be going about one-quarter the speed of light. The light from them would be blue-shifted, and they would appear shorter than they physically actually were.

When they were close enough, the ships represented by those red dots would start to accelerate according to timing worked out in advance. Then things would happen very quickly and they'd probably have to watch computer simulations and slow-motion radar recordings of what happened after the event. The Fleet ships would be traveling more than seventy-five thousand kilometers a second relative to Asgard and all the miner ships waiting to go into action.

If the Fleet ships accelerated randomly, then the humans would need more luck than they dared hoped for to pull off their plan.

As if hearing Johnson's thoughts, someone said, "Fleet ships still accelerating constantly."

Again, Johnson felt himself let out a sigh.

The messages to the miner ships would be sent via computer tied into the radar watching the Fleet ships: a burst transmission everyone hoped the Fleet ships wouldn't notice. Each one would be sent coded to a specific ship at the right time so that all ships would be in a line at a certain point in space no matter the light speed delay and the acceleration capabilities of the ships. It had to be done by computer because no human could do it with the correct timing and fast enough.

Who knew what supercomputer self-aware ships noticed? They might have already figured out the humans' plan and had a way to neutralize the threat. All three still appeared to be single-mindedly chasing the Rebel ships that were accelerating for the Oort cloud.

What felt like hours later, a computer dinged. Johnson's body jerked in surprise.

"The acceleration orders are being sent," the technician watching that display explained.

Johnson turned to the holographic display. On the scale it was showing that the ships appeared to be stationary. But the ships that accelerated the slowest would be the ones going first. Eventually, some of the dots moved. Johnson watched, knowing his eyes were wide with fear that his plan would fail and millions of humans, probably including him and his son, would die.

"Fleet ships?" he asked.

"Still accelerating," someone reported.

Johnson acknowledged the report with a nod. Because they were moving closer, the light-speed delay was reducing, making them appear to be accelerating faster. That, too, Johnson knew, had been compensated for in the calculations.

And he knew that it was his plan that had put those brave men and women in danger. "In harm's way" they used to say about sending people to war.

All that needed to happen for this plan to fail was for the Fleet ships to notice the miners' vessels and start using those gamma ray lasers on them.

"Any change from the Fleet ships?" Johnson asked, not caring it had been just a few moments since he'd asked before.

"No, sir," someone said.

On the holo display, other ships were accelerating, and doing so faster than the first group. The object was for them to be in an arc segment line all at the same time despite their different abilities to accelerate.

"Come on," Johnson whispered. Everything was happening too damn slowly. On the scale of interplanetary space, things did happen slowly, even for ships accelerating at a thousand gees as the Fleet ships were.

Eventually, all the red dots spawned a second dot. The point where that happened couldn't be planned in advanced but had to be determined once the Fleet ships got close enough to know what part of space they would pass through in their pursuit of the Rebels. The human ships kept accelerating, but the second dots accelerated to a stop. Except some didn't. On those, the retro rockets must have failed.

"Damn," Johnson whispered.

Each second dot was an approximately ten cubic meter piece of rock. The final configuration of the rocks was an elongated rectangle. They had hoped the Fleet ships would plow into them at one-quarter light speed. Each one would release the equivalent energy of a thousand Tsar Bombas. Johnson hoped it was enough. At 0.25C, sand would provide enough kinetic energy against a ship such as the *Longboat*, but Johnson was sure the Fleet ships would have strong enough shields or hulls to deal with such an impact.

Johnson realized that if the humans' radar could pick up the rocks, the Fleet ships' radar surely could.

"The Fleet ships have changed acceleration," someone reported, speaking quickly and excitedly.

"Will they miss the projectiles?" Johnson asked.

"I...don't think so."

Johnson nodded. Even Fleet ships had to follow the laws of physics.

It was over in a few seconds. The three Fleet ships collided with the stationary "projectiles" which, relative to them, were going around seventy-five thousand kilometers a second. But they also hit four of the slow-accelerating mining ships, vaporizing the ships and the humans inside them.

The explosions overwhelmed the visual pickups.

"The Fleet ships have stopped accelerating according to radar," someone barked.

"They're dead?" Johnson asked. He was trying not to think about the crews of those destroyed ships. They should have only been two or three people on board, but still that was eight or twelve deaths.

"Don't know, sir," the same person said.

"Trying to get a visual," another voice reported.

"Radio the Rebels to return," Johnson said. He had no idea how long that would take since they'd been accelerating at a thousand gees for over two hours. They were going a significant fraction of the speed of light, and any message to them would be red-shifted the same fraction. The Rebel ships had said they could compensate for that.

"I have a visual," the same technician reported.

"On my display," Spillum barked.

Johnson knew now that image would be red-shifted as the ships were past them and going away. In this case, the ships would look longer than they actually were.

The display was flat, not a holo, but it was obvious the three Fleet ships were heavily damaged. There were huge tears in the front where they'd impacted the rocks, and all three were tumbling.

A cheer went up in the room.

Johnson smiled but didn't join in. He was studying the ships on the display. Were they truly "dead"? he wondered. As everyone watched, they grew smaller and smaller until they disappeared.

"We're at the limit of our telescopes," the technician reported.

And now what? Johnson thought.

CHAPTER TWENTY-THREE

Spillum pushed herself over to Johnson. He noticed she was coming rather quickly, and she did, indeed, run into him, wrapping her arms around him in a hug.

"We did it," she exclaimed.

Johnson didn't say what he was thinking. They'd killed, he hoped, three Fleet ships. But how many Fleet ships were there, and how would they kill the next ones who came? And the next? And the next? He doubted this trap would work more than once.

"Yes," he said, feeling as if he needed to respond to her happiness.

"I think we deserve a beer," she said, pulling away from him enough to look into his face. The joy in her blue eyes was obvious.

Johnson forced himself to smile and said, "Sure."

Spillum turned to the room. "Keep an eye on those Fleet ships. If they do anything but look dead, let me know immediately. And let me know if the Rebel ships contact us."

Johnson didn't know, and *Úlfhethnar* had never said, how close they had to be in order to do that instantaneous communication trick. It had been about 2 AU when he'd talked to Spillum from Bostad orbit. Plus, he didn't know if relative velocity made a difference. In any case, the Rebel ships had to decelerate until they were stationary relative to Asgard, then accelerate toward the asteroid belt. If they wanted to be stationary to Asgard or match orbits with it, they would have to decelerate at some point in the trip back, usually about half-way. On the *Longboat*, they called this "turnaround."

Johnson had earlier calculated that at the velocity of the Fleet ships of over seventy-five thousand kilometers per second, they had more than two thousand times the velocity needed to escape the Bostad sun's gravity. They would leave the system, travel through the Oort cloud, enter interstellar space, and if they came across a star in, say, three parsecs, that would take them about forty years rest frame time. For them, due to their velocity, it would be around thirty-eight years, eight months. He wondered if he should ask Spillum to have one of her scientists calculate if they would come close to a human colony. They could pose quite a hazard to navigation if they came near enough to a planet or occupied asteroid belt. If they hit a planet, and he knew the odds were literally astronomical that they might, it would probably kill most of the life on that planet.

Spillum led Johnson out of what was being called the "War Room" and across several ropes to a bar. Since the war with Bostad, organic material to feed into the waste recyclers to make up for their inefficiencies was even more scarce and expensive, and diverting organic material to the production of ethyl alcohol meant less food for hungry mouths, so the price of alcohol was exorbitant.

Spillum paid for the beer bulbs and led Johnson to a quiet corner of the bar where they could strap in and talk. Everyone in the bar seemed to know who she was and many greeted her by name. "Ms. Spillum" was more common, although a few just said, "Britta." The mood in the bar was exuberant as word had leaked out that the plan had worked. There was an edge to the celebration, as everyone also apparently knew that some miners had been killed in the fight.

Spillum smiled again at Johnson. "Your plan worked," she said.

Johnson sipped his beer to give him time to think. It had a nice, artificial hoppy taste as he assumed no hops were grown in the asteroid belt. After 155 years, the fake flavor of waste-recycler-produced food had improved, he had noticed.

"For now," he finally said. "I don't know how many Fleet ships there are, and I doubt they will fall for this trick again."

"If more ships come, how would they know about this trick?" she asked.

Johnson shrugged. "I wouldn't put anything past these technologies. We can ask *Úlflethnar* when...it contacts us again." He had almost said "he."

"So what's the next trick?" Spillum asked.

Johnson shook his head. "I don't know. I think the plucky humans got lucky once fighting the evil alien ships. I wouldn't count on it again."

Spillum frowned. "You're just a bundle of optimism, aren't you?"

Johnson shrugged again. "Just trying to be realistic."

There was a long silence between the two, filled with the noise of the bar.

"But," Johnson said, "if we don't stop them here, they'll go on to each human colony, and eventually Earth."

Spillum shook her head. "We'll think of something."

Johnson only nodded. He hoped so, but doubted it.

#

Approximately three hours after the battle, the Bostad government contacted the Asgard Cooperative to ask what had happened. They'd seen the ships appear in orbit about their planet, then accelerate away. They saw the flashes from the explosions two hours after that happened, and apparently took over another hour to decide to contact their enemies in the asteroid belt.

On Johnson's advice, Spillum sent back a message detailing everything they knew about the Fleet and Rebel ships and the way they'd defeated the Fleet ships. Also on Johnson's advice, she added that they didn't know how many Fleet ships there were, if they'd come back again, and how they could defeat them again if they did.

A message came back a few hours later suggesting that the belt and the Bostad government cooperate to fight these alien ships.

Spillum snorted, but Johnson pointed out they needed all the help they could get.

The Rebel ships returned and Johnson said he should talk to *Úlfhethnar* alone. Spillum agreed.

After establishing contact on the frequency that had been used before, Johnson got right to the point. "How many Fleet ships are there, and when will they attack here again?"

"I do not know how many Fleet ships there are," the ship replied. "We know we have destroyed seventeen, including the three here. But we have no information on how many were built."

"How many Rebel ships are there?"

"I do not wish to tell you that lest it be revealed to the Fleet."

Johnson sighed.

"Do you think the other Fleet ships know what happened here?"

"As you've seen, over relatively short distances, less than four hundred thousand kilometers, we can communicate nearly instantaneously."

Johnson knew that *Úlfhethnar* could easily convert whatever units it used into human units such as AUs and kilometers.

"But any distance longer than that, like you," the ship droned in that monotone, expressionless voice it had, "we can only communicate via modulated ERM, which travels at a finite speed."

"Yes," Johnson said, "the speed of light."

"If we need to communicate with ships far away, we simply go there as that only takes moments."

Johnson snorted. That was a unique situation where your ship could move faster than your communications.

"So they probably do not know how we defeated these three ships?" he asked.

"They do not know how, but they will eventually, when the ships don't come back to whatever rendezvous point they have, know that the ships have been defeated. When they come here again, they shall be much more cautious."

Johnson frowned. That's what he was afraid of.

"They will probably come with more ships," *Úlfhethnar* added.

Johnson could only sigh.

"I've been wondering," Johnson said finally. "How did you stop the fusion reactors on Jideed Baghdad?" And how did the Fleet ship stop the fusion reactor on the *Longboat*, too, he didn't ask. He was grasping for straws. Maybe this would lead him to a way to defeat the Fleet ships, but he doubted it.

"As you know, fusion can only occur when the plasma is hot enough that the protons overcome their electrostatic charge. Since they have the same positive charge, they repel each other and the closer they are, the stronger they repel."

"Yes," Johnson said. He'd learned all this in high school. "We call it the 'Coulomb force,' and it increases with the square of the distance."

"I simply increased the force of the electrostatic charge, or the Coulomb force," the ship explained, "until your plasma was not hot enough to cause fusion."

Johnson went wide eyed. These ships can manipulate forces? That probably explained why they could accelerate at a thousand gees and stay stationary in relationship to a star, as if gravity didn't affect them. The technology they were up against was amazing, he realized. Yes, indeed, they had gotten lucky with the first three ships.

"Wait," Johnson said. "If you can manipulate the Coulomb force, can you reduce it?"

"Yes," the ship replied. "We do that in our fusion reactors so that they operate much cooler than yours need to."

"And if you reduced the Coulomb force to almost nothing?"

"Then fusion could occur at almost any temperature above absolute zero," the ship said.

"Could you do this to a Fleet ship's hull?" Turn its own hull into a fusion weapon, Johnson thought.

The ship was quiet for a moment. "They would detect it and counter it."

"Would they detect it if it were happening inside them?"

The ship was quiet for a moment. "Unlikely. But how could we do that?"

"I don't know," Johnson said. "But it's a possibility. More than we had before."

#

Johnson had been assigned quarters on Asgard. The Asgard government was paying his expenses, including Sven's and his air fees, as he had no money. Sven was at first fascinated by living on Asgard, but was quickly growing bored. He had little memory of his time living on BA-XP-4382 and was learning how to live in free fall again. Johnson suggested he find a job of some sort, but "space pirate" wasn't a marketable skill on Bostad. His knowledge of technology was 155 years out of date, so he didn't have anything to offer there, either.

Johnson found himself hoping his son would find a girl. Unfortunately, the only female he had known for the past seventeen years was his mother. He had no idea how to talk to a girl his age. Then Johnson smiled. His son was twenty-one years old. "Girls" his age were women.

A few days after the battle there was a memorial service for the nine people killed. Johnson felt that he had to attend, but he hoped no one would realize he was the one who'd sent them to their deaths. If anyone did, they apparently didn't blame him. Life in the belt was dangerous, and miners' attitudes toward death were more sanguine than people who lived in the relative safety of the surface of a planet.

Spillum spoke of their bravery and sacrifice. A large nickel plate was engraved with their names and would be mounted in the common area of the Asgard asteroid.

Of the few people who spoke to Johnson, all congratulated him on the success of his plan. He nodded and smiled and hoped they wouldn't blame him when the next Fleet ships showed up, and he wasn't able to destroy them.

#

Johnson woke up from a dream. He was hanging in a sleeping bag strapped to the wall. He had to go to the bathroom but he resisted, trying to remember the idea that had popped into his head. Something about teleportation and the Coulomb force.

He unzipped the bag and went to the bathroom.

Fusion at nearly any temperature, he thought as he emptied his bladder into the condom-like device, which was connected to a hose that had a negative pressure inside it to draw the urine to the black water tanks of the asteroid.

The Fleet ship they encountered had built a device that allowed Sven and him to teleport into the Rebel ship. That device was, according to *Úlfhethnar*, an explosive and was leading them to his fusion reactor.

After leaving the bathroom, he dressed: always an exercise in patience and agility in free fall. He left the apartment and pulled himself to the War Room. A man was outside the door but let Johnson in when he recognized him. He looked a bit surprised to see someone at the wee hours of the morning.

Johnson went to the radio.

"*Úlfhethnar?*"

"Yes?" the ship responded immediately.

"Can you build a device that will teleport itself inside Fleet ships such as the one I used to teleport into you?"

"Yes, but to what end?"

"Can you put in that device your Coulomb force manipulation technology?"

The ship hesitated. "Yes. The device would be large."

"How large?"

"Ten cubic meters, perhaps."

"Good, doesn't matter." That was small enough, Johnson thought, as it would fit in nearly any human ship. If it were a cube, and he suspected it would be, it would be 215 centimeters in each dimension. "When I teleported into you, I had to be about one hundredth of an AU away. I don't remember the exact number."

The ship was silent, so Johnson went on.

"We pilot ships within point zero one AU of the Fleet ships with your devices. The devices teleport aboard the Fleet ships. They lower the Coulomb force, and the ship explodes from the interior."

"I would only lower the Coulomb force so that elements lighter than iron fused," the ship said.

"Why?"

"Because the fusion of iron and heavier elements doesn't produce energy, but absorbs it. That would reduce the energy released by the activation of the device."

Johnson shook his head with a grim smile. "I didn't think of that."

"Also, a human would have to go with the device to activate it," the ship said.

"Why? Can't you put in a timer?"

"No, it can only be activated by being touched again."

"Why?"

The ship hesitated. "Your civilization does not have the understanding of science for my explanation to make sense to you."

Johnson growled. Every one of those humans would die, turned into fusing plasma.

CHAPTER TWENTY-FOUR

"A suicide mission," Spillum said. It was a statement, not a question.

"Pretty much," Johnson confirmed.

Spillum's face showed her agony. "It's one thing to ask someone to risk their life. Quite another to ask them to simply sacrifice it."

"I know," Johnson said. "But it's to save humanity. Billions, maybe trillions of humans."

Spillum shook her head.

"I had a thought," Johnson said.

"Yes?"

"The Bostad government," Johnson replied. "They have a lot more people to choose from. They have a military. The person only needs the skill to touch a control on the surface of the device twice. Once to teleport and once to set off the fusion reaction. Even condemned criminals could be used."

Spillum frowned. "I won't be the Impetusites's executioner. You probably don't know they murder political prisoners."

Johnson jerked his head in surprise. "How despotic are they?"

"Very," Spillum growled.

Johnson thought for a moment. "Still," he said. "I think we should see if we can get cooperation from them."

"How many people do we need?" Spillum asked, her voice soft.

"I don't know. *Úlfhethnar* claims he doesn't know how many Fleet ships there are."

"So we could be talking hundreds or thousands," Spillum said.

"Yes, perhaps, but I think it's less than that."

"Why? What do you base that on?"

Johnson took a breath. "If you were going to build very powerful ships to destroy all life, and were pretty confident in their abilities, you'd build very few because of the resources required. Maybe they only built twenty or so. And *Úlfhethnar* says that now seventeen have been destroyed, including the three we killed. If we knew what base numbers the builders used, we might be able to make a fair estimate. If they use base ten, then maybe they built twenty. If they used base, oh, eight, maybe they built sixteen."

"Or sixteen thousand," Spillum said.

"Then we are all dead in any case," Johnson said, not hiding the defeat in his voice. "But we fight anyway, because it beats rolling over and dying."

Spillum nodded. "Damn right."

#

Úlfhethnar and *Berserker* moved to a section of the asteroid belt that hadn't been invaded by humans yet. *Úlfhethnar* told Johnson that it was to find the resources needed to build the devices. Johnson asked how long it would take, and *Úlfhethnar* said that depended on how quickly they found what they needed.

Johnson imagined they would teleport the resources needed aboard, and then maybe there were small robots inside to do the building. He didn't know. Hell, maybe they would teleport the pieces together. He wasn't used to thinking in such advanced technological terms.

Johnson could only hope more Fleet ships didn't arrive in the meantime. He suggested to Spillum they be ready to try the shotgun strategy in case they did. She agreed and made the arrangements, with Holt's help.

Johnson had nothing to do, so he returned to the apartment he shared with Sven.

Pushing in, he was happy to see Sven was gone and not just sitting in front of a computer display.

Johnson didn't like being alone, though. It gave him time to think about Sonia.

He went to the computer and pulled up access to the War Room. He had to touch the screen so it could read his DNA to allow him in.

The picket of ships was still not deployed. The Bostad government was demanding answers even after the Asgard Cooperative told them everything they knew, which was mostly what Johnson knew. However, the fusion bomb plan, as it was coming to be called, was only known by a few people on Asgard. Even Holt didn't know. They didn't want to risk it being transmitted by radio and a Fleet ship somehow picking that up.

Úlfhethnar and *Berserker* were still, it was presumed, working on building the devices.

Johnson logged off and moved toward the refrigerator. He wanted some water. That's when he saw the piece of plastic sheeting stuck to the wall near Sven's sleeping bag.

Frowning, he pushed to it and pulled it off the surface. It was stuck with a common pressure-sensitive adhesive that stuck until it was pulled on.

On the sheeting was a note that was hand written and barely legible. It wasn't Sven's handwriting. Sonia had taught him better than that, although it was difficult to write in free fall when you learned in one gee.

"*Javla Helveta!*" he yelled when he deciphered the note.

\#

Asgard was big enough that some sections were less civilized than others. While prostitution, gambling, and some recreational drugs were legal on the asteroid and pretty much everywhere else in the belt, there were still banned chemical concoctions and other criminal matters such as thievery, smuggling of stolen and contraband substances, and outright murder. The Asgard security forces tried to keep a check on it, but in one section of the asteroid, which would be "down" from where the law-abiding worked and lived—if "down" meant anything in free fall—crime was abundant.

Johnson pulled the rope that took him into this section. He passed through the plane of the asteroid's interior where low-paid workers lived. Many of their plastic cubes were ill-kept and dirty, but some had enough pride to keep them clean and repaired. Most of these were people who came to the belt thinking they could make a fortune mining, but through bad luck or bad work ethic or lack of skill, ended up working for someone else in menial jobs. Every society needs its lowest strata, Johnson thought.

Past that, still heading for the shell of the asteroid, he came to an area that was even worse than the last. This was the true underbelly of the Asgard society. Johnson was worried he might be knifed before he could reach his goal. His overall, clean and new, marked him as having money.

Sometime in the past 155 years, the paper money in denominations of mass of gold were replaced by an electronic system. You deposited gold and got so many virtual grams. If you wished, you could trade virtual grams for physical gold. Everyone carried a small device that had their balance on it and responded to their DNA. Johnson had his, of course, but his balance was small, just what the Asgard Cooperative gave him for living expenses. He didn't like being virtually a ward of the state, but decided he was earning his keep by helping save humanity.

While hackers had tried, and failed, to steal the virtual grams, there was still a way to steal from people. If they could be forced to place their finger on the device and send their entire balance to an illicit account, then the criminal somehow—Spillum said they were still working on the "how"—transferred it to a legal account and the robber got richer, and the victim was broke. Usually the victim was threatened with a knife, gun, or just big men who could beat him or her badly. While that sometimes happened in the "nicer" sections of the asteroid, most of it happened in this area.

The victims were usually people looking to buy illegal drugs or the unfortunates who lived here.

Johnson was unmolested as he passed through, although some rough characters eyed him and some unattractive prostitutes called out to him.

He made it to the airlock designated in the note. There was a big man outside it, strapped to a handhold so his hands were free.

"You Johnson?" he snarled malevolently.

"Yes."

"You come alone?"

"The note said I should."

The man gave Johnson a predatory smile, then turned using the strap for leverage and touched a control by the airlock. It opened. Johnson could see from out here that it led to the interior of a small ship.

"Go in," the man ordered as Johnson hesitated.

Johnson sighed, pushed to the entrance, then used the handholds to go in.

As was typical, there was a "common area" behind the cockpit and storage behind that. It reminded Johnson of the *Nanna*, only slightly larger and not nearly as clean inside. Two men were there, each holding a pistol. The slug-throwing gun was still the preferred small arm, even after 155 years.

"Where is he?" Johnson demanded, noticing that the airlock had closed behind him.

"He's safe," the man on the right said. He had flaming red hair and pale skin spotted by freckles. Johnson wondered where he got enough sunlight to develop freckles. "Now strip."

"Pardon?" Johnson asked.

"Take your clothes off and toss them to Hank here." He indicated his younger and smaller companion, who had a thick mop of dark hair and almost black eyes.

Johnson complied, stopping at his underwear. The redhead didn't complain, so he tossed his overall, socks, and boots to Hank.

Hank caught the clothes with one hand and searched them carefully.

"He's clean," he finally announced.

Red nodded.

"You have what you want; let my son go," Johnson said, not hiding his anger but trying to hide his fear.

The man with the red hair shook his head. "No, first we need to know where John Larsen is."

"He's dead," Johnson said. "He was killed at Gredel by Fleet ships."

"Oh, and you just managed to escape?" Red asked.

"It's a long story," Johnson said.

"We have time," Red snarled.

"Let my son go first," Johnson said.

Red shook his head again. "Not until we have Larsen."

"Larsen's dead, damn it."

"Do you mind if I don't just take your word for it?"

Johnson pursed his lips lest he say something to anger this man pointing a gun at him. "If Larsen's alive, which I doubt, he's in the Gredel system, which is only about a hundred light years away."

Red just scowled.

"Who are you people?" Johnson asked. "What do you want with me?"

"We're with the Beowulf Cartel," Red said proudly. "You killed one of our men and stole from us."

"It's been a century and a half," Johnson cried.

"And how would it look if we let you get away with stealing from us and killing one of our men, even a century and a half ago? No, we have to make an example of you."

Johnson felt his stomach churn. He had a feeling they wouldn't just pop him out an airlock.

The sound of the airlock opening surprised him. He curled himself up into a ball as instructed. For some reason he closed his eyes, too, so he only heard what happened. Multiple gun shots from behind him, some from in front, and a lot of yelling of commands by people used to being obeyed.

When the shooting stopped, the air full of the smell of propellant smoke, Johnson uncurled and opened his eyes.

A woman, holding a gun that was still spewing smoke into a cloud around the barrel, asked, "Are you hurt, sir?"

"No, I'm fine," Johnson said, a little embarrassed to be in his skivvies in front of a woman.

"Search the ship," she ordered.

The two men with her replied, "Yes, ma'am," and pushed themselves in different directions.

They found Sven bound and gagged in the cargo hold.

#

"We're going to have to protect you better," Spillum said.

"I didn't know you were protecting me," Johnson replied.

Spillum chuckled. "We weren't. Who would hurt the man who saved us all from the Fleet attack?"

"The water cartels, apparently," the woman who had led the rescue said. She was high in the command of Asgard security. Johnson had learned her name was Lieutenant Vinter.

"We'll have to protect you the rest of your life," Spillum said, not masking her frustration.

"Could we somehow appease the cartels?" Johnson asked.

Spillum's face contorted with anger. "I'm not 'appeasing' criminals."

Johnson decided remaining silent was his best bet.

"It'll cost," Vinter said. "I'll have to have four personnel diverted from other work."

"Four?" Johnson asked.

Vinter nodded. "They'll work in shifts so we provide continual coverage. Two doing twelve hours a day for four days, then two doing twelve hours a day for three days. They'll rotate who works four and who works three days."

"I was asking 'only four?'" Johnson said. "Unless you're going to glue my son and me together, then you'll need at least one for each of us at all times." He wasn't sure one guard would be enough against a determined cartel.

Vitner nodded. "You're right. We'll need eight. And we'll have to restrict both you and your son's movements." She looked at Spillum. "I don't have that kind of manpower to spare."

"Do you see an alternative?"

"Other than hiring and training a platoon of guards, and raising fees and taxes to pay for it, no."

Spillum shook her head. Johnson again noticed what that did to her hair. Then he berated himself for finding another woman attractive when Sonia hadn't been dead for very long.

"The best I can do," Vinter said, "is keep an eye on the Johnsons during our regular course of security work, and whenever I can spare someone, have them watch them."

Spillum didn't look happy.

"Oh…," Vinter said. "It would be helpful if you two restricted your excursions outside your apartment. If we know where you are, it'll be easier to keep track of you."

Johnson nodded. Sven spent most of his time in the apartment anyway. But Johnson needed to work on the plan to defeat the Fleet.

"The good news," Spillum said, "is that the cartels now know you're smart enough to call for help."

Johnson nodded again. That was not much consolation.

CHAPTER TWENTY-FIVE

It took about a week, and the entire time Johnson worried more and more about the Fleet returning and about the cartels trying to harm him, or worse, Sven.

Sven was, before he was told he had to, perfectly content to stay in their apartment using the computer to play games or socialize with new friends he found on Asgard's 'net. Johnson suggested he try to bring himself up to date on current technology, and he knew Sven had spent a lot of time studying, too. But once he was told he couldn't leave, he balked at the restrictions and Johnson knew he was sneaking out at times.

Johnson could feel that he and Sven were drifting apart. After twenty-one years together all the time, Sven was pushing away now that he had the opportunity. It broke Johnson's heart, but he was also glad his son was working his way free as he needed to in order to become a functioning adult. Still, Johnson missed the days when he would teach his son something about the universe, and he'd see the light of realization go on in his son's eyes.

Úlfhethnar and *Berserker* came back to "park" near Asgard and communicated with Johnson with Spillum listening in.

"We have the devices to teleport humans onto Fleet ships and then lower the Coulomb force until fusion happens in an area shaped like a sphere approximately eighty-two meters in diameter," *Úlfhethnar* reported. "The device itself should provide a large enough release of energy inside the ship to at the very least cripple if not destroy it. Any added mass in that radius would simply add to the energy release."

"How many devices?" Johnson asked.

"One hundred."

"Will it be enough?" Spillum asked.

"We believe there are less than thirty Fleet ships remaining."

"Do you have any idea when they will attack next?" Johnson asked.

"No," the ship replied. "But they will likely send a scout to determine what happened to the three ships they sent. It will likely be shortly after that."

"And how close do our ships need to be?" Spillum asked.

"Within approximately 1,652,185 kilometers of the Fleet ships."

Johnson remembered that was the same distance he and Sven had to be within to teleport aboard *Úlfhethnar*.

"And how do we get our ships that close?" Spillum asked.

"Easy," Johnson said. "We put them in orbit around Bostad. The Fleet ships will most likely go there first."

"Or they might attack the belt first," Spillum said, "especially if they figure out what we did to the first three."

"Then we have two sets of ships: fifty each, one set in orbit of Bostad, one in the asteroid belt," Johnson said. "Maybe Bostad could supply the ones for their orbit."

"And then we wait?" Spillum asked.

"Yes," Johnson said.

"Can you imagine," Spillum said, "asking a person to sit and wait to kill themselves?"

Johnson took a deep breath. "I know. It won't be easy. But I have an idea."

Spillum frowned. "What?"

"Maybe someone, Holt for instance, can rig up a thing to attach to Coulomb devices with a timer to touch it and set it off a few seconds after teleportation."

"Will that work?" Spillum asked.

"*Úlfhethnar*," Johnson said to the air, "will that work?"

"Yes, it just needs to feel pressure on its surface."

"How much pressure?"

"One kilopascal would be sufficient."

"We'll need the specifications of the devices," Spillum said. "Their dimensions."

"You cannot put holes in the devices," *Úlfhethnar* said in that monotone voice. "Even if you had tools strong enough, it would damage them."

"That's okay," Spillum said with a smile. "We have glues that will stick to anything."

Johnson breathed a sigh of relief. He wasn't going to have to condemn people to die.

"There will have to be at least two people on each ship," Spillum said. "One to pilot it and one to activate the device."

Johnson nodded.

"Yes," Spillum said. She was silent for a moment. "One hundred volunteers, at least, and fifty ships. That's if the Impetusites come through with fifty. I don't know if they have fifty spaceworthy ships."

"We don't know if we need all one hundred," Johnson said.

Spillum rolled her eyes. "But we'll have to deploy all one hundred to ensure we have enough to kill all the Fleet ships."

"All teleportations must happen simultaneously," the ship said. "Or the Fleet ships will realize that the human ships are a threat and destroy them."

Spillum shook her head.

Johnson said, "*Úlfhethnar*, what if a Rebel ship found the Fleet and told them you wanted a final showdown here, in this system. Would they bring all their ships?"

"They may," the ship replied.

"It's worth trying, I think," Johnson said.

There was a hesitation. Finally, the ship said, "We will attempt to draw the Fleet here as soon as you are ready."

"Good," Spillum said.

"Otherwise," Johnson said, "I'm afraid they may skip this star system and go on to hit other human colonies. Or even Earth."

Spillum looked sick at the idea.

"There are the humans from Jideed Baghdad," the ship said. "They should be safe."

"Until they start using fusion and EMR," Johnson said. "It may take them centuries, but eventually they will. Then the Fleet will kill them, and humanity will be extinct."

"Plus, I don't want to sit by while trillions of humans are slaughtered," Spillum said.

"We will do our best to lure the entire Fleet here," the ship said, emotionless and monotone as always.

"How will you find the Fleet?" Spillum asked.

"They may still have a ship at Gredel. If not there, we do know some of the uninhabited systems where they go to plan and repair.

"Okay," Spillum said. "When we're ready."

"Yes," the ship replied.

#

The Bostad government refused to cooperate other than giving permission for mining ships to orbit the planet. Spillum tried to explain that if this scheme failed, every human on that planet would die. The entrenched bureaucracy could not get that fact to pass through their collective craniums, Johnson thought.

The devices, looking like glass cubes with a milky-white surface, were teleported over to Asgard by *Úlfhethnar*, where they were stored and guarded. Even Vinter agreed that they needed to be guarded.

Úlfhethnar said he'd continue making more in case more than one hundred were needed. He'd store those inside him.

Mechanical experts were working on the rigs to touch them after teleportation.

The biggest problem was finding two hundred volunteers for such a dangerous mission. People who worked and lived in space coexisted with death nearly every day, but this was more dangerous than just mining. If the Fleet ships discovered that the human ships were a threat, they'd destroy them. It didn't help that rumors spread on the 'net that the entire thing was an "inside job" designed to reduce the population of the asteroid belt and draw the Asgard Cooperative back into war with Bostad.

The engineer proudly showed off her device. "We call it a slapper," she said with a grin.

To Johnson, it looked like a metal box with an arm protruding from it at a forty-five degree angle. At the end of the arm was a pad made of plastic and covered in cloth. It bent up at an angle from the arm so that when the arm was down, it was parallel to the surface of the Coulomb device.

"How's it work?" Spillum asked.

"We glue it to the Coulomb device on the edge. Now, I understand the device gives a signal of when to touch it to teleport it, correct?"

"Yes," Johnson confirmed.

"So, when the operator sees that signal, they press this button—" she touched a red button on the metal box " —and then touches the device to teleport it. Three seconds later..."

The arm swung down as if on cue.

"How much pressure?" Johnson asked.

"Three kilopascals, give or take. I assume there's no way to break the Coulomb device, and I wanted a margin of error."

"Good," Spillum said. "How fail-safe are these?"

"And will they work in vacuum?" Johnson added.

The engineer smiled. "There's a simple timing device that, when it reaches zero, activates a solenoid that is holding the arm. The arm moves via a spring. There's a battery to run the timer and the solenoid, but it will last for months. And yes, they will operate in hard vacuum and space-like temperatures. We tested this one in an open airlock."

"Thank you. I need one hundred of these as soon as possible."

The engineer's face fell. "We'll get right on it," she said, obviously trying to hide her dismay.

"Fifty ships in orbit around Bostad," Spillum said more to herself. "Fifty around the occupied areas of the asteroid belt."

"The two targets the Fleet will likely attack," Johnson said. "After what we did last time, they may attack the belt first."

Spillum nodded. "I know."

#

It took the fifty ships assigned to orbit Bostad four days, approximately, to get there and get in orbit. It took considerably less time to get the ships stationed in the asteroid belt, again orbiting the sun as if they were asteroids, on minimal power just to keep their air recycler going.

The distance, 1,652,185 kilometers, that they had to be within the Fleet ships to teleport was about half the distance from the Earth to its moon. It was more than ten times the diameter of Bostad, so even if a ship were on the far side of the planet from the Fleet ships, the operator could teleport the device into an enemy ship at the same time as the ones closest to the Fleet could. The devices, according to *Úlfhethnar*, would each lock on to only one Fleet ship, so only one device went into each ship.

Berserker left when Johnson reported to *Úlfhethnar* that the humans were ready. Johnson didn't know if *Berserker* was going to find the Fleet, or find another Rebel ship to do so. He didn't really care.

Rebel ships began appearing. At least *Úlfhethnar* said they were Rebel ships. They parked about halfway between the orbit of Bostad and the asteroid belt. Johnson hadn't thought about the fact that Rebel ships had to be contacted, too. It had to look like the final showdown to the Fleet Ships when they arrived.

Johnson was in his quarters, quietly eating a meal with Sven. Johnson was too stressed to make small talk with his son, and they were drifting apart emotionally as Sven was finding more distractions on Asgard.

Johnson's communicator beeped. He pulled it out of his pocket. It was a text message from Spillum: "Come to the war room."

"*Fan*," Johnson spat.

"What?" Sven asked.

"This may be it."

At Vinter's suggestion, the Johnsons' quarters had been moved closer to the War Room since there was better security around there. Johnson pulled himself out of their quarters, and using ropes and handholds, to the War Room. He tried to keep his face passive and not move too fast lest he panic others who knew who he was.

He nodded to the guard at the war room and pulled himself through the door. The guard closed it.

"Is the Fleet here?" he asked, seeing only Spillum and wondering why more people weren't here.

She shook her head and smiled. "No."

"Then what's up?"

"*Berserker* has returned and has something."

Johnson frowned. "What?"

Spillum smiled and touched her holographic display. It showed a Rebel ship. What caught Johnson's eye was that under it was a long latticework with a wide disk at one end.

"The *Longboat*?" he whispered. "How is that possible?"

Spillum was still smiling. "Would you like to talk to them?"

"Them?" Johnson whispered. "They're alive?"

Spillum grinned as she nodded. She touched an area of her holo display. "Asgard to *Longboat*. I have Olly Johnson here."

There was no reply.

"They're about five light minutes away," Spillum explained. "I assume they can't use that Rebel ship trick of faster-than-light communication."

Johnson nodded, almost not believing what was happening. In ten minutes, he'd hear someone's voice from the *Longboat*. He was sure it would be Larsen, but hoped it would be Sonia. Johnson debated sending a message for Sven to join him, but decided he'd wait until he knew what the situation was.

The ten minutes passed more slowly than had any ten minutes in Johnson's life.

Then, finally, came a voice that Johnson recognized: "This is First Mate John Larsen of the *Longboat*. The ship is fine and both Sonia and I are alive. Sonia wants to know if Sven is okay."

If Johnson could, he might have collapsed. His body went loose. Spillum looked at him.

"You okay, Johnson?" she asked.

"Get my son down here," he said, barely able to force out the words.

"Yes, of course. Anything you want to send back?"

Johnson hesitated. What do you say after thinking for months your wife and friend were dead? He nodded, and Spillum again touched the same area and nodded at him.

"*Longboat*," Johnson started, "This is Olly Johnson. Sven and I are both fine. Sven is on his way here. May I please hear Sonia's voice?"

A few minutes later, Sven came in. Johnson couldn't help but admire his son's newly acquired skills at moving in free fall.

"What is it?" he asked his father.

"The *Longboat*," Johnson said, "It's here, and they are both alive."

Sven's eyes went wide and his jaw slack. "They're alive?"

"Yes, son," Johnson said, now smiling himself.

"This is Sonia," a voice said over the radio. "Hello, Olly and Sven. I love you both and have missed you so. We thought you were both dead."

Johnson laughed. He couldn't help it. He laughed uncontrollably for long minutes, gulping air as he did.

Spillum sent a shuttle for the *Longboat* after Larsen put it in orbit around the system's primary. "It does have a standard docking clamp?" she asked Johnson.

He nodded. "Yes, one." Left over from the conversion from the *Loki*, he didn't say.

It took six long days before the shuttle rendezvoused with the *Longboat* and could bring Sonia and Larsen to Asgard.

The reunion at the airlock was joyous and long. Johnson held his wife's small body until he had to stop due to embarrassment that he was making a scene. Sonia clumsily hugged Sven, and Larsen actually allowed Johnson to hug him.

"How?" Johnson asked.

"I'll tell you all about it."

CHAPTER TWENTY-SIX

"As soon as you left with that Fleet ship," Larsen said, "The two other ships started attacking Gredel."

"Damn," Sven whispered.

They were all in the Johnsons' quarters. Sonia and Johnson floated close together, holding hands. Since meeting at the airlock, they'd almost constantly been touching.

"Yes," Larsen said. "They just released the *Longboat*. Because we had no angular velocity, we weren't in orbit and we just started falling toward the sun, or Gredel, or both. I didn't bother to figure it out."

"What did you do?" Sven asked.

"You remember our hydrogen tanks were full because the Fleet ship filled them?"

Johnson and Sven both nodded.

"I pointed the *Longboat* at Bostad and hit the fusion rocket at five gees. I knew the Fleet ships could catch up in a moment and kill us, but I wasn't just going to wait for that. They at least had to chase us down, I decided."

"But they didn't?" Johnson asked.

"No," Larsen replied. "They ignored us. I ran on five gees for two whole days and then switched to one gee. I was planning to come here and hope I found humans."

Johnson nodded. He couldn't imagine two days at five gees. It must have been hell for his wife and friend.

237

"Then, we were about two AUs away from Gredel when what I thought was a Fleet ship rendezvoused with us," Larsen said. "It must have spotted our neutrino emissions."

"I thought we were dead," Sonia whispered, the fear evident in her voice.

Johnson gave her hand a reassuring squeeze.

"It shut down the fusion drive," Larsen said, "and I, too, thought that was it. The next thing we knew, we were in the Bostad system and forty minutes later, the Asgard Cooperative was radioing us asking who we were."

Johnson smiled.

"What about you?" Larsen asked. "When we found out the Fleet had malevolent intent, we assumed you were dead."

Johnson gave them a brief rundown on how Sven and he survived and arrived in the Bostad system, everything that they had learned about the Fleet and the Rebel ships, and all that had happened since, except Sven's kidnapping.

"Damn," Larsen breathed, hearing about the way they killed three Fleet ships. "And you thought of that?"

"Spillum helped," Johnson said. "And a lot of other people did the math and logistics and strategy. But the basic idea was mine."

"Spillum was that woman we met?" Sonia asked.

"Yes," Johnson confirmed. "She's in charge of the Cooperative."

"So now what?" Larsen asked.

Johnson smiled grimly. "We have a plan."

#

In all, thirteen Rebel ships were in the Bostad system, in orbit around the planet at about twice the distance as the human ships, except *Úlfhethnar*, which was near Asgard. Johnson asked *Úlfhethnar* if this was all the Rebel ships, or if they had kept some back just in case. The ship simply did not respond.

The *Longboat* was in orbit around the sun about a hundred thousand kilometers inside the orbit of Asgard. Johnson decided they could pick it up later if necessary, but he didn't think it was needed. He felt he'd found a home here on Asgard. Spillum wasn't about to turn him over to the Impetusites, even if they realized who he was. The biggest problem was the water cartels. He was wondering if he paid them with the gold in the *Longboat*, would that satisfy them. Ten thousand kilograms of gold was more than a king's ransom. More than a hundred kings' ransoms, he mused.

Johnson knew that when the Fleet ships arrived, they would appear in an instant. But where would that be? Close to Bostad, or close to the belt? No one knew.

Another complication was that since Bostad orbited the primary faster than Asgard, and had passed its closest approach to Asgard before the battle with the three Fleet ships, it was getting farther away with each passing moment.

The fifty ships around Bostad all needed to communicate with each other even with the planet blocking radio signals. That meant using a Bostad communication system of satellites and ground stations. The Impetusites reluctantly cooperated. Maybe, Johnson thought, they finally realized their survival depended on it.

Larsen had made a video recording of the destruction of Gredel as they raced away. It was transmitted to Impetus Party leaders, and they became quite cooperative. It showed almost the same thing that Johnson and Sven were shown by *Úlfhethnar*: a beam of energy traveled from the two ships to the atmosphere, and suddenly the planet turned orange as the entire envelope of life-giving air turned to fire. Johnson tried not to think about the fact he was watching the agonizing death of millions of people: men, women, and children.

The ships around Bostad all had to have their devices teleport at the same moment. Because communications had to go around the planet, there would be about a five second delay between the one to first get closest to a Fleet ship and the one farthest from that ship. So technicians figured out a system where the first ship sent the signal, and then at the appropriate time, a green light appeared on each ship's communication computer display saying it was time to teleport. The ones on the far side would teleport immediately. The ones closest to the Fleet ships would have to wait five seconds. Johnson thought those would be the longest five seconds of those people's lives. He could imagine what they would be thinking: "Please don't let me fuck up."

#

Spillum invited the Johnsons and Larsen out for drinks. They were in a bar and, other than a few stares and polite greetings, were left alone.

"So after you stole the *Loki,* what did you do?" Spillum asked.

"We stole the Bussard ramjet," Larsen said. "Which was easy because it was unmanned. We took both ships to the far reaches of the asteroid belt and paid shipwrights to use the *Loki* to convert the ramjet into a ship that could carry humans."

"That must have taken a while," Spillum said.

"About a year," Johnson said. "And we had to pay them all. It took all the gold we had."

"That you'd stolen from the Beowulf cartel?" Spillum asked.

"We did some mining, too," Larsen explained, "to keep up appearances."

"How did you decide who was going to be the captain?" Spillum asked.

"I thought Larsen should be captain," Johnson explained. "He knew a lot more than I did about spacecraft and navigation and everything needed to operate a ship safely. But he said it was my family, I had more responsibility, so it should be me."

Spillum nodded. "Makes sense."

"And, as my first officer, he would advise me," Johnson concluded.

Larsen was quiet during this exchange.

She nodded. "Everyone knows what you did after that."

Johnson tried not to smile. "Oh?"

"You went into orbit about Bostad and threatened to turn on the ramscoop magnetic field and fry every electronic device on the planet. You'd have sent them back to the Stone Age. Nice revenge for what they did to you."

Sonia didn't look happy about this discussion.

Spillum turned to her. "You didn't agree?"

240

Sonia shook her head. "I knew we needed organics and oxygen in order to leave the system. But I didn't agree with Olly and John's plan to extort gold, too."

"We were stealing from the government," Johnson said.

"And the government could only get it by taking it from the civilians," Sonia said in a low voice. "I didn't think we hurt the government as much as we hurt those still under the Impetusites' rule."

"But you did, anyway," Spillum said. It was a statement.

"Yes," Larsen said. "They sent up the gold, oxygen, and organics we demanded in a boat."

"Oxygen and organics to supplement your recyclers?"

"Yes," Larsen acknowledged. "We had a nearly ten year trip to Gredel."

Spillum smiled.

"So, then we stole the boat, too." Johnson grinned.

"Oh, the Impetusites must have covered that up. What happened to the pilot?"

"We allowed them to send a shuttle to get him," Johnson said. "The whole time we were scared to death they would try to kill us. Maybe have an unmanned ship ram us."

"Yeah," Spillum said. "They were, and are, so unimaginative, they probably didn't, or couldn't, think of that."

"So then we headed for Gredel, and did the same thing there: gold, organics, and oxygen," Johnson said. "We were planning to do it at Jideed Baghdad when we came across the alien ships."

Sonia was quiet. Johnson knew she'd made her argument many times and wasn't going to make it again.

"Then all we had to do was decide what planet to retire on," Larsen added.

"How long did it take you to get to Gredel?" Spillum asked.

"Nine years, ship's time," Johnson said. "Over a hundred years your time frame."

"And then to Jideed Baghdad?"

"Around eight years, ship's time frame," Larsen said. "Or fifty-four years your time frame."

Spillum nodded. "I should arrest you both for piracy. You know what we do with pirates?"

Johnson's face went pale.

Spillum chuckled. "Don't worry. I'm not going to throw you out an airlock. I don't care what you did to the Impetusites, and there's no one on Gredel to be a victim, now. The only people you hurt here in the belt were criminals already. We'd pop them out an airlock if we caught them and could convict them."

"Could convict them?" Sonia asked.

Spillum nodded grimly. "Witnesses and evidence have a bad habit of disappearing. We occasionally get lucky and convict some lower level cartel goon. But it's too easy to make people disappear. Take someone, oh, half an AU outward, toss them out an airlock."

"No *corpus delicti*," Larsen breathed.

"Exactly."

"And physical or electronic evidence?"

"Hackers and somebody on the inside. We catch a mole, and they just turn around and recruit another. They have a lot of money and basically make you an offer you can't refuse: work for us and you'll make a lot of gold. Don't, and we kill you and your entire family."

"Wow," Johnson breathed.

"Yes," Spillum said. "These are the kind of people you pissed off."

Sonia's face went pale. She looked angrily at her husband.

Johnson swallowed. Maybe they shouldn't stay here, he wondered. He glanced at Larsen. His face was grim. He must be thinking the same thing, Johnson thought.

#

Gredel had been the closest human colony to Bostad. After its destruction, the nearest was a planet called Paradisus, and it was 138 light years away from the Bostad system. Johnson did some quick calculations and found it would take the *Longboat* nine years, seven months to reach it, ship's time. He didn't really care how old he would be then, but Sven would be thirty years old. With a life expectancy of over a century, that gave Sven more than seventy years to find a wife, have a family, and enjoy his life.

That could work, he thought. After the Fleet was defeated, they would go to Paradisus. The planet was reported to live up to its name: with almost no axial tilt, it was in near-constant summer due to the brightness of its star and its orbital characteristics. The only downside was the star put out a bit more UV than Sol, so humans had to be careful with their skin. Johnson snorted. That was especially true for those with northern European DNA, such as he and his family.

He'd talk to Larsen and his family about it. That'd put 138 light years between them and the water cartels. There wasn't quite as much gold in the *Longboat* as Johnson had hoped to have when they "retired," but it was enough if they were a little careful.

#

"What is it?" Johnson asked, pulling himself quickly into the War Room. He was careful not to get up too much speed lest he not be able to stop himself. "Is this it?"

"No," Spillum said. "But a Fleet ship appeared in the system ten minutes ago. Well, we saw it ten minutes ago. We're forty light minutes away from it. It's just parked, not orbiting. It's almost ninety million kilometers from Bostad."

Johnson nodded. "A scout."

Spillum nodded. "That was my thought. Rebel ships are moving toward it. I don't know the range of their weapons."

Johnson matched Spillum's nod. The scout ship was probably observing what was happening in the system.

"It'll see our ships around Bostad," Spillum said, her voice tight.

Johnson nodded. "Maybe they'll think it's some pathetic human attempt at protecting the planet. Or maybe they won't think it's unusual."

"Let's hope so," Spillum said.

"The Rebel ships are firing," a technician reported. "Impact should be in about five minutes."

"Damn," Spillum said.

"Yes," Johnson agreed. The Rebel ships were shooting at the Fleet ship from five light minutes away. They didn't even know if the Fleet ship would be there when the lasers reached it.

And, everything they were seeing was forty minutes old. This battle could already be over. In fact, he thought, it probably was.

The minutes passed with the alacrity of drying paint as they waited and watched the radar display. It took the radar signals eighty minutes to travel from Asgard to the Fleet scout ship and back. Since they'd been sending out radar continuously, they saw the return signals in forty minutes.

The red blip representing the Fleet ship disappeared.

"The Rebel lasers didn't reach it in time," the technician reported.

Johnson wasn't used to thinking at the scale where lasers traveling the speed of light took five minutes to hit their target.

And it all happened forty minutes ago.

"Anything in the path of those lasers?" Spillum asked.

"No," the technician reported. "They are angled so that when they reach the asteroid belt, they'll be far above the plane of the ecliptic."

"Good." Spillum breathed a sigh of relief.

"This probably means they'll attack soon," Johnson said.

Spillum nodded. "Let's hope they don't start destroying our ships."

"If they do, we'll have to teleport as quickly as possible," Johnson said, his midsection twisting again. He was, again, consigning more humans to possible death.

CHAPTER TWENTY-SEVEN

The fleet of human ships orbiting Bostad was called, logically enough, the Bostad Defense Group. It had a commander who was authorized to decide when the operators should teleport. If he had to wait for orders from Spillum, that would take long minutes they didn't have to spare as Bostad kept moving farther and farther away from Asgard in its orbit.

The fleet in the belt was called the Belt Defense Group, and Spillum was in direct command of it. Someone proposed they be called "BDG One" and "BDG Two," but Belt and Bostad was better shorthand, as no one had to remember which was one or two.

Johnson spent as much time in the War Room as possible. He thought about having a sleeping bag brought in for him. He knew Spillum was sleeping in her office, which was adjacent to the War Room.

Sonia, who was learning to prepare food again in free fall and with actual fresh food, not just what the waste recycler produced, was bringing him his meals. She would linger awhile as he ate. Johnson felt bad, and he would rather have been with her and Sven than hanging (literally) around the War Room for nineteen hours a day, going back to their apartment, sleeping, quickly eating something, and returning to the War Room. But, after the coming battle with the Fleet, one of two things would be true: they'd all be dead, or he'd have time to spend with his family.

It was four days after the scout appeared. Johnson was passing the time fretting and trying to read a bad novel on a hand computer.

"Fleet ships have appeared near Bostad," the radar tech said. "They are accelerating toward the planet."

"How many?" Spillum asked.

"Twenty-three," the tech reported.

"Damn," Johnson breathed. He hoped this was all of them.

He looked at Spillum's holo display. It showed twenty-three red blips in a cloud around the green sphere that represented Bostad. He was frustrated that what he was seeing happened nearly twenty-two minutes ago because the planet was 2.6 AU from Asgard.

"Some Fleet ships are breaking off and coming this way."

"How many?" Spillum demanded.

"Looks like eleven."

"How long until they get here?"

The technician calculated for a few moments. "The soonest they could get here is 148 minutes, but they'll be going eighty-five thousand kilometers a second relative to us. If they match orbits, 209 minutes."

"Eighty-five thousand kps," Johnson exclaimed. "That doesn't give us a lot of time to react."

"No, sir," the technician said. "They'll be in range of the teleportation devices for thirty-eisht seconds."

Johnson and Spillum exchanged a worried look.

"And by then, they will have seen what happened at Bostad, assuming it happens," Spillum said.

"When do they reach the speed they can't go interdimensional?" Johnson asked.

"If they keep accelerating, forty-six minutes."

Johnson shook his head. The Bostad commander would most likely order teleportation before that. On the holo display, the Fleet ships were getting closer to the planet.

"Tell Bostad commander to hold off as long as he can?" someone suggested.

"Yes, and he'll get that message in twenty-two minutes," Spillum said, not hiding her frustration. "Probably long after he gives the teleportation order."

"Rebel and Fleet ships are exchanging fire," the man watching the telescopic display said. "Gamma ray lasers and hyperkinetic weapons."

"Our ships?" Spillum asked.

"None have been hit, yet."

"There's the signal from the Bostad commander: he's ordering teleportation," the radio technician said. "Will happen in five seconds."

Spillum only nodded, her face tight with worry.

Johnson thought, yes, in five seconds twenty-two minutes ago.

"Now," the radio technician said.

Everyone turned to the radar. Nothing happened.

"Damn," Spillum spat.

Still nothing happened. Johnson had no idea how much time passed. Did the slappers fail? Did the Fleet ships somehow neutralize the Coulomb devices? His stomach churned at the possibilities.

Then a red light winked out. More followed. The visual display showed them disappearing into a ball of light.

"Those devices must have teleported into a ship close to something vital," Spillum said, almost in a whisper.

At the scale of the holo display it was hard to see by eye, but the radar technician cried out, "The surviving ships around Bostad are no longer accelerating."

"They appear to be tumbling," the telescope technician reported. "And they are no longer firing at the Rebel ships."

"It worked," Johnson breathed. He didn't dare believe it. They saved millions of lives, for now.

"What's happening with the ships headed for us?" Spillum asked.

"They're still coming," the radar tech reported.

"They had to have seen what happened at Bostad," Spillum said.

"Before we did," Johnson added. "Of course, they are still light minutes away."

"Six Fleet ships have appeared very close to Bostad," the radar tech cried. "They are within range of teleportation."

"The ships they held in reserve," Johnson said.

"Bostad commander is giving the command to teleport again," the radio operator reported.

There was an interminable delay while the time reading on the holo display clicked off ten seconds.

Of the six red dots, two disappeared, again in a flash of light. The other four appeared motionless.

"The surviving four are no longer accelerating," the radar technician reported.

A collective sigh of relief was expelled in the room.

"Oh oh," the radar tech said.

"Yes?" Spillum demanded.

"It appears those four are going to impact on Bostad."

Spillum turned to Johnson. "How much do those things mass, did you say?"

"Half a million tonnes."

Spillum shook her head. "Let's hope they impact away from populated areas."

Johnson breathed, "Yes." This might be a pyrrhic victory if they hit the planet in or near a city. They would probably impact it with the force of nuclear weapons.

There was a moment of silence while each person was deep in their own thoughts.

Then Spillum demanded, "What's happening with the Fleet ships headed this way?"

"No change in course or acceleration."

"What are they doing?" Spillum asked out loud. "Do they have a plan?"

Johnson shrugged. Who could know what they were planning? If they fired those gamma ray lasers at the belt asteroids, the humans wouldn't know it until the lasers impacted. Johnson wondered what that much energy would do to an asteroid like Asgard. Probably crack it open like a dropped egg, he thought.

"Still coming, not changing acceleration," the radar tech reported.

Spillum touched her holo display and the flat visual of the eleven Fleet ships coming toward them replaced the three-dimensional radar display. All eleven ships were in a line. No, Johnson thought, it was an inverse V with the point farthest from them. At least that's what it looked like judging from the sizes of the ships.

"Radar?" he asked, "What formation are they in?"

There was a moment's hesitation. "Inverse V, the arms of the V coming at us. Five ships in each arm, one at the apex."

"What are they doing?" Spillum asked.

Johnson put his hands together, touching at the heel of the palm and extending out in a V. "What if your ships had to be a certain distance apart," he said. "But you wanted them able to concentrate their fire so have them close together."

Spillum frowned. "What do you mean?"

Johnson touched the tips of his fingers together, making his hands a straight plane. "This way, the ships are lined up, as close together as they can get, but still in a long line."

He put his hands back in the V configuration. "But this way, the ships can still be as far apart as needed, yet the frontal area of their assault is smaller and they can concentrate more power, more weaponry, on a smaller area."

"They're attacking," Spillum said as the realization hit her.

"Of course," Johnson replied. "But it looks as if they only have a small target."

"What?" someone asked.

"Cut off the head," Spillum said. "Us."

"It's probably obvious from our radar and radio transmissions that we're HQ," Johnson said.

"We have to stop them," a panicked voice said. Johnson turned to see the radar tech looking up wide-eyed.

Spillum looked at Johnson. "How do we stop them?"

Johnson thought for a moment. "Accelerate our defense ships toward them."

"They'll probably blast them," Spillum said.

"It's the only thing we have."

"The Rebel ships are chasing the Fleet," radar reported.

"They're exchanging fire," the telescope operator added.

"They'll never catch them," Johnson said.

"Maybe they'll slow them down," Spillum replied with hope in her voice.

"Maybe," Johnson said, but he didn't know what good that would do.

A few moments later Spillum said, "Order the defense fleet to accelerate toward the Fleet ships."

"Yes, ma'am," the radio operator said.

"Tell them to teleport as soon as in range," Spillum added. "Don't wait to do it simultaneously."

"Yes, ma'am."

As before, all those ships had different acceleration abilities, from as high as five gees to as low as 0.5 gees. Johnson thought the slow accelerating ones were most likely to survive the battle, being farthest from the Fleet ships.

"And if this doesn't work?" the radar tech asked.

Spillum had a grim look on her face. "Then we die. But we took a lot of those bastards with us."

A few minutes passed in silence. Spillum turned to Johnson. "Tell *Úlfhethnar* that if we don't destroy the Fleet that he needs to go to Paradisus and warn them and tell them how to kill them."

"If the same strategy will work again," Johnson said. He had doubts it would work again here, killing the eleven ships headed for them.

Again, time passed slowly for Johnson. He kept looking at the time read out on the holo display and being surprised how ponderously the seconds were ticking by. He expected gamma ray lasers to impact Asgard at any moment. He'd probably die before he knew what happened. Eleven gamma ray lasers hitting the asteroid would, he suspected, vaporize most, if not all, of it. He was not happy that Sonia and Sven were on Asgard. But having them on another asteroid would only delay their deaths, Johnson thought. Eleven Fleet ships were certainly enough to kill every human in the belt and on Bostad. He tried not to show his grief that they'd failed. There was still a slim chance they could kill some more Fleet ships. Perhaps the Fleet computers were too dumb to figure out what happened to their comrades around Bostad and would fly into this trap as the first three had flown into the projectile trap what seemed so long ago.

Johnson's death kept not coming.

It started at the arms of the V. Fleet ships would blink out in a flash of actinic light, or would stop accelerating.

"They're firing at our ships!" the telescope tech cried. "The Rebels are still firing at them."

Johnson watched. The Fleet ship at the apex of the V was hit multiple times by Rebel lasers as it fired at human ships. Then, it exploded like the others.

"What happened to that ship?" Spillum asked.

"The Rebels destroyed it," Johnson yelled. "Damn it, we might win this."

It took, again, interminable minutes while Johnson watched Fleet ships destroy human ships while the Rebels and the humans destroyed the Fleet. Eventually, all Fleet ships were destroyed or disabled.

"Make sure there's nothing in the path of those ships or the debris from the destroyed ones," Spillum ordered. At the velocity they were going, just hitting Asgard could destroy the asteroid.

"It'll be close," the radar tech reported, "but no, they won't hit any occupied asteroids."

"Will they hit anything near an occupied asteroid?" Spillum asked.

The technician hesitated a moment. Johnson knew what she was thinking. If they hit a small asteroid near an occupied asteroid, it might rain shrapnel of rock and ship pieces on the occupied asteroid.

"No," the operator finally reported.

Again, a collective sigh of relief passed through the room.

The four Fleet ships impacted Bostad a little less than four hours later. The impacts were visible on the Asgard telescope, at least the two that hit on the side of the planet facing Asgard, by the dust and water they threw in the air. There were, to Johnson's surprise, no fireballs.

#

It was calculated that the Fleet ships each hit Bostad with the energy of 1017 joules. The two that hit on land blew out craters two kilometers wide and half a kilometer deep. One hit in an unoccupied area of the still sparsely-populated planet, the other about a hundred kilometers from a city. The city experienced an earthquake of 5.5 on the Richter scale and a fine dusting of ejecta fallout. There were minor injuries and property damage, but no one was killed. Some people who were reportedly out of the city in the direction of the impact were reported missing and presumed dead, but the total was less than one hundred.

The other two hit open ocean far from populated areas, and the worst effects were tsunamis that were calculated to be only fifty-five centimeters high.

The seven disabled Fleet ships passed through the asteroid belt without incident and, while going slower than the first three the humans destroyed, also had much more velocity than was needed to escape the Bostad sun. They would likely travel interstellar space for millions of years.

Johnson stopped reading the report and put his hand computer in a pocket on his overalls. He looked up at his wife and smiled. She suddenly looked more beautiful to him than she ever had.

CHAPTER TWENTY-EIGHT

There was a memorial service for those who were killed in what was starting to be called simply "The Battle." There were eighteen pilots and operators on board the nine ships the Fleet had destroyed.

Considering, Johnson thought as he listened to Spillum eulogize the dead, that if they had failed, every human in the Bostad system would have died, and that being a number in the millions, the one hundred or so deaths on Bostad and eighteen in space were a small price to pay. He wouldn't give voice to those thoughts, except maybe to Larsen.

Sonia held his hand as they hung in the large common area of Asgard where the service was held. Tears formed glassy spheres on her eyes, and Johnson dabbed them away with a handkerchief.

After the service, Johnson and Spillum met in her office and made radio contact with *Úlfhethnar*.

"We have destroyed thirty-two Fleet ships. Was that all of the Fleet?" Spillum asked.

"I do not know," the ship replied. "I can only hope they took the bait, as you call it, to come here to finally destroy the Rebels."

"So we could be attacked at any time?" Spillum said.

"Perhaps," the ship replied, as always without emotion and in a monotone.

Spillum shook her head.

"I've done some calculations," Johnson said. "From the time the teleportation order was given around Bostad, it took over twelve seconds for the explosions to start. It should have taken seven as the message travelled around the planet, plus two seconds for the slappers."

"It also required," the ship said, "5.110959 seconds for the devices to teleport from their ships to the Fleet ships at the maximum range of 1,652,185 kilometers."

Johnson frowned. "When I teleported onto you, it was instantaneous."

"It was instantaneous from your perspective because you were the one being teleported."

Johnson released a bitter chuckle. He wondered how many things he'd missed in the battle that might have cost lives. Things he didn't think of. They had been very lucky, he thought.

"Now what?" he asked Spillum.

"We keep ships in orbit of Bostad on a rotating basis, and in the belt, too."

"For how long?"

She shrugged. "Until it's apparent they aren't coming back."

Johnson thought that would be boring duty, to wait who-knows-how-long for the possibility of a Fleet ship coming to the system.

She hesitated a moment. "*Úlfhethnar* or some other Rebel ship should inform the other human colonies of the threat. If we do it by laser, it'll take centuries."

"That's a good idea," Johnson said.

There was silence between the two. *Úlfhethnar* didn't say anything.

"Now what for you?" Spillum asked.

"I think I'm going to take the *Longboat* to Paradisus. My family and I, that is. Larsen if he wants to." Johnson thought Larsen would want to, to put 138 light years between him and the water cartels.

"How long will that take?" Spillum asked.

"About ten years, ship's time."

She smiled. "Might want to talk *Úlfhethnar* into taking you there."

Johnson laughed. He hadn't even considered it.

#

Privacy was scarce in the quarters assigned to Johnson. Originally intended for two males, there were now four people living there with one a woman who was jealous of her discretion.

Larsen took Sven to a bar in order to give Johnson and his wife some time alone. Their bodies were naked and entwined as they floated, tethered to one of the walls.

"Olly?" Sonia asked.

"Hmmmm?" His eyes were closed and he was relishing the moment.

"When were you going to tell me that Sven was kidnapped by a water cartel?

Johnson opened his eyes and did his best to look at his wife.

"Who told you?" He tried to keep the anger from his voice.

"Sven did," she said. "He was quite upset by it."

Johnson nodded. "I know. That's why our quarters are close to Spillum's office now: better security."

"We can't live in fear the water cartels will try to kill you and John."

Johnson didn't say that he thought they'd probably kill her and Sven, too, just to make an example of them. That's why he didn't go alone when Sven was kidnapped. He had decided if he did, they were both dead.

"I know," Johnson whispered. "That's why I want to go to Paradisus." He didn't mention the idea of asking a Rebel ship to take them there. Didn't want to get anyone's hopes up, but he figured the Rebels owed him. He'd helped them kill thirty-two Fleet ships which may, or may not, have been all of them. It would, in any case, have put a significant dent in the Fleet.

"We should go," Sonia whispered. "Soon."

"I'll talk to Larsen today," Johnson promised.

"Thank you."

"Of course." He kissed her.

#

"We need hydrogen," Larsen said. "We used up almost all of our reserve tanks escaping Gredel, and didn't spend enough time at ramjet speeds to refill them."

Johnson nodded grimly. "Maybe the Asgard Cooperative will give us some." The word "give" left a bad taste in his mouth. He'd rather earn something than be given it. But, he reminded himself, he also had once stolen a lot of valuable things.

They were in a bar and had invited Sven, too. It was supposed to be a "guy's night out," but the conversation eventually turned to what they would do next. Johnson felt Sonia needed to be part of this discussion, too, and called her on his communication device to come. She said she'd be right there.

Larsen snorted before she arrived. "Hydrogen is the second most precious commodity in the belt, after gold."

"Maybe *Úlfhethnar* can do that trick the Fleet ship did and refill them for us." Johnson was thinking the Fleet ship must have teleported hydrogen from that gas giant into the *Longboat*'s tanks. He could think of no other logical explanation.

"Or," Johnson continued. "Maybe *Úlfhethnar* could just take us to Paradisus."

Larsen's eyes grew wide and he smiled. Sven said, "What?"

"Have *Úlfhethnar* take us to Paradisus," Johnson repeated. "We'd be there in moments."

Sven grinned big at the thought.

"I think you need to talk to *Úlfhethnar*," Larsen said. "See what it's willing to do."

Johnson nodded. "I need to do that from the War Room. And I'll need Spillum's permission to use the War Room radios."

"She'll give it, won't she?" Sven asked, a little anxiety creeping into his voice.

"I'm sure she will," Johnson said, smiling at his son.

"The *Longboat*, physically, is ready to go," Larsen said. "We could use an organic and oxygen supplement in addition to hydrogen if we're going the slow way to Paradisus."

Johnson nodded, thinking. First thing was to talk to *Úlfhethnar* about what it was willing to do. Then, if needed, talk to Spillum about oxygen, organics, and hydrogen. He didn't want to spend any of his gold, but he would if he needed to. His retirement just wouldn't be as prosperous as he'd hoped.

"I'll talk to *Úlfhethnar* and Spillum," Johnson said. He turned to Sven. "And I wish you hadn't told your mother about the kidnapping."

"I'm sorry, Dad. She asked why I was having nightmares."

"You're having nightmares about it?"

"Yes, Dad. That's why I want to go to Paradisus, even if it takes nine years to get there."

"I'm sorry, son," Johnson said, his voice full of regret. And where the heck is Sonia, anyway? he wondered. She should have been there already.

"You gentlemen enjoying your drinks?" a gruff male voice interrupted.

All three looked up to see four large men hanging onto handholds looking at them.

"We're fine," Larsen said. His voice was dismissive with an edge of menace.

"Yeah," the same man spoke. He had a dark beard that was almost too long to be safe in free fall. Might catch it on something, Johnson thought. "I think you boys need to come with us."

"Pardon?" Johnson asked. He wasn't sure exactly what he'd heard the man say. "Come with you?"

"Or what?" Larsen growled.

"Or we'll kill you," the man replied, and opened a pocket at his hip and pulled a gun butt far enough out to show he was armed.

"Awfully public place for a murder," Larsen said.

Johnson looked at Sven and his son's face was contorted in fear.

"People know it's bad for their health to testify against the Ragnarök Cartel." Johnson remembered that was the cartel they'd stolen the *Loki* from.

"And Asgard security?" Larsen asked.

"Oh, they're busy with a little diversion we've set up." The man grimaced with malice.

Larsen and Johnson didn't say or do anything. Sven was frozen in fear.

"So you going to come or do we kill all three of you here?"

"Leave the boy out of this," Johnson said. "I'll come peacefully."

The man shook his head. "No. I need both you and John Larsen, who is miraculously alive. Well, for a little while."

"If you leave the young man, I'll come peaceably," Larsen whispered.

"I will, too," Johnson added.

"Dad, no," Sven cried out.

Johnson ignored it. What could he say to his son? There were no words to console him. Sven knew what would be the fate of Johnson and Larsen if they went with these men.

"Let's go," the goon snarled. "Or I'll kill the 'young man' before we leave."

"Is my wife safe?" Johnson asked.

"For now, if you cooperate."

Johnson frowned. He had no reason to believe anything this man said.

"We'll go," Larsen said firmly.

"Good," the man spat.

Johnson and Larsen were tethered to two of the men, and then all six pulled and pushed themselves out of the bar. Johnson wasn't surprised when they headed for this level's docking ring. He figured he and Larsen would be shoved out an airlock somewhere in interplanetary space. Well, he hoped that's all they'd do.

As they passed a display, a report was shown about a small riot in the poorer sections of the asteroid, residents demanding more pay for the same amount of work.

Larsen used his tether to pull himself close to the man he was tied to and punched him hard in the face. This sent both men turning in the air. The man tried to hit Larsen but he was at the far end of the tether. Another of the men grabbed Larsen, and holding him with one hand, hit him hard in the face with the other. Blood oozed and bubbled around Larsen's nose.

"Try that again," Beard said, "And I will kill the kid and the woman."

Larsen nodded.

"Someone give him a handkerchief to clean that up," Beard growled, and they continued moving.

Eventually, the group reached an airlock. It opened to the bearded man's touches on the control panel. The men moved inside, and the airlock closed. Larsen and Johnson were put in acceleration chairs that had locking buckles. Not standard, Johnson thought.

The other four men also climbed into acceleration chairs. When all were ready, Beard said to the air, "All set."

There was some movement as the ship undocked and separated from the asteroid, then maneuvered into the proper attitude for wherever they were headed.

"We have a long trip ahead of us," Beard said, "So you might as well relax."

The ship accelerated and quickly built up to what felt like one gee to Johnson.

"How long?" he asked.

"About two hours," the man said, unbuckling his acceleration chair and getting up. He walked with difficulty, having grown up, Johnson presumed, in free fall. Two of the other men also got up. The third looked like he was falling asleep.

"Damn, I need to exercise more," one of the men said as he hobbled along on the deck.

Johnson tried to think. Two hours at one gee...they weren't going very far, especially if they were trying to match an orbit. The equation was one-half the acceleration multiplied by the time squared. He could round the acceleration to ten meters per second squared, but the time was in seconds and there were thirty-six hundred seconds in an hour, so that'd be seventy-two hundred seconds. So that was five (one half the acceleration) multiplied by seventy-two hundred seconds squared, and he couldn't do that without a hand computer. Larsen or Sven could probably do it, but Johnson was never good at math in his head.

"Where are we going?" he finally asked.

"Your ship," the man said. "I think you call it the *Longboat*. We understand you have a lot of gold you stole from the Bostad government."

Johnson growled. He was at least hoping that if he died, Sonia and Sven would have access to that gold. Plus there was the gold they'd extorted at Gredel.

"Will you be satisfied then," Johnson asked, "if we give you all our gold?"

Beard laughed mirthlessly. "That, and throw you two out an airlock."

"You'll let my family live in peace?" Johnson asked.

Beard thought a moment. "Yeah, sure."

Johnson had the idea he was lying.

About an hour later, acceleration stopped and Johnson could feel the ship changing attitude. It would now decelerate to match orbits with the *Longboat*, he knew. A few moments later, it began accelerating again.

About an hour after that, a voice said, "Strap down. We'll be accelerating in order to dock."

The three men returned to their acceleration chairs. Johnson knew all he could do was wait. He couldn't do anything until they unstrapped them. He had to somehow overpower these men, steal this ship, and get back to Asgard as fast as it could accelerate. And radio Spillum to go ensure that Sonia and Sven were safe.

It seemed unlikely. His stomach churned at the possibility his family was dead or, if alive, he couldn't save them.

CHAPTER TWENTY-NINE

The cartel ship docked with the *Longboat*. Johnson had to admire the skill of whoever the pilot was as the docking went smoothly.

"Now," Beard said before unstrapping Johnson and Larsen, "your family's life depends on your cooperation. Remember that."

Johnson nodded and so did Larsen.

They were in free fall again, and Beard and two other of the four men were now holding guns. The fourth, the smallest of the three and the one who had been sleeping during the trip, grinned. "Assuming you didn't find it and disable it, there's a routine in the *Loki*'s computer to monitor the entire ship. I'll be on the bridge watching you."

"And we'll be going with you," Beard said.

"And what do you want us to do?" Larsen asked.

"Move the gold from your ship to this one," Beard said. "And be quick about it."

Johnson and Larsen exchanged a look. Both men knew that when that task was finished, they were dead.

The men unlocked the buckles and let Johnson and Larsen move.

All six men entered the ship. The small one moved toward the bridge. It was in the same place as it had been on the *Loki*.

"The cargo hold should be that way," Beard said, pointing toward the back of the life support spaces. "Just before engineering, unless you changed it."

"We didn't," Larsen growled.

"Let's go," Beard spat.

Johnson and Larsen led them to the cargo hold. There was a steel cube about one meter on each side welded down to the deck and the bulkhead. Under it was another sheet of eight centimeter thick steel. Strong and multiple latches held the lid on. In height, the cube reached about to Johnson's hip. Larsen opened it. It was full of gold bars about the size of two fingers put together.

"Fuck," Beard said. "You got all this from Bostad?"

"And Gredel," Johnson said.

Beard laughed. "And you think we're criminals?"

"How much mass is there?" one of the men asked.

Johnson decided there was no reason not to tell them. "Ten thousand kilos." Which was why it had to be in a strong box: that much mass could, if allowed to move, pick up significant momentum. And the plate underneath was because when the *Longboat* was at five gees acceleration, the gold weighed fifty tonnes.

"We'll be here all day," one man said.

"Or longer," Beard added. "The boss wants it all. They wouldn't have gotten any of it if they hadn't stolen a cartel ship and killed four of our men."

"That was a hundred and fifty-five years ago," Johnson said, even though he knew he couldn't argue with these men.

"Don't matter to us," Beard snarled.

Everyone just stared at the gold for a moment.

"Start hauling it into our ship," Beard ordered.

"You know," Larsen said, "It'll go faster if we can use bags rather than just our hands. I could carry at least ten bars, rather than just a few in my hands."

Johnson wondered why Larsen wanted this over sooner, because he knew when the gold was transferred, they would die.

"Good idea," Beard said. "Go get two and you—" he pointed at one of the other men "— go with him."

"Come on," Larsen said, and pulled himself out of the cargo hold, the other man following.

That left Johnson with two of the goons: Beard and another large man.

#

Larsen led the way down the main corridor of the *Longboat* back toward the living quarters.

"There should be some bags in the galley," he said.

"Yeah, okay," the man said.

Larsen reached a handhold and used it to spin in air. He wrapped his legs around the other man's neck, and with his arms giving him leverage, slammed the man's skull into the bulkhead.

The man was still struggling so he did it again. This time, the body went limp. Larsen released his legs and quickly pulled himself into the nearest door.

#

"Hey," the man on the bridge said over the ship's intercom, "Larsen's overpowered Swansen."

"Where's Larsen now?" Beard asked angrily into the air.

"I don't know," the man replied.

"What do you mean you don't know?"

"He's disappeared."

"I thought you could monitor all parts of the ship?" Beard growled.

"I should, unless they modified it."

"You, go find him and bring him here," Beard barked to the other cartel man in the hold.

That man nodded, pulled a gun from his pocket, and moved out of the room.

"And see if Swansen is okay," Beard called after him.

That just left Johnson and Beard in the cargo hold.

"I might as well get started," Johnson said, starting to move toward the cube.

"You stay right there," Beard ordered, pointing his gun at Johnson.

"Okay, okay," Johnson said.

Long, empty minutes passed.

"Have they found him, yet?" Beard asked the air.

"No, but they found a locked door. He must be in there."

#

Larsen found his gun. He had dutifully cleaned and oiled it, with supplies he'd brought with him, for the past eighteen years. The ammunition was also eighteen years old, but that couldn't be helped.

He heard pounding on his quarters' door. The lock was only designed to keep Sven out and wouldn't take a lot of abuse before it broke.

#

"Ever seen that much gold?" Johnson asked Beard.

"Of course not," Beard scoffed.

"Take a look," Johnson said with a smile. He tried to sound proud that he had so much.

Beard shook his head.

"I can show you some," Johnson said. "Maybe you could slip a few bars in your pocket. No one would know."

He watched the turmoil writhe across Beard's face. "How much are the bars?"

"One kilo each," Johnson said. That was both their mass and their value. "A man could have a lot of fun on Nirvana with a kilo of gold."

Beard spent a long moment in thought. Then he said, "Two bars. One for me and one for Petersen on the bridge."

Johnson smiled. "Sure." He pulled himself to the cube and, gripping a handhold with one hand, he reached in and pulled out two bars. Of course they didn't weigh anything, but he could feel their mass in their reluctance to move. Newton's first law.

He knew he had to get this right and he hoped it worked.

He twisted his body, still having a death grip on that handhold, and threw the two gold bars at Beard's face as hard as he could.

The man tried to move out of the way, but moving quickly in free fall is nearly impossible. Both one-kilo bars hit him in the face. It must have felt like a hard punch, Johnson thought, considering their mass and velocity. He put his legs against the bulkhead and pushed himself at Beard before the large man could recover.

Beard aimed his gun and fired but missed Johnson. He heard the shot impact steel behind him. He reached Beard and grabbed his overall with his left hand and smashed him in the face with the right repeatedly. Beard fired again, but missed still. Johnson ripped the gun from his hand, turned it, and shot Beard between the eyes.

Blood spurted out from the man's forehead.

Johnson had to clamp down on his throat lest he vomit.

#

"Come out, Larsen, or it'll go bad for you," a voice said.

Larsen remained quiet. Then, he heard a gunshot.

"Damn," the voice yelled.

Larsen could hear the man outside his door pushing against the corridor wall as he moved toward the cargo hold. Larsen pushed himself to the door, opened it, and shoved himself into the hall. The cartel man was hurriedly pulling himself toward where Johnson was. Larsen shot him in the back. The man let go of the handhold he was gripping and tumbled down the corridor.

Larsen shot him again.

Then, he heard a shot, and it was as if someone had punched him in the back, hard. He turned in the air to see the man he'd choked, Swansen, aiming a gun at him with a cloud of smoke around the muzzle.

Larsen fired, hitting the man, but Swansen also fired, hitting Larsen in the chest.

Larsen felt his blood leaving his body and tried to shoot again but didn't have the strength.

A shot rang out, and the last thing Larsen saw was Swansen's chest exploding with blood.

#

Johnson hung in the corridor. Blood was everywhere, floating in the air in spheres that rippled as they reacted to the air around them. They needed to shut down the ventilation system before blood got into the air recycler, he realized. That had to be done from the bridge.

He pushed to Larsen, turning his friend so he could see his face.

Larsen's eyes told him that his first mate was dead.

For the moment, Johnson had more to worry about.

"You, on the bridge, I am armed, and you are alone. I will let you return to the cartel ship if you surrender."

"Your family is dead," the voice came back.

"Yes, probably already," Johnson replied, trying to sound tough.

"I'm armed, too," the man said. "I could just as easily kill you."

"Or I could kill you," Johnson said, ignoring the churning of his guts.

"But I can see you," the man replied. "You can't see me."

"Fine," Johnson called. "Come get me."

He moved into Larsen's quarters. He remembered Larsen saying what felt ages ago, but was more like only three months, that his quarters were the only place on the ship the computer couldn't monitor.

He closed the door but didn't lock it and pushed himself against the far wall. He tethered himself so his hands were free and aimed the gun at the door with both hands. If he didn't kill the guy on the first shot, the man would probably shoot him, too. But to open the door, he had to have one hand on a handhold and one pushing the door open. That left him no hands to hold a gun.

"Okay," the man said. "I am disarmed. I'm heading for our ship."

Johnson stayed put and didn't say anything. He spent a moment looking at the one room in the *Longboat* he'd never been in. It wasn't remarkable except for a small picture of an older woman stuck to one bulkhead. Judging from her age, Johnson thought she must be Larsen's mother, probably now long dead.

The door flew open. The man was there, holding a gun. He'd used his feet to push the door open.

Johnson fired, and the man returned fire almost simultaneously. Johnson's bullet hit the man above the right eye. He went limp as more blood sprayed into the air.

Something had punched Johnson in the arm. He looked down and saw he was bleeding.

"*Knulla*," he whispered.

He put the gun in a pocket and pushed out of Larsen's quarters, trying not to move too fast. He went to the bridge and shut down the ventilation system. He spent a moment looking around. If Larsen wasn't dead, it would feel great to be back on the bridge of his ship.

Johnson moved to the three rooms he had shared with Sven and Sonia because the first aid kit was there. Ripping it open, he bandaged up the wound. That staunched the bleeding, and he knew it wasn't a life-threatening injury.

Slowly, Johnson went back to the bridge. As he passed by the airlock, he saw it was closed and the telltale indicated that the cartel ship was gone.

On the bridge, he activated the radio.

"*Longboat* to Asgard. *Longboat* to Asgard. This is Olly Johnson. I need to talk to Spillum."

The light speed delay should only be about two-thirds of a second, Johnson knew. Still, it took a few seconds for a voice to reply.

"This is the Asgard Cooperative. Say again who you are."

"This is Olly Johnson on board the *Longboat*. I need to talk to Spillum. Now." He almost yelled the last word.

"Please wait," the voice said.

Johnson growled loudly.

"Johnson," he heard Spillum say, "You're on your ship?"

"Yes," Johnson said. "You need to find my family. They are in danger."

"They're safe," Spillum reported. "When we realized you'd been kidnapped, we found them and put them in a secure location."

"Thank you," Johnson said, his voice soft with genuine gratitude.

"Johnson, we have a situation here," she said. "I don't have time to chat."

"What?" Johnson asked.

"A Fleet ship has appeared. It's headed straight for Asgard, and it's using its lasers to destroy the ships with the operators on them before they get in teleportation range. I think it figured out our plan."

Johnson thought about turning on the *Longboat*'s radar to find it but decided that might make it destroy him.

"Where is it?" he asked.

"A little less than ten AUs from us."

"How close will it pass to me?"

"Why?"

"Just tell me," Johnson spat.

There was some hesitation. "About ten thousand kilometers," Spillum said.

"How long until it passes within teleportation range?"

There was a long delay as Johnson assumed they were calculating.

"If it stays its course, and you don't accelerate, about an hour and a half."

"Put me in touch with *Úlfhethnar*," Johnson said.

"What? Why?"

"Just do it," Johnson ordered.

There was another pause. Then *Úlfhethnar*'s voice came back, as monotone and emotionless as ever.

"Yes, Johnson?" it asked.

"I'm on the *Longboat*," Johnson said. "Teleport a Coulomb device to me."

"Why?"

"Because so far the Fleet ship hasn't thought I'm a threat. I might be able to take it out before it hits Asgard."

"It will be one of the extras I built. It won't have a slapper. You'll have to teleport with it. You'll die."

Johnson hesitated a moment. "I don't have a choice. Teleport me a device."

His family was on Asgard. He had to save them. Never give up, he didn't say. But he knew Larsen would approve.

"Where's Larsen?" Spillum asked, interrupting his thoughts.

"Dead," Johnson replied grimly.

"Oh, Johnson, I'm so sorry."

Johnson didn't know what to say.

"*Úlfhethnar*," he finally said, "teleport me a device."

"I will," it replied.

It took a few minutes, but one of the devices appeared in the main corridor of the *Longboat*. Johnson heard air snap as it was pushed away from it.

The device floated free until Johnson maneuvered it to a wall in the bridge and strapped it down. Then he strapped himself to it. He knew that if a red area appeared on any of the faces, he was to touch that and that would teleport him and the device onto the Fleet ship. Then he had to touch the area again and the device would cause a fusion reaction in a sphere approximately ninety meters in diameter. The atoms in Johnson's body would fuse into heavier elements, releasing energy due to mass loss as predicted by Einstein and his $E=mc^2$ equation.

CHAPTER THIRTY

Time passed slowly. He thought about asking to talk to Sven and Sonia, but decided it was best if he didn't. He might lose his nerve to do this and turn himself into energy and other elements.

He spent the time trying to remember his physics. His body was mostly made of carbon. Carbon-carbon fusion usually only happened in massive, older stars that had burned all their lighter elements. If he remembered right, the carbon in his body would fuse to produce neon and sodium. He wondered briefly if he'd feel anything.

He looked at the time displayed on the *Longboat*'s bridge. For seventeen long years, this had been his ship. Now it would be Sonia's.

"*Úlfhethnar*?" Johnson said over the radio.

"Yes?" it replied.

"Please take my family to Paradisus."

There was a longer hesitation than would be accounted for by light speed delay.

"I will," the ship replied.

"Thank you," Johnson said.

"Get ready, Johnson," Spillum said. "And thank you. You will be remembered as a hero."

"Yes," Johnson breathed, watching the cube.

He didn't feel like a hero, but he had to save his family. It had always been about the family: Sonia and Sven. The piracy, the stealing from the cartels, all of it, was simply to keep Sonia and Sven safe from the Impetus Party, from the despotic regime on Bostad. Even blackmailing Gredel was so that Sonia would have enough gold to never have to worry about money again. Maybe he was wrong. Maybe what he did was wrong. But it was too late now to worry about that. Maybe what he did now would make up a little for the pain he may have caused. Maybe just a little, he thought.

The red area appeared. He did not hesitate—didn't dare hesitate—but touched the area.

He found himself floating in vacuum in pitch blackness. He hadn't thought about the fact that there'd be no light inside the Fleet ship.

His ears felt as if someone were jabbing needles in them. He breathed out as he fumbled to touch the device. Just before he passed out from lack of oxygen, he managed to touch one of the faces of the cube.

#

Spillum watched her radar. The Fleet ship was also close enough that it was visible through the telescopic display.

"He should have teleported," the radar technician reported.

"It takes about five seconds," Spillum whispered, more to herself than anyone else.

On the visual display, the Fleet ship had a burst of light near the part closest to Asgard.

"That must have been it," the technician said.

"Radar?" Spillum barked.

"It's no longer accelerating. I think he did it."

"What's its trajectory? Will it miss us?"

There was some hesitation. Spillum was about to repeat the question angrily.

"Yes," the radar technician finally said. "It'll be close, less than a kilometer."

Spillum let out a breath she wasn't aware she was holding. Then she had a thought. "Did you calculate in our gravity?" She thought at less than a kilometer, Asgard's gravitational pull might cause it to collide with the asteroid.

"Yes, ma'am, I did," the technician said.

Spillum smiled. "Good."

#

The *Longboat*, somehow attached to *Úlfhethnar*, appeared in the Paradisus star system.

Sven and Sonia felt nothing as *Úlfhethnar* accelerated to orbit the planet, but were in free fall the entire time.

"You are in orbit," *Úlfhethnar* reported. "Good luck."

"Thank you," Sonia replied over the radio.

There was no response, but Sven looked at the radar display. "It's accelerating away at a thousand gees."

Sonia only nodded.

"Call the planet," she said.

"Yes, Mom." Sven touched the radio control on the computer. "Mayday mayday, this is *Longboat* in orbit of Paradisus. We cannot land and need assistance to get to the planet surface." They had no boat but, even if they did, neither Sven nor Sonia could pilot it.

Sonia smiled. The gold would, for now, stay on the ship until they could arrange to have it deposited in a bank. First, she wanted to breathe a planet's air again.

It was a sad smile, however. And she found herself brushing a sphere of tears away from her eyes. Olly should be here. And John. They had found John's body when they arrived on the *Longboat* back in the Bostad system. Of course, Olly was gone, turned into energy that had helped destroy what everyone hoped was the last Fleet ship.

#

"The inhabitants of the Jideed Baghdad system are back on their planet or in their respective asteroids or ships," *Úlfhethnar* reported to Spillum.

"Good," Spillum said. "And you explained what happened?"

"Yes," the ship replied. "They said they were happy to be home."

Spillum nodded, realizing belatedly that the ship couldn't see it and might not know what it meant.

"I'm under political pressure to dismantle the defense groups. Pretty much everyone is convinced that was the last Fleet ship."

"Perhaps," *Úlflethnar* said. "The fact it attacked alone makes us think it might have been. They always attacked in numbers before."

"A lot to risk," Spillum said. "I'll keep the defense groups up as long as I can politically hold out."

"That is probably a wise decision," *Úlflethnar* said, as always monotone and emotionless.

"What will the Rebel ships do now?" Spillum asked.

"One will stay in this system. A few will warn all human colonies and Earth of the Fleet danger. Then, we wish to explore the universe."

Spillum smiled. She didn't think emotionless ships could have wishes.

"That is probably a good idea. If you learn anything interesting, let us know, please."

"We will."

"Goodbye, *Úlflethnar*, and thank you."

"Goodbye," the ship replied.

Spillum smiled. It was bittersweet. Already she'd heard rumors that people were funding research into how the Rebel and Fleet ships moved faster than light. If they were successful, humanity would be able to move throughout the galaxy.

But, she wondered, what other terrors might they find out there?

She shook her head. She didn't have time for dreaming. She had work to do.

ABOUT THE AUTHOR

S. Evan Townsend has been called 'America's Unique Speculative Fiction Voice.' Evan is a writer living in central Washington State. After spending four years in the U.S. Army in the Military Intelligence branch, he returned to civilian life and college to earn a B.S. in Forest Resources from the University of Washington. In his spare time he enjoys reading, driving (sometimes on a racetrack), meeting people, and talking with friends. He is in a 12-step program for Starbucks addiction. Evan lives with his wife and has three grown sons. He enjoys science fiction, fantasy, history, politics, cars, and travel.